This Far by *Faith*

This Far by *Faith*

STACY HAWKINS ADAMS

KENDRA NORMAN-BELLAMY

LINDA HUDSON-SMITH

THIS FAR BY FAITH

A New Spirit Novel

ISBN-13: 978-0-373-83024-4
ISBN-10: 0-373-83024-6

Copyright © 2008 by Harlequin Books S.A.

The publisher acknowledges the copyright holders
of the individual works as follows:
MY MOTHER'S SHADOW
Copyright © 2008 by Stacy Hawkins Adams
A CRACKED MIRROR
Copyright © 2008 by Kendra Norman-Bellamy
HONOR THY HEART
Copyright © 2008 by Linda Hudson-Smith

www.kimanipress.com

Printed in U.S.A.

CONTENTS

MY MOTHER'S SHADOW

Dedication

I dedicate this story to mothers and daughters who are struggling in their relationships, with the hope that it helps them realize how God's guidance, an open heart and a willingness to forgive can heal most rifts. I also dedicate this story to the memory of my beloved mother, Dorothy A. Hawkins, with whom I had a loving and special bond until her departure for Heaven in April 2005. Her spirit lives on through me, as I nurture my own children.

Acknowledgment

I sincerely thank Glenda Howard for including me in this project; my fellow authors, Kendra and Linda, for their friendship and support; and my family and friends for their continuous encouragement in my writing endeavors.

Chapter 1

It had taken years, but today here I stood, staring into her eyes.

The moment I met Diana Edmonds, I understood why the Tony Award- and Oscar-winning actress captivated me and thousands of other fans. Diana was the reason I had become an actress, now three weeks shy of college graduation and striving to land a job on Broadway.

"So nice to meet you," she said, giving me the once-over. I smiled and prayed that my makeup had concealed the acne on my chin. But Diana zeroed in on it and frowned.

"Good luck," she said coolly, before moving on to the next actor, singer or dancer who stood in line, waiting to audition for a part in the musical she would be headlining. I hoped I looked calmer than I felt; my stomach was turning flips.

When I was in second grade, my parents had taken my sister, Charlene, and me to see *Azula,* the touring musical in which Diana had a starring role. Then Diana had released an album and played a recurring role on a hit TV show. She was everywhere, and as often as possible, I reminded my mother that I also wanted to act and sing, just like Diana Edmonds.

Mom and Daddy believed in me and had provided for everything from dance and voice lessons to regular visits to regional theater productions and to the national touring shows that came to Baltimore. For my sixteenth birthday, they treated me to a trip to New York to see *The Lion King*.

It wasn't easy, on teachers' salaries, but they knew what corners to cut to make their girls' dreams come true. When Charlene decided in ninth grade to become a chemist, they helped her make that happen, too.

Despite the many years I had followed Diana's career, today was the first time I'd ever been this close to my "inspiration." I laughed at myself for being so excited. Most of the hundred or so actors and singers surrounding me were probably feeling the same way.

We had gathered at this theater on Forty-fifth Street to audition for spots in *Then Sings My Soul,* Diana's upcoming Broadway musical. The stars of the cast had already been selected, but the chorus line was still being formed, and out of that, several lucky actors and actresses would garner bit parts.

Daddy, Mom, Charlene and my church family in Maryland had already prayed me into a prominent role. I didn't know what it would be, but Mom had assured me when I talked to her this morning that something special was going to happen after today's audition.

"God has smiled on you your entire life, Jess," she said. "This won't be any different. Go in there and just trust Him to anoint your singing and whatever lines you have to recite. You're so close to graduation. I just know that this is going to be your first job. I feel it in my spirit."

I had smiled as I gripped the cell phone with one hand and brushed my teeth with the other. Mom's spirit was always speaking to her, and usually whatever God was saying was on target. I tried to listen to Him, too, but I hadn't mastered the practice yet.

While Diana continued to weave her way through the crowd of actors to extend greetings, I spotted a couple of my classmates from New York University. We exchanged waves before turning our eyes toward the stage, where a production assistant announced that we were about to start. The elimination process was about to begin.

Diana walked to center stage and stood there silently for about thirty seconds, inhaling deeply, and then exhaling, to prepare for the solo she was about to render as a warm-up for our auditions.

It was unusual for her to even be here. Most directors worked with a panel of judges or the playwright to decide who should fill each slot. Rarely was the star on hand.

However, the industry rumor mill indicated that this was Diana's legacy-making performance. She wanted absolutely every detail and person in the production to be handpicked, down to the members of the chorus. Which explained the time she had devoted to personally greeting everyone who had come to audition.

When the legendary director, Palmer Jordan, rose from the table and motioned for silence, a hush fell over the Imperial Theater. Following his cue, a tall, thin man walked regally to the piano and seconds later, music floated through the air, in dramatic crescendos and decrescendos.

Diana closed her eyes. With her arms loosely before her and her fingers laced together, she poured out the song that we would accompany her on as a full chorus.

Her voice was so powerful, yet controlled, that it gave me chills. Watching her was rewarding: her vibrant brown eyes, the perfect curve of her full lips and bronze cheeks, the flawless skin that put mine—twenty years her junior—to shame.

I glanced at the people to the left and right of me. I wasn't the only one spellbound.

After Diana sang, each of us was called, one by one, to perform two songs for her and for the director, both a song we had selected and one of their choosing.

Listening to the competition had its pluses and minuses. When someone belted out a Jennifer Holiday–like performance, I counted how many slots in the chorus would be left to insure I still had a chance. When someone missed a note or butchered their selection, Diana showed no mercy. Palmer would glance at her, and if she delivered a quick headshake, that yielded a polite, "Thank you. We'll call if we need you."

I had number thirty-one. By the time they called me, I thought my heart would leap from my chest. I walked to the center of the stage, gently cleared my throat and bowed my head for a few seconds to breathe in and focus.

When the music for "Somewhere Over the Rainbow" swelled, I closed my eyes and forgot where I was until I sang the final note. I was greeted with silence, which left me trembling.

Is this good or bad?

The seconds in which that thought flitted through my mind seemed like an eternity. When I finally raised my head, Palmer Jordan, his assistant directors and several of the stagehands simply looked at me.

"No need to do a second song, Jessica Drake," Mr. Jordan said. "You'll receive a call from us soon."

A thirty-something woman who had auditioned just before me and had also received a promising response was gathering her belongings as I came down the hallway.

"I heard you sing and thought you were great," she said, and zipped her lightweight jacket.

The woman strolled toward the door and I called after her.

"Um, thanks. What's your name?"

She chuckled and continued walking, without turning toward me.

"You're new to this game, aren't you? This is not a business where you take names and form friendships, sweetie. You take names to know who you need to out-perform at the next audition."

She opened the door and turned for a final look.

"I'm Mara," she said. "See you soon, at rehearsal."

I smiled at her confidence and prayed that she knew what she was talking about.

Chapter 2

I slid into my short blue jean jacket and exited through the same door Mara had used. It had been a long morning and I was starving, but I had to call Mom to fill her in on the audition.

I pulled my cell phone from my jacket pocket just as I stepped outside. Before I could dial, Mara caught my eye. She was standing a few feet away, gesturing vividly and talking fast to a tall, café-latte brother. He held a long, skinny notebook, but he was also armed with a miniature digital tape recorder.

They noticed me and Mara motioned for me to join them. I tucked the cell phone back into my pocket and strolled over. The man tipped his cap and extended his hand.

"Quentin Grey, *Times* reporter. Great job up there on the stage today. I was standing at the back of the theater during your audition."

"Thank you," I said, determined to keep my eyes neutral, despite his good looks and the intense stare he leveled at me.

"Quentin writes for the *New York Times'* Sunday magazine," Mara explained. "He's planning to write a profile of Diana and share backstage details about the cast of the new musical and what goes on during rehearsals for a major stage production."

I read the *Times'* Arts section and Sunday magazine regularly and was familiar with his name. Still, I decided to tread cautiously.

"That's great," I said. "Have you already interviewed Ms. Edmonds?"

He nodded.

"Several times. The director has given me the okay to talk to the cast, sit in on rehearsals and capture some behind-the-scenes action. I'm talking to some of the folks who auditioned today, to get a sense of what it felt like and how hopeful you are about your chances."

"Good luck with your story, but I'm not interested in talking, especially before I know whether I've got the job," I said. "See you later, Mara."

I spun on my heel and strode in the direction that would take me to the nearest subway station. He thanked Mara for the interview and bade her goodbye, then trotted along beside me. He thrust a business card in my face.

I read it and continued to walk. *Quentin F. Grey, staff writer, New York Times.*

I looked at him again.

"Thanks, but Mara just introduced you."

He smiled and my heart involuntarily fluttered.

"You're probably a great actress, Ms. Drake, but your suspicions were written all over your face a few minutes ago."

I shrugged.

"I've been taught that it's bad luck to plan for something before you have it in your hand, that's all. Don't want to ruin my chances with Ms. Edmonds or Mr. Jordan."

"Don't worry," he said. "A lot of the interviews I'm doing now are for background information. This piece won't run for several months, until the weekend after the show premieres.

"If you're in the cast, then great, I'll have some 'before and after' quotes from you," he said. "If you aren't, you may or may not be quoted about what it felt like to audition in front of the great Diana Edmonds."

He paused and cocked his head to one side. I stopped because he had piqued my curiosity.

"What?"

"You kind of look like her, you know. A younger, fresh-faced version."

I shoved my hands in my pocket and leveled my eyes at him.

"You can't come up with a better line than that?"

He laughed and walked toward me. I had reached the subway stop I was planning to take to the Village and was about to trot down the stairs.

"No, I'm serious. You really do favor her. It's uncanny."

I sighed.

"You're entitled to your opinion. I guess I should be flattered. I mean, I am her biggest fan and I've always considered myself a 'plain Jane,' but hey, a *New York Times* reporter has spoken! I'm hot!"

I laughed at myself and extended my hand.

He tucked his notepad in his pocket and shook it.

"Off the record? You are hot, Ms. Drake."

Now that was pretty forward. I blushed and grew flustered.

"I need to catch a train. Gotta go."

He nodded.

As I descended the stairs to the subway, he called after me, "You've got my card. Give me a ring when you've been hired and let me know how it feels. It would be great for the story."

Now he had me confused. Was this work-related flirting or sincere interest?

Either way, I had to go home and think about it. If actor Hill Harper wasn't available, there was at least one look-alike brother to ease the pain.

Chapter 3

Quentin had been right. I got a call from the staff of *Then Sings My Soul,* but it wasn't what I had expected.

Instead of offering me a spot in the chorus, Palmer Jordan's assistant left a voice mail two days after my audition, requesting that I return for another tryout, this time wearing business attire, with my hair braided into a long ponytail.

This could mean any number of things. I decided not to fill my brain with speculation. Instead, I called my number-one prayer partner. She assessed the case immediately.

"They're auditioning you for one of the bit parts," Mom said. "They're trying to put you in character. Call back and ask for the specific lines you should rehearse from the script, so you'll be able to read the part with a sense of connection to the character."

It was such a blessing to have parents who understood the theater industry. Not only did they teach drama at the high school level, Mom and Dad had appeared in off-Broadway productions years ago, before Charlene was born and they felt the need to provide her with a more settled, stable environment. I didn't join the family until ten years later, and by then, their theatrical careers were long over.

"I don't know, Mom. I'm afraid to call back and ask for anything," I said. I had worked during the summers in regional or traveling theater productions, but this was the big time.

"Besides," I said, "they probably want me to do a cold reading. The assistant who called would have mentioned the lines if practicing were an option. And I wouldn't want Diana to hear about it and think I was worrisome."

I climbed off the twin bed in my university studio apartment and began tidying my desk while we talked.

Mom paused.

"Even if Diana is a diva, with a capital *D*, her work still inspired you to do what you're doing. Be respectful, but look out for yourself, Jessica. I gotta run because I've got a roast in the oven."

After the usual "I love you's," I hung up and wondered what tomorrow's audition would entail.

Chapter 4

I arrived for my second audition forty minutes early, just in case they'd changed their minds about not letting me see the script. I sat there with two other women about my age, who had tried out for the chorus earlier in the week.

At one o'clock sharp, the director called my name.

I inhaled deeply and walked onto the stage, trusting that whatever I had been brought here for, I would achieve.

One of the assistants passed me the script, with the ninety-second monologue I needed to recite highlighted.

As soon as I read the second line, my confidence began to wane. Could I do this? Could I breathe life into this character without ripping open a part of my past that I'd tried to tuck away and forget?

I stood there for several minutes, until one of the directors coughed. Palmer Jordan leaned forward and tried to look into my eyes.

"You up to this?"

I nodded eagerly and straightened my posture.

"Yes, sir. I'm ready."

I uttered the lines with the hurt and lack of understanding I had truly felt at one point in my life.

One of the codirectors read the lines that Diana would speak during the play.

"I'll always love you, but I need to take care of me right now, Melanie. I need to get over your father's death the best way I know how. You'll be safe at boarding school. You're going to be fine."

It was my turn again.

"You haven't taught me everything, you know, I'm twenty, but I still don't know how to be a woman. I still don't know how to make it in this world."

I started yelling as the tears streamed from my eyes.

"What kind of mother would give her child away?"

I fell to my knees and sobbed.

"What kind of mother are you? You aren't one! You care more about yourself than me!"

I had completed the highlighted section and could rise and leave, but first I had to stop this flow of tears. One of the directors brought me a tissue. I looked up at Palmer Jordan, embarrassed and worried that he might view the emotion as overacting.

He sat back in his chair and stared at me.

"Wow. I wasn't expecting that."

My heart leapt.

"Where did that come from?" He leaned forward in his chair.

I couldn't tell him the truth; not now, anyway. I shrugged.

"NYU trains the best, I guess," I said, trying to regain my composure and stop the sniffling.

"NYU trains the best," he repeated. Just as quickly as he had seemed entranced, he snapped out of it. "When do you graduate?"

"Three weeks from tomorrow," I said.

"Thank you, Ms. Drake. We'll be in touch."

I smiled and thanked him. As I walked offstage, I saw Quentin, sitting in the back of the theater.

Wonder what he thought this time.

If he put my audition in his story, I might have to hurt him.

Chapter 5

Quentin met me in the foyer of the theater and gave me a hug.

"How did you do that?"

His eyes held deep respect. I raised my chin toward him and smiled, embarrassed that my eyes were still red. When I didn't answer, he raised his hands to feign surrender.

"That was an off-the-record question, I promise," he said. "I couldn't help but ask. You were amazing."

"Thank you, Quentin. That means a lot," I finally said. I still didn't answer him.

"Let me treat you to lunch."

I chuckled. "There you go again. I still haven't landed the job."

He held the door for me as we left the building.

"Trust me, you have the job," he said. "Which part is it, by the way?"

I gasped. I'd been so focused on getting through the scene that I had failed to ask. I was sure it was still a small part, but who wouldn't want to know?

"If they call with good news, I guess I'll find out," I said.

Quentin paused and laughed heartily.

"You mean to tell me you're not sure?"

He noticed my embarrassment and leaned down to give me a light hug. His muscles clung to the outline of his shirt.

"Don't worry—you'll find out tomorrow. Let me take you to dinner this evening, to celebrate."

Now it was my turn to laugh at him.

"What are we celebrating, my ability to cry on cue?"

He nodded.

"That's a feat. Besides, I know you've impressed the directors. If nothing else, let's celebrate that."

I wanted to say yes, but after causing all of those painful memories to resurface for the audition, no felt safer.

Quentin sensed my indecision and paused.

"You're right—I can't compromise my integrity with this magazine piece. Can I treat you to dinner in exchange for an interview?"

This man was persistent. I understood how he had landed his job.

"Interview about what? I'm not part of the cast yet, remember?"

He stopped and grabbed my arms, turning me toward him.

"Tell you what, as soon as you get the call, let me know," he said. "I'll take you to dinner to discuss life as a budding actress who has landed her first gig on Broadway, okay? As long as I don't promise to keep anything pertinent to the story off-the-record, or accept any bribes, we should be okay."

He pulled out another card and wrote his cell number on the back. Then he walked in the other direction.

"Call me," he said. "I don't bite! And congrats again on your stellar audition. You've chosen the right profession."

I watched him until he turned the corner. I had come alive onstage today, but at what price? The longing to find my birth mother was seeping back into my spirit.

I had buried it several years ago, when I had packed my bags for college. Otherwise, I would have driven myself crazy, combing New York City for someone whose name and other personal information I didn't even know.

I stopped pressing my parents about it because I didn't want them to feel threatened. They'd been so good to me. Having their love and full support should have been more than enough. Today, I reminded myself that it had to be.

Chapter 6

When I wanted to, I could joke with the best. My alarm went off at 6:00 a.m. and thirty minutes later, after sipping a cup of tea, I dialed Quentin's number. He picked up after four rings, sounding like his mouth was full of cotton.

"Good morning!" I sang.

"'Xcuse me?"

I pictured him rubbing his eyes and trying to discern my voice.

"It's me, keeping my promise! What's for dinner?"

I was loving this. The poor man hadn't been anything but a perfect gentleman—a fine one at that—and here I was torturing him.

For the first time, I wondered if he was dating someone, if he was there alone. He didn't seem like the type of guy to pursue one or more girls when he already had one, but one never knew.

"Jessica? You got the call? This early?"

He impressed me again.

"Actually, there was a message waiting for me yesterday, when I got home. I called back and accepted their offer. I'll have a small role in the play, as the best friend of Melanie, the daughter of Diana's character. The exciting part is that I'll also be the understudy for the role of Melanie. Vivian Holmes is the lead actress in that role."

The normalcy returned to his voice.

"Congratulations! We need to meet for lunch."

"What time and where?"

"Want me to pick you up?"

"Sure. I'm in a campus dorm on Cliff Street."

We agreed to dine at a popular Chinese spot in the Village.

Five hours later, at a table filled with wonton soup, sesame chicken and shrimp with lobster sauce, we got to know each other better.

"You look pretty young," I told him as I sipped my tea with honey. "How did you get a reporting position at the *Times* so early in your career?"

He smiled modestly.

"I interned there. Worked hard in school. Howard and Columbia. It paid off. From the weight of your audition yesterday, looks like you know something about that."

I turned my head to the side and gave him that "Now you know better" look.

"Don't try to steer the conversation away from yourself through flattery," I said. "I know you're trained to do that, but I want to know more about you."

He chewed the bite of food he'd just popped into his mouth.

"Whatever you'd like," he said.

"You know that's plagiarism."

"What?"

"Eddie Murphy's *Coming to America,*" I said. "That's where that line came from."

"Oh, so you're an actress *and* a movie buff?"

"Always have been," I said, between bites. "Welcome to my world."

"Whatever you'd like."

We laughed. I was having fun with all of this posturing, but I really was curious. I tried another avenue.

"How'd you get interested in journalism?"

"My high school English teacher in Indianapolis realized that I could write well and encouraged me to enter some of my essays into several statewide writing contests," Quentin said. "One of the prizes was a weeklong summer writing camp that exposed me and the other students to a variety of careers for writers, from journalism to TV sitcoms. Journalism stuck and I joined the school newspaper the following year. Once you get bitten by the bug, it's hard to let go."

I could relate.

"That's how I feel about acting. I'm a totally different person when I'm onstage, in character."

"What do you think it's going to be like, working with Diana? You know she has a reputation—"

I thought about her lukewarm greeting the first time I auditioned. I wondered what her reaction would be to the understudy news.

I looked at Quentin. If anyone could make me sing like

a canary, it would probably be him. His neat dreadlocks nicely complemented his mellow brown complexion, and his bright smile exuded charm and confidence.

Those broad shoulders, long legs and massive hands seemed more suited for caressing a professional-quality football rather than scribbling furiously into a notepad with a pen.

"I don't know," I said thoughtfully. "You've seen her onstage. She has enormous talent. I'm really looking forward to working with her."

I pulled my cell phone from my purse and glanced at the time.

"Gotta be somewhere?" he asked.

I shook my head no.

"Not really. I'm expecting a call from my parents about a trip home this weekend. Just wanted to make sure I had my ringer on."

"Good," he said. "'Cause I still don't know much about you."

I leaned back in the seat and began the spiel, conveniently leaving out details about my adoption or my long-term search for my birth mother.

"Let's see. I grew up in Owings Mill, a suburb of Baltimore. When I was about seven, I saw Diana Edmonds in a musical and I was hooked on the possibility of someday being able to perform on a grand stage."

I shook my head. The memory of that young-girl desire was still fresh and thrilling. I couldn't believe I was standing on the threshold of making it a reality.

"I did the dance and voice lessons, and even a youth

drama camp," I said. "I got accepted into the Baltimore School of the Arts and learned from some of the most talented people on the East Coast. Those years transformed me from a dreamer into an artist. The training there helped me land a partial scholarship to NYU."

"Any brothers and sisters?"

"A sister, ten years older, who's married and has an infant son," I said. "You?"

"I'm the youngest of three boys," said Quentin. "My poor mother had us back-to-back."

"Ah, she's the queen of the castle, for sure," I said. "So what is it that you like about writing? What draws you to it?"

"Look, who's interviewing who?" He raised an eyebrow, then considered the question.

"What draws me? Hmm. I guess as a reporter, it's having the opportunity to see into another person's soul and helping readers understand that even though we're all different, at the core of our humanity, we're really the same."

I chewed on a spring roll. What would he reveal to readers in the magazine article he was preparing on the *Then Sings My Soul* cast? Could he see similarities between Diana and me?

He must have read my mind. Quentin reclined in his seat and stared into space.

"I want to capture the essence of who you guys are, each of you, outside of your particular character. I mean, most people come to the theater or go to a movie to escape, to get outside of themselves for a few hours. But I want to know how you transform yourself into Melanie's best friend, or for that matter, Melanie, and make her a believable character. How does Diana leave herself in the dressing room and become Marian? If I can effectively answer those questions for readers, or make them feel as if they're in the room with me during the interview, then I'll be giving them a broader perspective of what it means to act, and the value of acting excellence. Tell me, what draws you to this art form?"

I leaned forward and rested my elbows on the table.

"I can't say that I chose acting," I said. "I really feel like it chose me. To paraphrase your quote, acting feeds my soul. I can't *not* do it. It's part of who I am. When I'm onstage, it's as if I'm drinking in sunshine or joy, or some combination of that."

"Get ready," Quentin said and took a sip of his drink. "You're starting at the top. Some of the secret doors in this industry will be opening for you soon."

"Secret doors?"

"The A-list parties and behind-the-scenes deals worked out for premiere roles," he said. "Diana has keys, so don't worry, you're on your way. She'll guide you through the process."

Quentin leaned forward and grabbed my hands, which were resting on the table.

"I'm happy to know you! Let me touch greatness," he said.

I smirked, but inside, I was a puddle of emotions. If only he knew. Knowing him was making my day.

Chapter 7

Quentin was becoming as much a fixture on the set of *Then Sings My Soul* as the cast.

Sometimes he pulled out his pad and jotted notes or whipped out his digital recorder to capture comments from someone involved with the production. But many days, he just lingered around, watching the rehearsals, the backstage interactions and the directors' near breakdowns when any little thing didn't unfold as they desired.

It was an easy way for me to watch him, too. I liked his style. He was cool, yet not arrogant. Smart but not pompous. Funny but not silly. And I wasn't the only member of the cast noticing.

"He's looking at you, too, you know," Vivian whispered to me one day as I sat eating a peach and gazing at him while he interviewed a dancer.

I gasped. "Am I that obvious?"

She laughed.

"Well, just a little. But it's mutual," she said. "He's trying to conceal his interest, too. I say go for it. I've heard nothing but good things about him."

She leaned against the wall behind the round folding table at which I sat and crossed her arms. We had become close, and even though she was a Tony-winning actress, Vivian had an easygoing personality.

I turned toward her.

"Heard?"

She shook her head in dismay.

"I have so much to teach you. He works for the *New York Times*, Jess. He's a minor celebrity. People talk."

I looked at Quentin, who seemed to be ignoring the dreamy-eyed look the petite dancer was giving him as he lobbed questions at her.

"What's the word on the street?"

"He seems to be a good guy. Hard worker. From a close-knit family," Vivian said. "Had a serious girlfriend at Columbia, but they broke up about a year ago."

My heart skipped a beat. So there was someone. At least there had been. It made sense that a guy like him would at least be dating.

"Has he asked you out yet?" Vivian asked.

I looked at her and raised an eyebrow. If anyone else had asked, I would have rendered my ready smart-aleck reply. But Viv was my girl.

"We've actually had lunch, if that counts. But dating someone featured in the story you're writing could be a conflict of interest. He's treading lightly."

Vivian nodded.

"Told you he was smart. But don't let him get away," she said. "Diana's story isn't worth all that, you know?"

She strolled away, humming the song she'd be singing onstage for the first time in a few minutes.

I rose to dump the remains of my snack in the trash when I heard the crash.

Everyone paused.

Diana came storming out of her dressing room, with her assistant trailing her. The girl looked terrified.

"I'm so sorry, Ms. Edmonds. I can order you something else."

"There's no time, you little twit," Diana spewed. "I asked for a specific tea, to prepare my vocal chords, and you come back here with some green tea brand that you probably picked up at your neighborhood Wal-Mart.

"Don't you know that I'm a professional? How do you think I got here? By doing what the average Joe does? If money was the issue, I could have fronted you the cab or train fare to get to the specialty store." Diana was still yelling. "Don't you ever come in here again trying to pass off something fake as the thing I've asked for!"

She put her hands on her hips and glared at Christina.

Then it hit her. She had given a full performance in front of everyone, including Quentin.

As she surveyed the crowd, most of them lowered their eyes. The only ones who dared glare back were Vivian and Quentin. When she turned toward me, I decided to do the same, to live in truth.

That was foolish. I wasn't her costar or a *New York Times* reporter. I became a fresh target.

"Who are you looking at so self-righteously, Ms. Drake? You ain't nothing, just a little understudy hick who thinks you can use me to get what you need and then move on, just like everyone does. Stop trying to play my biggest fan. I don't fall for that anymore and I don't let anybody use me. I got mine, you get yours."

She stalked back to her dressing room and slammed the door. Somehow Palmer Jordan had learned about the commotion and came trotting toward the break area backstage.

He was thirty seconds too late, or he would have seen my public scolding.

Determined not to cry in front of everyone, I turned away and began walking toward one of the exits. I wasn't planning to leave; I needed to compose myself privately.

Vivian called out to me but I waved without turning toward her.

"I'm all right," I said, trying to control the tremble in my voice. "Just going to grab a little fresh air."

Once outside, I leaned against the brick building and looked toward the sky.

Before I could get my bearings, a body leaned next to me.

"Talk about a performance."

I looked to the right, into Quentin's deep brown eyes.

"Talk about humiliation," I responded.

"She made a fool of herself, not of you. You okay?"

I nodded.

"I just needed to gather my thoughts and get away from all those curious eyes, taking it all in."

I laughed out loud.

"What?" Quentin asked.

"The best part of all of this is you being there," I said. "She's going to be mortified that her beloved *New York Times* reporter saw her outburst."

"Beloved?"

"Trust me, her beloved."

Quentin leaned against the wall and looked upward, in the direction I was gazing. His shoulder touched mine, but he didn't move. A smile coursed through my body.

The moment was stolen before I could enjoy it. Palmer Jordan's assistant poked her head out of the door. I prayed that she wouldn't go back and report seeing me and Quentin standing there, all cozy.

"We're about to start again. Palmer wants you in position."

I stood up straight and moved away from Quentin.

"I'm on my way," I told her.

I turned to bid Quentin goodbye, but he grabbed my forearms and pulled me toward him. Before I could speak, his lips had captured mine. The deep, wet kiss left my insides feeling like Jell-O.

Reluctantly, I pushed him away. I touched my lips with the back of my hand. He turned his head away and stepped back.

"Sorry," he said huskily. "Couldn't help it."

I didn't know what to say. I looked at him, wanting to feel his lips on mine again, but I tried to suppress that thought. My boss was waiting inside for me; I had to go.

"Don't be sorry," I said softly as I trotted toward the entrance. When I reached the door and pulled it open, I paused before going inside, wanting to lighten the mood.

"I hope that was 'off-the-record,' Mr. *Times* reporter."

He shoved his hands into his pockets and turned to walk down the alley.

"Maybe it was, maybe it wasn't, Ms. Drake," he called out before turning the corner at the end of the block. "I'm still writing the story."

Chapter 8

Thank God it was Friday. So much had happened during the week that I planned to enter my apartment tonight and stay there until the alarm clock jolted me awake Monday morning. It had felt strange coming into a place I could call my own just a day before graduation and officially moving off campus, but I had quickly grown accustomed to the privacy.

I set the small pizza I had picked up from the corner restaurant on my coffee table and trotted to my bedroom to slip into a T-shirt and sweats. I pressed the speakerphone mode on my cell, which was the only phone I used, and while I changed, I listened to the three voice mails awaiting me.

One was from Quentin, whom I had finally given my number a few days ago.

"It's me," he said. "About today, I— Just call me, as soon as you can."

Hearing his voice made my face grow warm at the thought

of his tenderness that afternoon. I hoped he didn't regret it too much. I didn't at all.

The two other messages were from Diana, and one had apparently been left while I rode the train home to Brooklyn.

"Jessica? Jessica, please call me. I don't know what got into me today. Please call me so I can make this up to you. I wasn't my usual self. Call my cell. I never give this number out, but you're special to me. It's 555-2229."

She didn't leave her name, but I'm sure she was convinced that wasn't necessary. How could I not know it was her?

I rolled my eyes. So now I was special to her. Maybe she had a conscience after all. It was more likely, though, that her publicist had advised her to make things right, and fast.

Her second message made me pause, with one pant leg on and the other dangling at my ankle.

"Jessica, it's me again. It is 5:42, according to my driver. I've obtained your address and I'm on my way to see you. I'd like to apologize in person and take you to dinner. Tonight. Please. I hope you get this message so we won't be waiting long. See you shortly."

I looked at my alarm clock. The neon lights glared 6:10 p.m. Assuming that Ms. Thing was calling from the city and had to fight traffic, she'd be here in another twenty minutes.

I started to panic, then I got indignant. Who was she to assume that I'd be home on a Friday night? Or, that I would make time for her despite the short notice?

On the other hand, here was my chance to sit down with Diana Edmonds and see whether this world-renowned star had any substance. I pulled off the sweats and rummaged through my drawer for a pair of black slacks. The shimmery gold, sleeveless sweater in the back of my closet and pair of black stilettos with ankle straps seemed perfect. I sat on my bed and slid them on.

By the time my doorbell rang, I was curled up on my red faux-suede sofa, reading the recent issue of *Essence.* I turned off my iPod and strolled to the door, with the magazine still in my hand.

Diana had called seconds earlier to let me know that Andre would be escorting me to her car. My indignation rose again. Who was she to think I was so readily available?

"Did you hear me, Jessica? Andre's on his way up, in the elevator."

"I heard you, Diana, it's just that I'm not—sure—"

I hated to make up a lie. I wouldn't even be able to repent, because God would know it was a bold-faced one.

I sighed.

"You really don't have to do this, Diana. Really," I said. "I got your voice-mail message earlier. Your apology is accepted."

Maybe she was doing this more for her than for me. After the way she had treated me today, she didn't deserve my compassion. But if I was sure of nothing else, I had no doubt that God had probably felt the same way about me, on occasion.

"I'll come down when Andre gets here, Diana."

I didn't feel the need to use the formal "Ms. Edmonds" anymore. She had lost a level of respect with me after her performance today.

Andre stood at the door now, waiting for me to accompany him to the car waiting outside. I remembered my scheduled dinner, sitting on the coffee table, and asked him to give me a second while I tucked the box of pizza in my fridge. It would be tomorrow's lunch.

Andre graciously led the way when I was ready. I stepped outside, under the fading sun, to find my neighbors strolling slowly past the black Mercedes with tinted windows that Andre had parked directly under the No Parking sign in front of the brownstone. He opened the passenger door and motioned for me to climb inside.

Before I could settle in my seat and say hello, Diana leaned toward me and embraced me.

"You were great today during rehearsal," she said. "Reminded me of my younger self, when I was first starting out in the business."

I tried to form my lips into a smile. Had her "younger self" told people off on whim, too?

She must have read my thoughts, because her eyes suddenly became somber.

"I am sincerely sorry about my outburst today, Jessica. I was so upset with Christina because it was the third order she got wrong this week. Plus it's that time of the month—"

I looked out the window as Andre sped away from my neighborhood. I must have heard her incorrectly; I know this woman hadn't just mentioned her monthly cycle. I coughed before changing the subject.

"How did you find my address?"

"A friend of a friend got it for me."

I turned to look at her.

"I convinced Casey, Palmer's assistant, to help me," she said.

I sighed. Anything could be bought these days.

"You really didn't have to come all the way here to apologize, Diana," I said. "Your phone call was enough."

A manicured hand fluttered at her chest.

"Oh no. Taking you to dinner was the least I could do after the way I behaved. I am truly sorry. There's really no adequate excuse. I'm taking you to one of my favorite restaurants. You'll love it."

I leaned back into the seat's soft leather and tried to relax. We made small talk on the way to the restaurant about nothing in particular.

"Where are you from originally, Jessica?"

Diana gazed at me intently, awaiting my answer.

"I grew up in Owings Mill, Maryland, just outside of Baltimore."

She nodded.

"I remember Palmer mentioning during your first audition that you attend Baltimore's School for Performing Arts. It has a great reputation. Have you always wanted to act and sing?"

I smiled, calculating whether I should tell her she had been my inspiration since childhood, or if she'd think I was simply trying to flatter her. I decided to tell her the truth and let her decide whether to believe it.

"I've had the acting and singing bug ever since I was seven, when I saw you perform in Baltimore, at what was then the Hippodrome Theater."

Her eyes widened.

"You're joking. What was the production?"

"You were one of the principals in *Azula*."

She smiled at the memory.

"That musical was one of the projects that put me on the map," Diana said. "It was a lot of hard work, but I learned so much from that cast. They were like a family."

I looked at her, wondering why I wasn't having the same experience with *Then Sings My Soul.*

She cast her eyes downward, as if the same thought had crossed her mind.

"Guess it was nothing like what you experienced today, huh?"

I looked out the window again before answering.

"We don't have to keep revisiting that, you know. You've apologized. It's behind us."

I turned to her and smiled.

"I've learned a lot of good things by watching you," I said. "It's been a good experience, overall."

"Thanks, Jessica. You're a good kid. I mean, young woman."

I surveyed her profile and admired the white-gold inset earrings that dangled just above her shoulders. A light dusting of blush covered her smooth, unlined and unblemished cheeks. Her black hair was pulled back into a bun, secured at the nape of her neck with a diamond butterfly hairpin.

She was simply elegant, with a beauty that silenced you, whether you wanted it to or not.

Andre pulled up in front of Maison La Petit, one of New York City's renowned French restaurants. I glanced at myself, wondering if my outfit was appropriate. I had grabbed a shawl on the way out of the door to drape across my shoulders, so I thought I might be okay.

"Don't worry," Diana said. "You look fine. Classy and

elegant. Besides, we'll be dining alone, for the most part. No one's going to ogle your attire."

I relaxed and followed her into the restaurant. I noticed how she elevated her chin slightly and swayed her shoulders back as she walked through the eatery's main floor, past diners who tried not to gasp or stare as she glided past.

The maître d' seated us in a room cordoned off with a blue rope.

When we were settled in our seats, it was my turn to ask questions.

"Where are you from, Diana?"

She shrugged and averted her eyes.

"A little here, a little there." She laughed nervously.

I wasn't sure how to react. The waiter brought white wine for her and the hot tea I had requested.

She gripped her goblet and took a sip.

"I was born in Detroit, but moved around with my parents a lot. I lived in Pennsylvania from the time I was ten, until I came to New York to pursue acting. The rest, as the cliché goes, is history."

Building a rapport with her wasn't going to be easy. She exuded charisma onstage, but clearly had issues with connecting with people on a personal level.

I decided to keep trying; we still had to make it through dinner. Plus, she knew enough about me now to write a script, if she wanted. The one detail she'd been spared was the fact that I was adopted. I wasn't up to the usual "Have you searched for your birth parents?" questions tonight, so I conveniently didn't mention it.

I tried to question her again.

"What part of Pennsylvania are you from? Do you have siblings?"

Diana looked slightly annoyed.

"Quite nosy, aren't you?"

I tried not to look taken aback. Hadn't she just given me the third degree? This was fair play.

On that note, I sat back in my cushioned chair. Our food arrived, as if on cue.

I tried to switch subjects.

"Any advice for me, since I'm just starting out in this business?"

She took a bite of her seafood and pointed her fork at me.

"Watch your back, especially with that handsome reporter, Quentin Grey," she said. "He might like you, but he loves his career."

Chapter 9

Quentin was the one person I wanted to talk to, though.

Diana's driver had delivered me back to my apartment by 9:00 p.m., and my first move after locking the door was to check my voice mail.

He had called again. I slid my heels off and carried them into the bedroom as I debated whether to call him back tonight or wait until tomorrow. Diana's advice ran through my mind.

She was right: I should be cautious, because Quentin still had a story to write about the cast.

On the other hand, she hadn't experienced the passionate kiss we had shared hours earlier. There was something there. I couldn't leave it hanging on the advice of a diva actress who was so fearful of losing her career that she didn't trust anyone.

I plopped in the center of my bed and tucked my legs beneath me before allowing the callback feature on my phone to dial Quentin's number.

He answered on the second ring and skipped a formal greeting.

"I've been waiting to hear from you. Did I scare you off this afternoon?"

I smiled again at the memory of the kiss.

"You didn't scare me, Mr. Grey. But I was surprised."

"I know. Me, too," he said.

Was he second-guessing himself?

"I wanted to get to know you better before I started groping you."

We both laughed and spent the next three hours chatting about my evening out with Diana, trading stories about life in New York and getting to know each other better.

His favorite ice cream was Rocky Road and he was a Trekkie, a major *Star Trek* fan. He was baptized when he was fourteen, along with his fifteen-year-old brother. His Dad, a minister, did the honors.

"What about your eldest brother?" I asked.

Quentin paused.

"He's twenty-nine now, and we're still praying for him. He comes to church for family occasions and sometimes during the holidays, but he's never given his life to Christ. That's one of my motivations to live right—so that I can be a light to him."

He asked about my sister.

"Charlene is ten years older than me and had been praying for a sibling when I came along," I said. "My parents adopted me when I was about three months old."

I knew he was going to ask the dreaded questions, but surprisingly, I didn't mind.

"Was that hard, not knowing who gave birth to you?" he said. "Have you ever thought about finding your birth mother?"

"Yes, to both questions," I said. "My adoption wasn't kept a secret. Our church family and people throughout the community knew about it, so my parents told me as soon as they thought I could understand, when I was six.

"But when I turned thirteen, those crazy hormones took over. I loved my parents, but I was angry about being given away. I wanted answers from the one person I thought would have them. I didn't have her name or any personal information about her, but I prayed everyday that God would lead me to her. Hasn't happened yet."

I don't know why I was pouring out my heart, but it was cathartic.

"Did you ever find her?"

"Nope," I said. "And eventually, I stopped looking. My parents were uncomfortable with it and I had no real leads. All I know is that I was born in Delaware, near Wilmington, and that my mother was in her late teens when she had me."

"Did you see the birth certificate?"

"My parents have kept it filed away, like it's top-secret property. This has been such a sensitive subject for them that I never asked."

His silence made me wonder whether he was trying to figure out how to end this call. He wasn't.

"You know I'm a reporter, and I've done some investigative work," he said. "If you want, I can help with your search."

Now it was my turn to ponder in silence. Was it worth angering my parents to have these lingering questions answered? Or, did they even have to know I was looking?

"Maybe I'll take you up on that offer," I said. "Let me give it some thought."

"Do that," he said, then lowered his voice. "While you're figuring that out, care to join me for a movie tomorrow night?"

I thought about Diana's warning and my plans to stay in all weekend. I really needed the rest so I could get up to speed on Vivian's lines. As her understudy, I needed to know them as well as she did. He heard the hesitancy.

"Don't worry about it," he said quickly, sounding embarrassed.

"No, no, it's not you," I responded. "It's just that, between the drama on the set of the musical drama and just plain being tired, I'm not sure this is the best weekend to get together."

I decided to be honest with him.

"I do want to see you though, to get to know you better," I said softly.

"The feeling is mutual," he said in that husky voice I had encountered earlier today. "And if you're worried about my magazine article being a conflict, that's pretty much wrapped up. A photographer will accompany me to the set next Tuesday for a group shot of the cast, I'll do a final interview with Diana and with Palmer and then I'll turn the piece in for editing."

"Am I in it?"

"Possibly." He was teasing me.

I decided to flirt a little.

"I'll give you another kiss if you tell me."

"You didn't kiss me—I did all the work," he said. "But I'm not complaining."

Neither am I, I thought. *Neither am I.*

Chapter 10

Diana supposedly made peace with me on Friday, but by Monday morning, her resentment of the entire cast, which included me, apparently had resurfaced.

She ignored me when I greeted her on the way to the cast dressing room and barely raised her eyes during the first run-through of scenes with Vivian and Griffin, the lead male actor.

This was a problem, given that the *New York Times* photographer would be coming the next day to take candid shots while we rehearsed and a group photo for the cover of the Sunday magazine.

Palmer called all of us together soon after we arrived Tuesday morning and lectured us.

"It's normal for there to be tension during a production of this weight, but it's time to put this behind us," he said.

We sat in the audience, close to the stage, where he stood projecting his voice.

"We have to stay focused on what we're here to accomplish," he said. "*Then Sings My Soul* is a story of faith, redemption and forgiveness. Think about that today, people, as you're performing your job, whether it's acting, singing in the chorus or making sure the sound functions properly. Our goal should be to unite to create something excellent. We have to be on the same page!"

He looked toward Diana, who stood just offstage, behind the curtain.

"That goes for all of us, from the lead actor to those with the least dialogue. We must be one."

Palmer's effort had rallied the troops. The rehearsal was one of the best yet, and Quentin came over to me during a break and said his colleague had gotten some great photos.

Just before lunch, the cast put on costumes and formed three rows, to pose for the magazine cover shot. Diana was front and center; I stood two places to her left, next to Vivian.

Diana smiled serenely for the camera, as if doing so would heal the rifts she had caused on the set last week. I wondered if Quentin had put any of that in the story, but I had decided not to ask.

When the photo shoot was over, Palmer was so pleased everything had gone well that he ended rehearsal early.

I joined Vivian and several other cast members for a late lunch at a bistro on Forty-first Street. Afterward, I was headed north, toward the nearest metro stop, when I remembered that I had left my script, with notes about scene positions and postures, in my dressing room locker.

I decided to trot over and pick it up before going home to do laundry.

When I entered the theater, the stage was dark and all was quiet. I turned the corner leading to the dressing rooms and found Diana's door slightly ajar. She stood in the center of the room, rehearsing the song she would sing in the show's grand finale.

I waited just out of view and watched her inhale, close her eyes and sing from the depths of her being. It was as if she believed the words she uttered could heal every hurting heart in the audience. I had no doubt they would. Chills ran through me as I listened.

When she finished, I stepped into view and applauded. She was startled at first, but then seemed miffed.

"Were you eavesdropping?"

I slowly entered and stood in the entrance.

"Your door was open. I couldn't help but hear you. It was beautiful. Why are you still here?"

She cocked her head to the side.

"The only thing separating me from any other forty-something actress with a pretty face and a decent voice is excellence. I can't rest on my laurels. Even if rehearsal ends early at a director's insistence, I can still train by myself for several more hours."

She turned away from me and sat in front of her mirror to remove the makeup she had worn for the photo shoot.

I couldn't figure out why she was being distant, but I wanted to know. I wanted to like her, to understand her better.

Why, I wasn't sure. But I knew there was a lot I could learn from her, and I knew that she needed a friend.

I walked over to the seat across from where she sat and asked to join her.

"Look, Jessica," Diana said, "I don't have anything to give you. No secrets to share and no favors to call in so you can be the next big star, okay? What you see is what you get. Take it or leave it."

That sounded like an ultimatum she had issued many times before, sometimes to her detriment.

I decided to try anyway.

"I don't want to use you, Diana, but I do have a lot to learn. You seem like a really nice person when we talk privately, but once we get on this set—another side of you comes out. I hope I'm not offending you. I'm just wondering if there's something I can do to help."

Diana smoothed moisturizer on her now-clean face and turned toward me. Without all of the cosmetics, she looked like a younger, almost innocent version of her lovely self.

"I'm sorry, Jessica. I'm a little stressed out, that's all," she said and sighed. "Quentin Grey and his photographer hung around after everyone left so he could get a few final details for the article. I got rattled when he started asking about things I don't necessarily want to revisit."

I leaned forward.

"Was he being rude?"

She shook her head and her eyes softened.

"I know you like him, Jessica. No, he wasn't rude or forceful at all," she said. "It's just that he's an investigative reporter, and he wants to revisit my past to add another dimension to the story. But I'm not one of Oprah's guests—I'm not ready to share my entire life with the world. I give one hundred and ten percent of myself on the stage. That should be enough."

I remained silent, not wanting her to think that Quentin had sent me to twist her arm for more details.

She picked up her comb and raked it through her thick black mane of hair. "People think I have a weave, but this is really all mine."

I smiled.

"I get that a lot, too," I said. "I couldn't possibly have this much thick hair, flowing to my waist, unless I bought it. Mine's real, too."

She laid the comb on the table and turned toward me.

"Quentin wants to know who groomed me for stardom. He thinks it was my family, but I wasn't as lucky as you," she said.

"What I don't want printed in the paper is the fact that I've been estranged from my family for a long time. My father and mother lost custody of me when I was eight. They were abusing drugs and neglected me to get money however and whenever they could. We lived in one place just long enough for them to rack up debts they couldn't pay, forcing us to move."

I tried to remain expressionless, but I was sure shock was registered all over my face.

"Remember me telling you I settled in Pennsylvania? That was the last place we moved. Mama and Daddy went out one night doing whatever it was they did in the evenings and left the TV to babysit me. This time though, they never came back. They never came back."

She seemed far away, lost in the memory of it all.

"What happened to you?" I asked.

She looked at herself in the mirror.

"Foster care. I wound up in the home of the Baxters.

They raised me from the time I was ten until I graduated from high school. They gave me a warm bed and hot meals, but very little else in the way of affection.

"Mama Baxter always had a problem with the fact that my looks won me more attention than my four foster sisters," Diana said, speaking as if she were recounting nothing more significant than the days of the week. "She told me I was vain for wanting to wear makeup and be the 'center of the universe' by becoming an actress."

I could see the wheel of memories turning in Diana's mind as she spoke in a near whisper. She was talking to me, but really to herself, as if releasing this story that she'd held in for so long would free her from the weight of carrying it.

"I was the middle child in the family, but most people said I was the most striking," she said. "Mama didn't know what to do with a pretty girl. And I never knew what to do with my longing to be loved. Until I took center stage in the tenth-grade play. That's when I discovered my place on this earth, where I could be adored.

"Despite my foster parents' objections, I participated in every school production I could and applied to university theater programs across the country, praying that I would get a scholarship."

"Did you?" I asked.

She shook her head no.

"My grades weren't up to par. But I didn't let that stop me. I decided to come to New York and get a job while pursuing a career in acting."

She hesitated, then rose from her seat, folded her arms and turned her back to me.

"I came to New York, found work at the makeup counter in Macy's and to be honest, made some really stupid choices.

"My foster parents were furious when I went home for a visit and they found out. I was nineteen by that time and technically no longer in their legal care, so they told me to go. But I wound up needing their help. They let me stay just long enough to make it through a tough situation.

"I came back to New York, determined to succeed and show them just how wrong they were about who I was," Diana said.

She faced me again and plopped in her seat. She wiped the single tear that trickled from her eye with a forefinger.

"While I was here working, something terrible happened back in Pennsylvania," she said. "I blamed them and they blamed me, and I decided to never go back. I threw myself into acting to forget about everything."

"Did it work?" I asked.

"Let's see, it's more than twenty years later and I'm still crying about it," she said. "Guess not, kid."

I wanted to wrap her in a hug, but I was afraid that might make her angry. Instead, I leaned over to touch her arm. Surprisingly, she didn't push me away.

"Whatever happened in Pennsylvania, that's what you don't want Quentin to know?"

"Some things are meant to be kept secret, Jessica. This is my one thing."

I sighed and sat back.

"You're right that Quentin and I are pretty good friends, Diana, but I have purposely not asked him about the story he is writing on the musical and on the cast, to keep both of us operating in integrity.

"You're also right that he's a good reporter," I said. "I don't know everyone he's spoken to. If I were you, I'd just ask him about it."

She looked at me incredulously.

"And give him a reason to go digging? You're so naïve, Jessica. You'll learn," Diana said. "Besides, I did let my guard down and tell him I was raised by foster parents in a community near Harrisburg. I'm hoping he'll consider that enough history for the story and move on."

I didn't have any other suggestions for her, but I knew who did.

"Can I pray with you?"

"No thanks," she said quickly. "If you want to pray for me on your own time, do whatever. But that's not my style."

"Do you believe in God?"

"Of course I do, Jessica. I'm just not comfortable praying to Him all up in the middle of the day," she said in exasperation. "That's not me."

I watched as she slipped into a mint-green leisure jogging suit and sneakers. She called Andre and told him he could bring the car; she was ready to be taken home.

When she was done, she walked me to her dressing room door and held it open for me.

"Thank you for listening, Jessica. I can't force you to keep this conversation just between us, but I'm asking you to, if you don't mind."

I hugged her lightly.

"Consider it done."

I wondered, however, if it was too late. She may have told Quentin enough to set him off on an unauthorized search.

Chapter 11

The roses waiting for me in my dressing room had the desired effect. Quentin couldn't attend tonight's premiere of *Then Sings My Soul* because he was away on assignment, but he didn't need to worry. I was smitten.

I hadn't asked questions about the story he had left town to report, maybe because I was afraid to know, in case it involved some research on Diana.

His article on the musical had been turned in and edited, he said, but it wouldn't appear in the *New York Times* Sunday magazine until three days after opening night.

Quentin and I had gone out to dinner twice in the week before he left for the assignment and before I became consumed with final rehearsals.

Mom, Daddy, Charlene, my brother-in-law, Greg, and my nephew, Todd, arrived two days before opening night. I had secured prime seats for them, to make sure they didn't miss a thing.

Tonight, the blinding stage lights prevented me from looking into the audience and seeing anyone, but as I sang with the chorus in most scenes and portrayed the best friend of Melanie in a few others, I could feel their love.

The night had been magical. Diana sang each of her numbers, and especially the tear-jerker finale, with a gusto that even stunned Palmer. He stood behind the curtain at one point with his hands at his hips, shaking his head in awe.

Diana might indeed be a diva, but she proved tonight that she was worthy of the title. After her third encore, the crowd finally dissipated.

Without going into details, I had shared with my mother a few weeks earlier that Diana and I had somehow become friends, and that it appeared I was one of very few. When Mom and the rest of my family came backstage, they had flowers for me and for Diana.

Not surprisingly, Diana's dressing room was full of fragrant blooms she had received from fans, colleagues and media personnel throughout New York and the nation. But I believed her when she grasped my mother tightly and told her that these red roses meant the most.

I looked at the two of them and smiled. They were about the same age and both were about five feet nine inches, just an inch shorter than me. My mother's smooth ebony skin contrasted deeply with Diana's, and my own, honey complexions. But Mom wore her complexion with the confidence of a woman grounded in her faith and in her beauty. I loved that about her.

It was a confidence that Diana seemed to lack, because based on what she had shared with me, her inner and outer beauty had never been fully valued. I was glad to see her soaking in some of the affection my family extended.

After Palmer and Diana led the cast in a champagne toast to celebrate tonight's successful debut, everyone left with their respective guests to continue celebrating elsewhere. I had reserved a private room for my family and friends from NYU at B. Smith's on Forty-sixth Street.

Once we were seated, with me at the head of the table to give me a full view of my guests, Daddy, who was seated to my right, rose and shushed everyone by clinking his fork against the side of his water goblet.

"I just want to thank everyone for coming out tonight to support Jessica in her first Broadway performance," he said in his booming voice. He'd never lost his native North Carolina accent, and I still found it endearing. "It's a blessing to know that she has the support of such wonderful friends. And I have to tell you, it was truly humbling for me to see my baby girl up there on that stage, working with some of the best actors and actresses in this country."

Daddy paused and looked at me as his bottom lip began to quiver.

"I remember it as if it were just yesterday, when she came home from school one afternoon and declared that someday she was going to perform on a big stage, under bright lights, and make everyone in the audience happy," he said. "God must have given her that vision. Tonight it became her reality. Congratulations, Jess. I love you."

I rose and hugged Daddy's neck tightly, as tears flowed from my eyes. When I sat down to dab my cheeks with my napkin, I looked around and realized everyone else at the table was doing the same.

I had a speech, too, but Daddy's was enough for now. Before we left for the evening, though, I wanted to thank everyone for their support and prayers. I had been under the spotlight this evening, but if it weren't for the support of most everyone in the room, I wouldn't have persevered.

Just as the first course ended, my purse, which I had placed under the table next to my feet, vibrated when my phone began silently ringing. I knew it was rude but I was curious to see who was calling.

I leaned down quickly and put the purse on my lap. By the time I had rummaged through it and reached my cell, the call had been sent to voice mail. My heart skipped a beat, though, when I saw Quentin's number lingering on the screen.

Wherever he was working, he was with me in spirit.

My mom gave me a questioning glance when she saw a smile cross my face as I put the phone away.

"I can't wait for you to meet Quentin, Mom," I said softly. "You're going to like him."

She gave me a worried look and then tried to smile. She patted my hand.

"We'll see, Jess. Let's talk about it tomorrow morning."

That odd exchange piqued my curiosity. Tomorrow seemed so far away. I didn't think I could wait, but the thrill of tonight's accomplishment soon made me forget anything but the ongoing celebration.

Chapter 12

By the time Mom, Daddy and I reached my apartment in Brooklyn, it was nearly 1:00 a.m. I knew they were tired, but Mom's comment at dinner still nagged me. Unless she explained, I would toss and turn all night.

Since my place was tiny, Charlene, Greg and the baby were staying in a nearby hotel.

Daddy went to my bedroom, which I had insisted they use, and took off his shoes. Mom was headed in that direction when I lightly touched her shoulder.

"Mom, I know it's late and you're worn-out, but I just have to ask you. What were you alluding to when I mentioned Quentin earlier tonight? Sounded as if something has gone on that I don't know about."

She looked at me and was about to speak, but hesitated. She looked toward the bedroom, as if she wanted Daddy to come out and rescue her.

"Let's talk tomorrow, Jess, okay?" She hugged me tightly. "I'm so proud of you and tonight was so special. My comment was out of line. Let's just regroup in the morning, okay?"

I wanted to protest, but I wasn't going to force her hand. I nodded.

"Okay, Mom. Whatever you want."

She could see that I was disappointed, but seemed relieved to have convinced me to skip a round of questioning tonight. She kissed my cheek.

"We'll talk in the morning, honey, after everyone's had a chance to rest. Go on and get some sleep. Dream sweet dreams about what a joy tonight was."

I couldn't help but smile. Mom knew just how to soothe my nerves. It worked—almost.

I curled up on my sofa with a blanket below and on top of me and thanked God for everything—tonight's performance, my parents' love, the talent to act and sing.

Then I closed my eyes and rested, wondering what daylight would bring.

Chapter 13

The answers came swiftly, after breakfast.

Mom had risen with the sun and prepared pancakes, bacon, eggs and hot coffee. We ate heartily, and I answered her and Daddy's numerous questions about the musical and about various members of the cast. They soaked in every detail, as if doing so would make them part of the experience.

Once the leisurely meal ended, the dishes were washed and my cozy kitchen area was tidy, we moved to the living room to wait for my sister and her family to join us. We were eager for them to arrive, because Charlene had agreed to bring today's New York papers so we could read reviews of *Then Sings My Soul*'s opening night.

I had suggested we spend the day shopping, but I wasn't surprised when my parents turned me down. Years of sacrificing their wants and even some of their needs to put two daughters through expensive colleges had trained them to be content with little.

For them, shopping would have been a chore. I had discovered that as a teen and had finally concluded that I was indeed adopted, because I would never understand. I longed to shop as much as I craved chocolate.

Daddy was reaching for the TV remote control and Mom had picked up a book when I realized I'd have my parents to myself for only another thirty minutes. I needed an explanation from Mom and now was the time to get it.

I cleared my throat as Daddy searched for ESPN.

"Mom, picking up where we left off last night—"

Before I could complete the sentence, Daddy turned off the television and sat up straight. Mom put down her book and moved closer to him. He took her hand.

My heart beat faster. I didn't know what was up, but something was.

They looked at each other and Mom nodded at Daddy, giving him permission to begin.

"Your friend Quentin the one who sent the roses?" Daddy seemed unusually nervous. I gripped the sides of the sofa chair and waited. "It just so happens that we've already met him. He came to Owings Mill last week."

"What?" I felt a mixture of anger and confusion. Why were they just telling me this now?

"You met Quentin? How? Why? What's going on?"

Daddy held up a hand to shush me.

"Calm down, Jess," he said.

"This is why I didn't want to get into this last night," Mom said, looking at me sympathetically.

I pursed my lips together and waited.

Daddy looked at Mom for reassurance and began again.

"We got a call from the principal of your high school three weeks ago, informing us that a *New York Times* reporter had interviewed him about the Baltimore School for the Arts and wanted to contact us, since you were an alumna and about to appear on Broadway.

"We told Mr. Ludlow to give the reporter our names and phone number and two days later, Quentin Grey called to request a formal interview," Daddy said.

"We agreed that he could come to the house and when we met him, your Mom and I were impressed by his questions and his demeanor. He told us right away that he knew you and that you were a friend of his, but he said you didn't know he was conducting this interview to include in the article—it would be a surprise."

Mom picked up for him.

"We told him about your childhood dreams of stardom, how hard you worked to succeed and how proud we were to be chosen as your parents."

I sat up straighter.

"You guys told him I was adopted?"

"Actually," Mom said, "Quentin said you had told him. We figured if you had shared that information, it was okay for us to talk about it."

Now I understood how families unknowingly betrayed their famous relatives. I'd have to give my parents and sister the speech about not commenting every time they were approached by a friendly reporter.

"What did you tell him?" I asked.

They traded looks and Mom sighed.

"That's what we needed to talk to you about," Daddy said.

"We told him how we got you when you were almost three months old. We told him how after your mom gave birth to Charlene, we had been unable to have more children. Your arrival was a joy to our entire family and to the congregation at our church.

"He started asking where you were born and if we knew anything about your birth mother," Daddy continued. "He wanted to know your birth date and which agency we had used to find you."

"Those are things we haven't even talked with you about," Mom said. "The conversation got heated and we asked him to leave. Before he did, however, he said has reason to believe he knows who gave birth to you."

I gasped and put my hand to my mouth. Time seemed to stop.

"What did you say?" I whispered.

Mom's eyes filled with tears.

"Quentin said he thinks he knows," she said. "After talking to you, he decided to try on your behalf to find some answers that you seemed to want. I accused him of using you to try to boost his career with a sensational story. He didn't tell me I was wrong."

I sat back in the chair and folded my arms, trying to stay calm amid the questions assaulting my brain and the anger choking my heart.

Was Quentin playing me for a fool? What had he learned about me that my parents weren't willing to reveal all these years? Their efforts to control and conceal the truth were going to end. Today. Turning the conversation to Quentin's motives wasn't going to work. I would deal with him later.

"What did you tell him?" I asked them.

Daddy shook his head.

"Nothing, really. The only thing he got out of us was that we adopted you when you were less than six months old, your birth date is June 23 and that your mother had been nineteen when she gave birth to you."

"Thanks for telling me her age, after all these years," I said slowly, trying to deflate my growing anger. "Now I want the rest of the story. The truth. All of it."

"We know, Jess, we know," Mom said softly. "We weren't going to leave New York without telling you."

Daddy looked down and seemed to be uttering a prayer. He raised his eyes and cleared his throat.

"Jess, the reason we've always told you that you were a gift from God and that God chose us as your parents is because we truly believe that," he said. "We didn't get you through an adoption agency.

"On Sunday, August 17, when you were about seven weeks old, your Mom and I arrived at Mt. Nebo about two hours before service was scheduled to begin," he said. "I was the head of the trustee board and wanted to make sure the church was cool enough, there was enough bread for communion and that everything was in order for the day. Your sister, Charlene, had spent the night with another girl from church and was scheduled to arrive with Tiffany and her family at 11:00 a.m.

"When we got to the church, we parked out front instead of in the parking lot as usual," he said. "For some reason, I told your mother I wanted to go through the sanctuary that morning instead of one of the side entrances.

"We walked up the steps leading to the church entrance and there you were, wrapped in a pink blanket, tucked deeply in a wicker basket with a note pinned to the inside of the newborn T-shirt you wore."

I leaned forward as if getting closer to my parents would help me comprehend what he was saying. I frowned.

"Are you saying I was abandoned as an infant, in front of the church? Are you saying you made up the few little things you've told me about my background?"

I felt numb. I had to be dreaming.

Mom reached across the small space between us and grasped my hands.

"No, Jess, no," she said in a pleading voice. "Yes, someone left you there, but they also left a can of baby formula in that basket with you. And there was a copy of your birth certificate also pinned to your T-shirt. It listed your birth mother's age, your birth date, your weight, the state in which you were born—Delaware—like we've always told you."

"What about my parents?"

"That's among the information that was missing," Mom said. "Whoever left the birth certificate took a pair of scissors and neatly cut out a lot of important details—both your mother's and father's names, the city and the hospital in Delaware where you were born and the serial number on the birth certificate.

"If we'd been really diligent, we probably could have taken the birth certificate to Delaware and found a complete copy in the vital statistics department," Daddy said. "But to be honest, we didn't want to. We had just enough information to know how old you were and to determine that you'd been born under a doctor's care and were probably healthy."

Mom picked up the explanation.

"We spent the next hour holding you and praying over you. We asked God to give us direction on what to do," she said. "The logical thing would have been to call the police, but we figured anyone who had gone to the trouble of editing your birth certificate so they could send it with you, along with providing a supply of milk and leaving you on the steps of a church, had been intentional in their actions. They knew what they were doing."

Daddy shrugged.

"And to be honest, we had been praying for God to bless us with another child for the longest time. It made sense to us that we would find you, with no strings attached, at a place where we devoted the bulk of our time," he said. "It was selfish, and even wrong, I know. We decided to keep you, and when people began arriving for service, we had agreed to introduce you as our adopted daughter, Jessica Lynn Drake."

This sounded like something out of a soap opera, but Daddy was telling me this was my life. That explained the years of evasiveness. It explained their refusal to give me details about where I was born and who my mother was.

It explained a lot, and yet it opened a whole new level of questions. I was too stunned to ask any of them right now, though. I had to focus on continuing to breathe, to keep my head from exploding.

There was one thing I needed to know, though.

"You gave me the name Jessica," I said. "What name was listed on the birth certificate?"

"That section had been cut out, too," Mom said, "but someone had written *Angel* in cursive ink at the top of the birth certificate. And that's what you were to us, Jess, an angel."

Chapter 14

I wanted my big break, but not at the expense of my friend. Yet, Palmer Jordan said I had heard him correctly: Tonight would be my debut in the role of Melanie.

Hours later, I stood center stage in the Imperial Theater, facing Diana and reciting the words of a forlorn daughter.

"What kind of mother sends her child away just because life gets hard? If Daddy didn't leave you enough money, go get a job! Better yet, we can both get jobs. I'm sixteen. Why are you doing this? Do you even love me anymore?"

Diana, in the role of Marian, turned her back to me and walked toward the edge of the stage.

"The truth is, I don't even know if I love myself. I don't even know who I am."

She turned toward me with a sorrowful look.

"If I don't love myself how could I possibly love you, Melanie? At least with the kind of love you need? That's why

I'm sending you away. Not to get rid of you, but to give you a better life. Your aunt and uncle are well off, they have other children and they care about you. They're happy to have you. Go spend some time with them. Let me figure things out."

Vicious sobs racked my body and I fell to my knees. I looked longingly toward Marian, who watched me stoically from across the room.

The tears that I shed as I sang were real. The emotion that poured from me into the lyrics was sincere. I purged much of what I had been carrying around by the time that scene ended.

After the song, I looked at Marian one last time.

"Love doesn't have to be perfect, you know?" I said softly. "It just has to—be."

We did three curtain calls that night, and when my name was called, the thunderous applause told me that I had nailed it. So did the kiss that Palmer planted square on my lips.

"This is your night, Jessica Drake," he said.

Everyone showered me with applause, and I soaked in the magical moment.

I emerged from the dressing room and expected to see Quentin. I hadn't talked to him since before he left for his reporting assignment, just before the musical's opening night.

He had continued to call me, but when I never picked up or called him back, he had surmised that my parents had informed me of his visit.

"It's not what you think, Jessica. I can explain. Just call me, please?"

I never responded, and after two weeks he'd finally left me alone.

I guess he hadn't given up, though. I wondered who had told him I was standing in for Vivian tonight.

It didn't matter. As I took in the sight of him, I wanted to go back in time, to the days I trusted him and felt safe in his arms. Whatever I felt, though, I wasn't going to let my emotions overrule wisdom.

For all I knew, Quentin wanted to interview me, to get another great story. We couldn't have a relationship if I was always going to second-guess his motives, so I guess that meant no relationship at all.

He watched me as I watched him.

"You were beyond fabulous tonight," he said and walked toward me. "Whatever you are thinking at this moment, it's wrong."

The closer he came, the more nervous I grew. My heart began to beat faster. I had to keep my cool, to stay focused or just plain mad.

I put my hand on his chest to keep him from invading my personal space. He tried to pull me toward him and I resisted.

"What do you want, Quentin? Don't you have enough information to write a blockbuster story? Now that I've done such a 'fabulous' job tonight, you can probably get it on the front page of the *Times*—'Dazzling understudy was abandoned baby.'"

His eyes widened.

As soon as I uttered the words I wanted to kick myself. I'd just told him more than he already knew. My parents hadn't shared the full story with him. I had landed myself in deeper trouble.

I turned away and sighed.

Quentin began walking toward me again, but stopped.

"Look, Jessica. I don't even know where to begin. Yes, I was doing some investigating on your background, based on your telling me you were adopted. Yes, I went to interview your parents without telling you first. I was wrong for that. But I didn't want them preparing for our meeting too far in advance and hatching a story that sounded good. I was trying to get at the truth."

I spun around.

"Really? For whom, Quentin? For me or for yourself?"

He flinched.

"I deserve that," he said. "To be honest, I don't know. Yes, I'm a dedicated reporter. But I also care deeply about you."

He paused to let those words sink in.

"I knew that I could help you find some answers. I knew your parents would tell you about my visit, but I foolishly thought they wouldn't expose me until I had more answers for you."

I shook my head. He wasn't making sense.

"Quentin, what are you talking about? I just spilled the beans on myself. Didn't your research reveal that most of the answers about my heritage are obscure?"

"They may be obscure, Jessica, but that's what I've been trained to uncover. I think I've found your birth mother."

Chapter 15

An awkward silence filled the space between Quentin and me on the drive to SoHo. Neither of us attempted to erase it.

Quentin took me to a restaurant far from the Theater District with the hope that we'd have some privacy.

The quaint Chinese-food place was nice, and even though it was Thursday, the beginning of the weekend in New York, there wasn't a large crowd.

We sat in a section in the back, in a corner to ourselves.

I was still angry with him, even more than before, because right now it seemed that he had the upper hand.

He had information that I wanted, so he knew I'd agree to accompany him. And I was still worried that he planned to use whatever facts he had uncovered in an explosive article.

"Why are you doing this?" I finally asked, after the waitress had brought us tea and had taken our order.

"What are you talking about, Jessica?"

"You didn't go to the trouble of uncovering whatever information you have just because you and I were dating and you wanted to help me find my birth mother. You went to Maryland to meet my parents as a reporter. Whatever other research you have done was also part of your job."

His silence told me I was correct. I continued.

"So that means you were using me. I trusted you with my private concerns and you took the opportunity to capitalize on them. Diana was right—you might care for me, but I don't stand a chance next to your career."

I spat the words at him.

His eyes widened as if he had been slapped. For several minutes he didn't speak. Then he leaned forward and rested his elbows on the table.

"I deserve that, Jessica, because you are right."

My face remained expressionless, but my heart sank. Part of me was still hoping I had been mistaken.

"We talked about you being adopted and my curiosity got the best of me. Secrets are a challenge for me. I was convinced that the answers to your heritage weren't as hard to find as you thought.

"And I reasoned that since I was working on a profile of the *Then Sings My Soul* cast, this would fit in somehow, especially if you were happy with what I learned," he said.

He reached for my hands and I pulled away.

"I was plain stupid for going to Maryland without telling you. Your parents grew suspicious during our meeting so I didn't get much out of them. The only jewel I found was your birth certificate."

My heart skipped. Had he seen the one my parents described?

"I went to the Maryland Vital Statistics Department and saw a photocopy of a birth certificate, but it listed the Drakes as your parents," he said. "I thought that was odd, but I didn't have time to research the state's laws about adoption and what certificates are kept on file after one has been finalized."

I caught my breath. How had my parents managed to get the birth certificate I'd been using for years, if their story about finding me on the church steps was true? I'd worry about that later. I tried to focus on Quentin's explanation.

"The week that *Then Sings My Soul* debuted, I flew to Pennsylvania."

I looked at him and frowned. He had researched Diana's past, too.

"I met with a woman there who said she was once Diana Edmonds's foster mother."

This time I sat forward.

"What? Have you told Diana this?"

He shook his head quickly. I could tell he wanted to finish his story. Before he could go on, our meals arrived.

We thanked the waitress and he continued.

"Laura Baxter's her name. She's eighty years old but her memory is as sharp as a tack."

Suddenly I wasn't hungry anymore. My hands got clammy.

"Okay, you were snooping around on Diana, too," I said impatiently. "Can you finish my story before you get to hers?"

He looked me in the eyes.

"Jessica, they are one and the same."

"What?" I had asked the question a little too loudly. Other

diners turned our way and peered at us before resuming their meals when they realized the commotion was over.

"What did you just say, Quentin?"

He sighed and reached for my hands again.

This time I slowly put my palms in his.

"Jessica, I believe that Diana Edmonds is your birth mother."

I gripped his fingers as he continued.

"Laura Baxter told me that she and Diana stopped talking years ago, after she did something terrible to Diana.

"Diana had moved to New York, seeking fame and fortune, and returned home a year later with a newborn baby. She had given birth to the infant in Delaware three weeks before her arrival and had come back to Pennsylvania to get help from Mrs. Baxter to care for the girl."

Against my will, tears slid down my face, into my food. Quentin held my hands tighter and looked around, to see if anyone had noticed.

"Want to leave?" he asked softly. "I can finish sharing the details in the car."

I shook my head no. I didn't really care where we were or who saw. I just wanted to hear the truth. I had been waiting years for it.

"Diana took the baby girl to Mrs. Baxter and begged her to care for the child while she returned to New York and earned enough money to get a decent apartment and properly care for the child," Quentin said. "But Mrs. Baxter said she was angry at Diana and had always considered her rebellious."

I remembered what Diana had told me about being resented because of her beauty. The two accounts seemed to be meshing.

"When Diana was gone, Mrs. Baxter decided that the baby needed a better home, one with two parents who weren't caught up in their looks and in entering the sleazy world of acting," Quentin said.

"She waited until Diana had been gone for two weeks and then she told Diana the baby died in her sleep."

I looked up into his eyes again.

Diana had mentioned something tragic happening, something that had led her to cut ties with the Baxters. This made sense.

"It wasn't true? The baby didn't die?"

Quentin hesitated. He rose from his seat and came around the table, to slide in the booth next to me. I wasn't fighting him anymore. I slid over to make room for him, so he could tell me the rest of what he knew.

He took my hands again and spoke softly.

"No, Jessica. The baby didn't die. One weekend, when her husband had taken the other foster children on a camping trip, Mrs. Baxter drove until she was out of Pennsylvania and looked for a safe place to leave the baby.

"She had purchased a large wicker basket and a fresh can of formula. She took the birth certificate Diana had left with her and carefully cut out the identifying information, so that whoever found the baby wouldn't be able to trace the child to her or to Diana."

I shook my head to clear my thoughts. This couldn't be real.

"Somehow she wound up in rural Maryland and by this time, it was early Sunday morning, before dawn. When her eyes grew too heavy for her to drive much farther, she started searching for churches," Quentin said. "She knew parishioners would be going to worship service, and since it was early August and fairly warm, the baby wouldn't be exposed for too long.

"Mrs. Baxter told me she couldn't remember the name of the church where she left the little girl just after 7:00 a.m., but it had steep steps, and from the road, you couldn't see the wicker basket she placed right in front of the door.

"She says she sat a few blocks away and watched, to make sure no stray animals bothered the child. About ninety minutes later, a nice-looking couple arrived. She saw the man climb the steps to open the door and yell to his wife when they found the baby.

"The man and woman embraced," Quentin said and smiled. "They seemed happy to have found the child, according to Mrs. Baxter. And she considered it a sign from God that she was doing the right thing. She hadn't known that it was an African-American church when she placed the baby there. The fact that it was and that this couple seemed willing to help eased her conscience."

I shook my head. I was stunned, but I also realized what this meant for Diana.

"She couldn't have had much of a conscience, though," I protested. "She told Diana that the child she had given birth to died. That was just plain wrong."

Quentin nodded.

"I agree, Jessica. But Mrs. Baxter is beyond right and wrong now. She lives alone and is cared for by a home health-care nurse. Her husband passed away a decade ago and she says her foster children never come to visit. Obviously, Diana wasn't the only one she ran away."

I sat back in my seat and stared at my cold food.

I couldn't believe it. I was Diana Edmonds's daughter. The diva who often couldn't stand to be around me, but at other times reached out to me, was my flesh and blood.

I couldn't believe it.

I remembered that Quentin was there next to me and I looked at him.

"I'm sorry," he said and stroked my cheek. He gazed at me tenderly as if he wanted to say more.

"For what? Helping me find the truth?" I sighed.

"Don't be sorry for that, Quentin. Thanks for your hard work," I said. "The big question is, what are you going to do with this information? And have you told Diana yet?"

"Diana doesn't know yet," he said. "I thought you might want to tell her. And what I'm going to do remains to be seen. I'm praying about that—and about us."

Chapter 16

The reviews the next morning were humbling.

"Superstar in the making." "A new star is born." "Jessica Drake steals the show." "Understudy, Diana look-alike, delivers."

Even the *Baltimore Sun* had run an article, pulled from the Associated Press wire. Their headline read "Hometown girl captures Broadway."

When the flowers began arriving and my phone rang nonstop, I knew my life was changing. I tried to enjoy the moment, but I was distracted by a recurring thought. I had to get to Diana.

"Diana, I need to talk to you. In person. It's important."

She was silent for what seemed like minutes.

"Hello?" I said.

"What's so urgent that it can't wait until we get to the theater?"

"It's private," I said.

I knew I had her. She was always paranoid about the cast or crew overhearing her personal business.

"How soon can you get here?"

Forty minutes later, the doorman of Diana's lavish apartment building in Manhattan sent me up to her twentieth-floor penthouse.

Elsie, the maid she always complained about, seemed startled when she greeted me at the door.

"*The Enquirer* is right—you're a dead ringer for Lady Di," she said before averting her eyes.

Lady Di? This was too much. I sat in Diana's foyer and waited for her to emerge.

My heart was racing and my palms were sweaty. Did I even want to have this conversation with her? Why hadn't I let Quentin do the honors?

I knew that would have been a cop-out. Plus, she was going to be mortified when she learned that he knew everything about her.

Diana strolled in about ten minutes later, wearing orange silk pajamas. Her hair was pulled up in a bun and she wore no makeup.

Seeing her and realizing that I had come from her womb left me breathless. Some of what I was feeling must have shown on my face. She stopped and stared at me.

"Are you okay?"

I looked at her and lost it.

"I'm not dead."

With those words, I crumbled. Tears flowed like lava as I recalled the nights I had lain awake, wondering what my birth mother could be doing. I thought about the regular entries I had made in my teenage diary during my daily subway rides to and from high school.

I reviewed what my parents and Quentin had told me about my early weeks of life and how I had become Jessica Drake. I cried for all that could have been, but may have never been, if I had remained Angel Diana Edmondson.

Diana stood there watching me, with her hand to her throat. She grew pale.

"Is this some kind of joke?"

I shook my head and managed to utter a few words between my tears.

"I'm your daughter, Angel."

She walked over and knelt before me and touched my wet face. But seconds later, she rose to her feet and began backing away.

"How could this be? Is this a cruel joke? Who told you about Angel?"

Anger and fear flashed in her eyes.

My tears began to dry as I saw snatches of the Diana I knew.

"It's okay, Diana. I don't want anything from you. I just wanted to know the truth. Quentin went behind my back after I told him I was adopted and began digging into both of our pasts."

She glared at me and put a hand on her hip.

"Didn't I tell you not to trust him? Don't you know I've been hurt by men I trusted?"

I looked at her curiously.

"How would I know that?" I snapped at her. "What does

anyone know about you, except the things you accidentally let seep out?

"I believe Quentin's account of what happened, though," I said. "You came to New York, got pregnant and then tried to dump me with the foster mother you hated."

She peered at me as if she were noticing me for the first time.

"Stop," she whispered.

But I couldn't. I needed to get it all out. She needed to deal with the truth, and with me.

"No, Diana," I said. "You stop for a change and listen."

She took my hand and led me upstairs to her bedroom. She closed the door behind her and directed me to a sofa in the sitting area.

"Why did you take me to Mrs. Baxter?" I asked.

I was impatiently seeking answers, but Diana wanted me to finish the story first, telling her how I had survived.

"Mrs. Baxter told you I died of SIDS, but in reality, she drove across state lines and left me on the steps of Mt. Nebo Baptist Church in Maryland, where the man and woman who became my parents found me.

"They told everyone they had adopted me, but they just happened to be the first to find me on that Sunday morning," I said.

Diana shook her head in dismay.

"She lied to me. How could she be so cruel? How could she hate me so much?"

"My parents never gave me much information about my birth mother because they didn't have it," I said. "Mrs. Baxter cut your name, the hospital where I was born and other information off of the birth certificate she left with me in the basket. But my birth date was correct."

"June 23rd?" Diana asked.

I nodded.

"My baby was born in Wilmington at 2:53 a.m."

Those details matched what was listed on the birth certificate my parents had somehow manufactured.

"Quentin interviewed Mrs. Baxter to get all of those details. Then he went to Delaware and found a record of the birth certificate. Your surname was listed as Edmondson and I was called Angel. There was no father listed."

Diana looked as if she had seen a ghost.

"She told me you were dead. I've grieved all these years, felt guilty for leaving my baby with her. How could she do that and live with herself?"

I sighed.

"According to Quentin, she waited to see who would find me on the church steps and then felt comfortable that the couple who did, my parents, would take proper care of me," I said. "She thought she was doing the right thing."

Diana's eyes turned hard.

"I'm sure she did. In her mind, I was some fancy-free starlet, stuck on living in New York. She didn't approve of me bringing you here, which was why I left you with her, with plans to come back when I had gotten settled. After she told me you died, there was no reason to go back. Not just to visit a tiny grave."

Now I grew angry.

"But you should have gone back," I said. "If you had, you would have known she was lying. Why wouldn't you want to visit your daughter's grave?"

Diana didn't like to be challenged. She stood up and began pacing the floor.

"How do I know this is the truth? What if you and Quentin are making all of this up?"

She stopped and glared at me.

"What do you want from me? Isn't it enough that you've taken over my show?"

I rose from my seat and stood face-to-face with her.

"That's what it always boils down to, doesn't it?" I asked between clenched teeth. "Your show. Your songs. Your reviews. Nothing and no one else matters. Seems to me like Mrs. Baxter did you a big favor. She helped launch your career. Had I been around, you might not be the diva you are today."

Smack!

She slapped my face so hard that I stumbled. If she hadn't been my elder, I might have swung back.

Instead, I balanced myself and held my cheek. If there was a bruise, I was going to have to wear an extra coating of makeup tonight. And how was I going to perform opposite her, anyway, now that I knew the truth?

"How could you give me away?" I whimpered. "And who is my father?"

She turned away from me and folded her arms.

"What is Quentin planning to do with this information?" she asked. "He didn't find all of this out for no reason. When will his story run? It could ruin both of our careers."

I stared at her back in disgust.

Nothing meant more to her than her precious career. Not even me.

"Do you even care that I'm alive, Diana? Doesn't it matter that your daughter has survived? I'm your flesh and blood."

I didn't mean to sound so hurt, but I couldn't mask what I was feeling. My emotions were spent and I was praying that I would be able to tap into these tender spots tonight, for the show. But how on earth was I going to stand opposite her character, Marian, pleading as Melanie, not to be given away?

This was just too much. I rose to leave.

She stopped me before I opened the door.

"Jessica?"

"Yes?" I responded without turning toward her. I prayed that she would ask for a hug, or for me to stay so we could work through this. But I should have known better.

"Can you keep this to yourself, until I figure this all out? And can you have Quentin call me? We need to keep this out of the newspapers for as long as we can."

I opened the door and answered before I walked away.

"Sure," I said. "Whatever Lady Di wants."

Chapter 17

God granted me grace.

Somehow I made it through Friday's shows without letting my personal issues affect my performances. If anything, the anger and hurt I felt over the recent discovery made my tears and my pleas for love more authentic.

The accolades continued. Critics commented on my and Diana's natural chemistry and on our uncanny resemblance.

I scoured the *Times* on Saturday morning in search of Quentin's revealing story, but there was nothing.

Pastor Evans and his wife had driven up from Maryland with my parents to see me in the role of Melanie. The four of them were leaving this morning after brunch at a soul-food restaurant near my apartment.

I didn't have the heart to blemish their visit with talk of my revelation. I had decided to save it for another time, when my parents were traveling alone.

Besides, my mother read everything she could get her hands on about my career. I knew she had heard and seen the comments about Diana and me being look-alikes, and it had to hurt.

I was hurting, too, from Diana's disdain. The truth hadn't changed anything. This was still her world and I was just the competition.

Was she afraid that someone would guess the truth? Or was she mostly jealous that she had to share the applause with me, even temporarily?

I didn't have time to figure it out. Vivian was still sick, so I'd be filling her role for at least four more shows, two on Saturday and two on Sunday. After that, who knew what would happen?

As we walked across the restaurant lot to my parents' parked car, Mom slowed her pace so she and I could have some privacy.

"You were amazing last night, baby," she said. "I cried for most of the show. And I see what they mean about the chemistry between you and Diana," she said. "Last night, the anger you expressed as Melanie seemed so real that I could almost feel it."

Where was this leading? Mom knew me better than anyone. She was trying to make a point.

"Maybe the anger was real, Mom," I finally said. "Diana is something else."

She took my hand and turned to face me.

"You know, Jess, you can't hold on to anger about things you have no control over," she said. "Diana may not be perfect, but God has a plan for her and for you. It's not an accident that your first role on Broadway paired you with your birth mother."

"How did you know, Mom?"

She smiled and touched my cheek.

"The emotion between you two last night was just too powerful. And the resemblance is more than just uncanny. There's no way you two could look so much alike without there being some biological connection," she said. "I realized that when I met Diana on opening night, but until you were ready to talk about it, I wasn't going to."

"Why now?" I asked.

Daddy, the pastor and his wife sat in the car chatting as they waited for Mom. She didn't hurry.

"I can tell you've found out something about your past, about your connection to Diana, and it's weighing on you," she said. "Your daddy may not have noticed it, but I could feel it in your performance last night. I'll be eager to hear the details whenever you want to tell me.

"In the meantime, just keep your ears open so you can listen and your heart open so you can love, Jess," she said. "Remember that your daddy and I made mistakes and questionable decisions, too, when we selfishly decided to keep you. We've asked God to forgive us and to continue blessing our family, but it doesn't change our past.

"I don't expect you to forgive Diana and love her overnight, but until you find your way there, you'll never really fulfill the purpose God has called you to.

"Diana has skeletons in her closet just like everyone else," Mom said. "You can't control how she reacts to her demons or to the fact that you're her daughter."

Hearing her acknowledge the truth again caused me to shudder.

"We've been afraid all of these years that if we helped you find her, we'd lose you," she said. "When we told you the truth a few weeks ago, we realized that instead of driving you away, we had deepened our relationship with you.

"Your dad and I know that you're angry with us, and that's to be expected. We're going to work through it. But we understand now that we can share you. It's okay."

I frowned.

"Share me? That's not necessary," I said. "You were the one taking care of me on the nights I was sick. You paid for the classes and showed up at all of my plays, dance recitals and vocal performances. You and Daddy prayed with me and taught me to love God."

Mom cradled my face in her hands and leaned her head toward mine.

"If I've taught you to love God, then I've taught you to love Diana," she said. "It doesn't mean you and she will have a close bond or that you'll ever publicly acknowledge your connection. It just means that you are going to refuse to let your beautiful life be consumed by hate and the inability to forgive.

"The way you're channeling your anger at her now, on the stage, is powerful and effective," Mom said. "To move forward and blossom in the path that's opening up for you, though, you're going to have to work through that pain and find a way to forgive me and Daddy and Diana."

I nodded.

"I know you're right, Mom," I said. "I just have to figure out how to get there from here."

She hugged me tightly and held me for a few minutes.

"Don't try to do it on your own, Jess. That's what God is for."

She kissed my forehead and pressed an envelope into my hand.

"I've got to go," she said. "Recite the verse on the Bible card in this envelope, for when you're having a tough time, and remember that no matter what, Daddy and I love you."

I hugged her again.

"I love you, too, Mom. With all my heart."

I waved until they turned the corner then used my thumbnail to open the envelope.

The pink and white card inside had a simple message, a Scripture that I suspected I would be relying on often.

Be even-tempered, content with second place, quick to forgive an offense. Forgive as quickly and completely as the Master forgave you. (Ephesians 4:32)

Chapter 18

The theater was dark on Mondays and I was glad there were no shows today. Diana invited me for lunch at her place, and I accepted. We needed to clear the air.

I took a cab to Diana's apartment building and the doorman walked swiftly to the car to escort me inside.

When I reached Diana's door, Elsie was already standing there. She nodded hello and gestured for me to enter.

Diana was waiting in the foyer. She held an apple martini in one hand and two newspapers in the other.

"Hi, there," she said and motioned for me to follow her into her study.

The room was both formal and cozy. A floor-to-ceiling palladian window filled the room with sunlight and provided a breathtaking view of New York's skyline. The walls were lined with books that I suspected Diana might have never read.

She motioned for me to sit on a sofa just in front of the

window. The latest fashion and celebrity magazines were scattered across a large ottoman that doubled as a seat or coffee table.

She held up her drink and pointed.

"Would you like one?"

"No thanks," I said.

I needed my thoughts to be clear for whatever this afternoon might bring. That obviously wasn't one of her concerns. She lifted another martini from the tray Elsie brought into the room and asked her to bring a pitcher of iced tea for me.

When Elsie was gone, she sat on the sofa next to me and curled her feet beneath her.

"I don't have a mole," she said lightly.

"Excuse me?"

"The only thing that keeps you from looking exactly like the twenty-three-year-old pictures of me in my photo album is that mole on your left cheek, near your nostril. I don't have one of those."

I didn't respond, so she continued.

"I guess that doesn't keep you from being my daughter, does it?" She said it regretfully.

I was surprised at my own disappointment. Part of me had wanted her to embrace me and welcome me into her life. I could see now that was wishful thinking.

"At least you don't have to deal with me onstage," I finally said. "Vivian's feeling better and will be back tomorrow."

She nodded.

"I heard. Good for her. And for you, I'm guessing."

"What do you mean?" I asked.

"Those few days of excellent reviews are going to carry you far. I wouldn't be surprised if Hollywood calls," she said. "That was a feat I never accomplished."

I sighed.

Was this always going to be what it boiled down to? Her ambitions, successes and failures? Her need to keep competing instead of enjoying what she had already achieved?

"Diana, what are you talking about? You have five Tony Awards and three Grammys," I said. "You were nominated for an Oscar twice. And besides, what does this have to do with me? Can you for once stop tying my personal connection to you to our professional one?"

She rose from the seat and walked over to the window, where she fixed her eyes on the blue sky.

I watched her from where I sat and tried to control my growing resentment.

Finally, she looked my way.

"I don't want to be your mother, Jessica," she said. "That's your adoptive mother, Lynn's, job, and she's much better at it than I could ever be.

"I'm too self-absorbed and focused on my work," she said apologetically. "But that doesn't mean I can't have some type of friendship with you. We can at least be friends, right?"

I frowned and walked over to her, so I could read her eyes and see if she was serious.

"I thought we were friends, Diana, before I found out any of this," I said. "At least I tried to be your friend, when you didn't push me away. But I don't think you want a friend any more than you want a daughter.

"The reason you never returned to Pennsylvania to verify

whether I had really died in infancy is because you were glad when Mrs. Baxter called and told you I was gone, weren't you? Weren't you!"

She inhaled deeply and then looked defiant.

"Maybe I was!" she said. "I got pregnant by a struggling actor I didn't love and knew I'd never have a future with. He was married and had no plans to leave his wife. She was his meal ticket while he sought fame."

Diana turned away from me but kept talking.

"The only place I have ever felt special or like I matter is when I am on the stage," she said. "I couldn't give that up for a baby who would have no father and could only snatch my future. I just couldn't."

She turned back toward me and took a sip of her drink.

"There was no guarantee that if I kept you, you would love me. I had more to lose by keeping you and halting my career than I did by placing you with a woman I thought could care for you as well as the other children who had been placed in her home," Diana said. "Mama Baxter hadn't loved me, but I never once thought that she would harm you."

I narrowed my eyes and kept looking at Diana as she paced back and forth in front of me. What I wanted to hear was some sort of regret for her choices.

Instead, I heard reasons why she hadn't wanted me then and didn't need me in her life now.

"I understand, Diana. It's obvious that I'm a burden and, in your mind, a potential threat," I said. "I know we won't be doing any mother-daughter cover shoots anytime soon. I guess I might as well go now."

I turned to leave, but she grabbed my arm.

I saw fear rising in her eyes.

"I didn't mean for you to leave, Jessica," she said, almost pleading. "I was just trying to be honest."

"I'm confused, Diana," I said. "If this is how you honestly feel, then why do you want me to stay? I can walk out of that door, and out of your life, right now."

She lowered her eyes.

"What about Quentin? He knows the truth and can reveal it at any time."

So that was what this was about. She had invited me to lunch to find out what Quentin was up to, whether he was planning to ruin her precious career.

"I haven't talked to Quentin since he shared this information with me last week," I said. "If you want to know what he's up to, call him."

She glared at me.

"You think this is funny, don't you? I guess in some odd little way, being my daughter, even one I won't acknowledge, could boost your career."

The more I listened to her, the harder I found it to stay angry with her.

Partly because when I looked at her, I saw an older version of myself.

I picked up my purse and headed for the door.

"I'm leaving now to go and put my time to better use," I said calmly. "I'm not walking out of your life. As far as I'm concerned, the door will always be open for us to be friends. You may never want that, but if you do, just know that you have at least one person you can call.

"In the meantime, I'll fulfill my contract with the musical

and stay out of your way," I said. "I don't know what Quentin has in store, but if he's planning a story, I won't cooperate unless you specifically ask me to."

She looked at me with no emotion and didn't speak. I couldn't tell what she was thinking, but I knew I had to stop caring.

"Goodbye, Diana," I said softly. "Take care of yourself."

Chapter 19

I emerged from the elevator in my apartment building and found myself face-to-face with my other dilemma.

"Need another quote for your story?" I asked Quentin.

He was leaning against the wall next to my door, reading a magazine and waiting for me.

"No," he said and looked down at me. "What I need to do is apologize—and be forgiven."

I sighed and tried to brush past him, but he grabbed my arm and gently pulled me toward him.

"Jessica, you can't deny that there's something between us," he said. "Not just a physical attraction, either. You are a special person, and I really don't want to lose you, not over an article that doesn't pass the test."

I looked at him curiously.

"The test?"

"A story about you and Diana would be the biggest news

in the entertainment industry for years to come," he said. "It would take my career to dizzying heights. In fact, I sat down and wrote it last night."

I inhaled and tried to keep my composure.

"I wrote it and printed out a copy," he said. "Then I deleted it from my computer and went home for the night, to talk to my dad and to God about it."

"And?" I was afraid to ask.

"And with their help, I realized that the story would be sensational, but it didn't pass my personal 'journalism with integrity' muster," he said.

"In other words, would telling this story meet a public need? Would it improve society in some way? Or would it enhance the community more so than if this information were never revealed?

"I thought about it and silently concluded that the answer to each of those questions was no. My life wasn't as important as the little bubble I lived in had made it seem. Nor was Diana's.

"There was a war going on in Iraq, the threat of continued terrorist attacks and numerous other critical issues that better deserved newspaper space."

Quentin extended a manila envelope toward me.

"If and when your and Diana's story appears in the *New York Times,* it should be in a more meaningful way," he said. "Only the two of you will know when that time comes."

I took the envelope and peeked inside at the typed article with Quentin's byline.

"It's the only copy," he said. "I still have my recorded and written interview notes, but I've locked them away."

I stared at him.

"Why are you doing this?"

He shrugged and stuck his hands in his pockets.

"Sometimes doing the right thing isn't the thing that puts you in the spotlight," he said. "It's doing nothing at all. Wasn't that how Jesus operated?

"Diana was wrong about me," he said. "I care about my career, but I'm beginning to believe that I care about you more."

I walked away from him, toward the elevator. When it opened, I turned toward him.

"Are you coming?"

"Where?" he asked without moving.

"To take this article to Diana," I said. "She needs it more than I do. Besides, I'm starving. You can treat me to lunch."

* * * * *

A CRACKED MIRROR

To **Rhonda**: Thanks for promoting me every chance you get and for helping me take my career to the next level.

To **Heather**: We've been friends for nearly three decades now. Can you believe it? I've gotta write a book that tells our unique story. What do you think?

To **Gloria and Deborah**: Some bonds never break. Ours is one of those.

To **Lisa**: Thanks for being loyal both professionally and personally.

Dama: I'm so glad to see your ministry expanding. This is only the beginning.

To **Vivi, Tia, Michelle, Norma, Shewanda and Vanessa**: Thank you for sharing in the vision that is the Anointed Authors on Tour. Seven cities, seven sisters…ONE message!

Clive, Emily and Gerald: I just wanted to give you all a shout-out for being such a vital part of the Cruisin' For Christ dream team. Y'all are just da bomb!

To my **Kimani (New Spirit)** family: Thanks for continuing to be a God-inspired vehicle that allows me to share my gift with the world. I'm enjoying the ride and I hope you are, too.

To **The Writer's Hut members**: You have given me no regrets for creating this online retreat for writers. I love each of you and continuously pray for your success.

To **Revival Churches, Inc.**: Through you, I learned how to fast, pray, trust and believe. Thank you for all that you've meant to me through the years.

To **Bishop Johnathan and Pastor Toni Alvarado and the Total Grace Christian Center family**: If God's anointing could be measured, my cup would run over every single time I worship with and among you. There is no place like Total Grace!

To **book clubs and other readers**: When I hear from you, saying that my stories have ministered to, touched, encouraged and/or entertained you, I know that my writing is not in vain. Thank you!

Lastly, to **Brian, Melvin, India, Israel and Boyz II Men**: Thank you for the music and melody that played in my head and in my stereo during the time I wrote this project.

Prologue

It was supposed to be just a quick errand, a brief visit to an upscale neighborhood grocery store to pick up the latest issue of *Men's Health* magazine. The plan was simple enough. But when Jaxon Tillman's eyes locked onto the front cover of the newest edition of *Ebony*, he couldn't tear them away. Nothing about the rest of his day was going to be quick, brief or simple. Jaxon knew that he was in for a long afternoon and an even longer night.

More than anything, he wished he could close his eyes and make one wish that would be granted instantaneously. There were a lot of things in life that Jaxon could ask for, but today, all he'd request is that one of the faces be changed on the front of the special edition release. It didn't even matter who they would place in her stead, as long as the image that belonged to Sariah Langston was superimposed by one belonging to some other model in her fifties that the world of high fashion and cosmetics still idolized.

Jaxon's eyes darted back and forth, scanning his surroundings. He didn't particularly want anyone to see him picking up the magazine. Although his indirect connection to Sariah wasn't common knowledge, he could never be too careful. Under the topic that read "Former Supermodels—Forever Super Beauties," sat Beverly Garvin, Aria and Sariah Langston, all looking better than most women half their ages.

As Jaxon flipped to the feature article, he couldn't deny the hype. Like the ladies who shared the cover with her, Sariah was strikingly beautiful. Her skin was flawless, her legs were shapely and for a woman who had given birth to three children, her body was taut. As soon as the last thought flowed through Jaxon's mind, his eyes fell to the closing sentence in the article beneath Sariah's photo, reminding him of why he wanted to make her part of the feature disappear.

Sariah Faith Langston, wife of successful restaurant mogul Geoffrey Langston and mother of two daughters, Gabrielle and Giovanna, continues to reside in metropolitan Atlanta, Georgia.

"Two daughters." Jaxon whispered the words as he silently reread the rest of the sentence.

He knew that those were the only words in the article that would mean anything to his wife whenever she got her hands on a copy of this month's *Ebony*. To LaShun, it wouldn't matter one bit that Sariah had cofounded a scholarship fund to help good students from low-income homes get the education that they deserved. It would make no difference that she had just been nominated Woman of the Year by one of the city's most respected nonprofit organizations. It wouldn't even be important that Sariah's husband had sent a check to Oprah's Angel Network to help with the ongoing efforts to assist victims of the infamous Hurricane Katrina and other natural disasters. All that would mean anything to LaShun is that her mother, the woman who'd birthed her nearly thirty-three years ago, had only acknowledged having two daughters.

Chapter 1

Five hundred dollars and fifty cents. In the last five days, that was the amount LaShun had spent on copies of what *used* to be her favorite magazine. The mission was frustrating, to say the least. Every time she emptied one shelf's supply, a day later, there was new stock. She'd noticed the raised eyebrows of the clerk at the bookstore she'd visited three times in as many days.

"These special editions sometimes go for good money on eBay," LaShun said as she handed the clerk her debit card, all the while avoiding eye contact.

Her words sounded foolish to her own ears, so LaShun had no doubt that the gray-haired woman behind the counter hadn't bought one word of her unsolicited explanation. If the inquisitive eyes that peered at LaShun could steal a glimpse into the Hefty bag that housed LaShun's trash, they'd find the truth. Now, as she took periodic glances toward the heap on her floor, shame threatened to sneak in, but every time it tried, LaShun would shoo it away. In her opinion, she'd carried enough shame because of Sariah. She wasn't about to give in to the nagging sense of embarrassment. In LaShun's opinion, Sariah was getting off too easily. She deserved worse than having a few copies of her photos tossed in the trash. *Much* worse.

"At best, a human incubator is all that you ever were to me," LaShun whispered. She didn't at all feel that she was disrespecting Sariah. After all, respect had to be earned and the fifty-year-old has-been model hadn't done a thing to merit an ounce of regard from LaShun. Not one single thing.

"You are kidding me, right? You have *got* to be kidding," Carminda Reynolds said, coming to a stop at LaShun's open office door and placing one hand on her hip as she eyed the half-open bag.

LaShun looked up at the short Hispanic beauty, briefly taking her eyes away from the paperwork on her desk and then refocusing. "Don't even start," she warned.

"Oh, I haven't even begun to get started yet. Not *even,*" Carminda forewarned, prompting LaShun's eyes to return to her.

Carminda was more than LaShun's assistant. She was also her best friend and probably the only person in the world who could talk to her in that tone of voice without suffering some type of repercussion. Carminda was also the only person outside of Jaxon whom LaShun had told about her estranged mother.

"Look at what you've done here, Shun. Just look at it. How much sense does this make, huh? Please tell me how much sense this makes. How many magazines do you have in there? How many?" When Carminda became excited, her words were rapid and repetitive statements were frequent. In addition, agitation caused the accent that she'd learned to suppress for the sake of corporate America to come forward full force.

Walking closer to the reinforced plastic bag, Carminda tried to lift the heavy load, but couldn't. Then she fully opened the top of the garbage bag and stuck her face inside. "Oh my goodness, Shun. Oh my goodness. There has to be eighty or ninety magazines in here. Eighty or ninety, *at least.*"

"One hundred and forty-three, but who's counting?"

"One hundred and forty-three?" Carminda pulled her face from the bag and looked at her friend in disgust. "Have you lost your mind? Well, have you? I can't believe you bought all of these magazines just to throw them away. I mean, honestly, Shun, what do you think you've accomplished? What? Do you know how many hundreds of thousands of these things they print each month? Literally hundreds of thousands, Shun. What did buying a few dozen copies of them accomplish?"

LaShun didn't feel like being preached at—not today. "That's more than a few dozen," she said, refusing to allow Carminda to rob her of her sense of triumph. "That's almost a dozen, dozen, so if nothing else, I made *me* feel better by doing it."

"I don't know why. All you really did was give the sales-to-date a boost. Boosted the sales, that's all you've really accomplished."

LaShun pretended to focus on her work, but Carminda's

words struck a nerve and resulted in a painful reality check. The satisfaction she'd gotten from purchasing the copies and throwing them in the oversized Hefty bag had now been overshadowed by the knowledge that she'd actually, in a roundabout way, helped Sariah. If magazine sales soared in the first week, it would be concluded by the fashion industry that the women on the cover of *Ebony* were still as marketable as ever. She hadn't thought of that during her blind mission.

"What if this month's *Ebony* shatters the record of their previously bestselling issue by exactly one hundred and forty-three?" Carminda challenged. "What then?"

The invisible knife that had been jabbed into LaShun's back at Carminda's first observation seemed to twist just a bit.

Carminda continued. "What if, at the end of the month, there would have been only one hundred and forty-three unsold issues left on the shelves, preventing the magazine from being a complete sold-out issue, and because you bought the exact amount needed to clear the shelves—"

"Okay, Carminda, you've made your stupid point," LaShun snapped, grimacing at her friend, who dramatically flailed her arms in the air while she outlined the hypothesis. "What's done is done. Besides, none of that stuff will be the case, anyway. You kill me with your what-ifs. Every time a situation arises, you've got to list a million and one what-ifs to go along with it. The magazine is not going to sell out and there won't be any records broken because I bought a few dozen copies."

"But that's more than a few dozen, remember?" Carminda grinned. "That's almost a dozen, dozen."

LaShun fumed on the inside. She felt as though her own best friend had turned on her, was making a mockery of her painful past, and was now taking sides with the woman who had inflicted the unhealed wounds. Outside of the office, Carminda, with her sharp wit and quick tongue, might have the advantage, but at LT, Inc., LaShun had the upper hand. And she determined that now was the time to exercise that authority.

"I'm sure you have some work to do, Carminda. How about you focus on that for a change?"

Carminda pulled one of the magazines from the garbage bag and began thumbing through it. Pursing her lips, LaShun stared at her in silence, wondering if Carminda had heard a word she'd just said. As one of a select few people who knew the story of how her mother had heartlessly given her up for adoption, LaShun expected her best friend to be a little more sympathetic. Instead, Carminda's eyes were glued to the pages, absorbing every word of the article in front of her. LaShun opened her mouth to speak again, but Carminda's words placed her on pause.

"She is so pretty. I can't believe she's fifty. I would say that they had the picture airbrushed, but she's always pretty—even when she was on that talk show a few weeks ago. You think she's had cosmetic surgery?"

LaShun bit her bottom lip to hold back the words that threatened to come gushing out of her mouth like an uncontrollable waterfall. A personal relationship with Christ had tamed her tongue years ago, but LaShun could taste the bile of her not-so-distant past creeping onto her palate. She didn't know whether or not Sariah Langston had ever had cosmetic surgery, but more importantly, she didn't care.

"What do you think?" Carminda insisted, looking at LaShun through clueless eyes.

Remaining unresponsive, LaShun returned Carminda's stare. She knew it was best that she not open her mouth too soon. It would be detrimental to both parties involved. It took a moment, but Carminda finally got the silent, but un-mistakably clear message. In doing so, she rolled her eyes to the ceiling and then released an exaggerated sigh before tucking the magazine under her arm and laying a blue folder on LaShun's desk.

"Here are the letters you asked me to type this morning," she said. "Your mail is also in there as well as a few telephone messages that you received during the time you asked not to be disturbed."

"Thanks," LaShun mumbled, opening the folder and flipping through the enclosed envelopes to see if any of the mail was important enough to give immediate attention. Most of them were bills that she didn't have the time or the funding to deal with right now.

Changing the direction of the conversation completely, Carminda said, "And don't forget that you and Jaxon are supposed to have dinner with Wendell and me after church on Sunday. I've decided not to cook, so I hope you guys are okay with going out. It'll be our treat."

Thank God, LaShun thought, taking special precaution to make sure that the same relief couldn't be seen on her face. Jaxon had been trying to plot a way out of dinner with the Reynoldses anyway. He hated Carminda's cuisine, citing that it was always overcooked and under-seasoned. Truthfully, LaShun didn't care much for it, either, and she was almost certain that love for his wife was the only reason that Wendell held his own opinions to himself.

"You're not let down, are you?" Carminda said, drawing LaShun's attention back to the conversation at hand.

Let down? Are you kidding? Girl, this is the stuff Sunday morning testimonies are made of. It's taking every ounce of self-control that I have not to start speaking in tongues and breaking into a shout. "Not too much," LaShun replied, trying to sound just a bit thwarted. "We'll just have to find a place that's not too crowded. You know how packed restaurants can be on Sunday afternoons."

"If we ride to Buckhead or Alpharetta, we should be able to find somewhere that's not overly crowded."

LaShun nodded. "I'm sure you're right."

Carminda turned to walk away and then paused. "I should stop being so lazy, shouldn't I? You cook for your husband just about every day of the week and Wendell is always picking up dinner on the way home so that I won't have to cook. He's spoiled me, hasn't he? I really should cook, shouldn't I?"

No, no, no, no, nooooooo! "You could," LaShun said in a level tone despite her horrified thoughts. "But the four of us haven't gone out together in a while. It might be fun to spend a Sunday afternoon dining out for a change. If you want to make the men happy, we could go to the ESPN Zone and let them watch the game while we eat. I'll bet both Wendell and Jaxon will forgive you for not cooking in exchange for that."

"Girl, that's a great idea." Carminda beamed.

"Yeah. It'll be fun."

"Thank you, Jesus, for me not having to cook whatever I was going to cook," Carminda said.

Thank you, Jesus, for me not having to eat whatever you were going to cook, too. "So, ESPN Zone it is?"

Carminda nodded as if the idea were her own. "ESPN Zone it is."

As she turned for the second time to leave the office, LaShun stopped her with a loud clearing of her throat. Carminda turned around and looked at her boss with inquisitiveness. Following the direction of LaShun's eyes, she traced them to the magazine that was still tucked under her arm. Grunting her disapproval, Carminda dropped the publication in the middle of LaShun's desk.

"Trash goes in the trash," LaShun said, her voice laced in warning.

"You know, you really need to pray about this animosity," Carminda said.

Without another word, LaShun raised her eyebrows and pointed in the direction of the plastic bag that still lay on her floor. Heeding the silent order, Carminda retrieved the magazine from the desk and disposed of it as directed.

"Thank you," LaShun sang.

"Humph." This time, the grunt was all the reply Carminda offered before disappearing on the other side of the door.

Chapter 2

"Mommy?"

Sariah heard the voice of her youngest daughter echoing in the hallway as the always-upbeat teenager made her way to her parents' room.

"Come on in, Giovanna," she replied, not interrupting her task of pinning up her hair as she prepared for bed. "What is it, honey?" Sariah said when the face of her baby girl appeared in the mirror as she stood behind her mother, who sat at her brass vanity.

"Disney World would be the perfect place," Giovanna exclaimed. Her eyes widened with excitement as she spoke. "Chris Brown is going to be there, Mommy. Can you believe it? *Chris Brown!*"

Sariah stopped her task and looked at her daughter's reflection in the mirror. While Giovanna shrieked, spun around in a circle and then fell backward onto the bed behind her, Sariah's mind raced to catch up. She knew that if she thought long and hard enough, she'd figure out what it was that Giovanna was talking about. Her youngest always did that—started conversations that picked up where others had left off. Sometimes her continuances were linked to discussions that had taken place hours, even days earlier, but Giovanna always spoke as though the dialogue was fresh and still in progress.

"That would be the greatest gift ever, Mommy!" Giovanna gushed while staring at the ceiling. "Do you think Daddy will go for it?"

It was the hint that Sariah needed to bring her up to speed. "You've been to Disney World before, honey. Why don't you ask your dad to let you have a sleepover or something? What about a pool party or a shopping spree with three friends of your choice? You could be like the Cheetah Girls for a day. That would be fun, wouldn't it? Wouldn't you rather spend your Sweet Sixteen party with your girlfriends?"

Sariah was highly pleased with the idea she'd come up with in such a short span of time. She would have given anything to have that kind of party for herself at sixteen and nothing would make her happier than to give her daughter what her mother couldn't give her…what her mother *wouldn't* give her. With a wide grin birthed by sheer satisfaction, Sariah quickly turned from the mirror only to find her daughter sitting up on the bed and looking at her, grossly appalled.

"*Friends?* Who needs friends?"

"Everybody needs friends, Giovanna," Sariah said. "You have plenty of time for boys. Christopher will still be there when you turn eighteen and if it's meant to be, you can spend your birthday with him then. Until that time, I'm not supporting any ideas of your spending time at Disney World or anywhere else with any boys. And your father won't condone it, either, so before you start getting any ideas in your head to ask him, I think you should…"

"*Christopher?*" Giovanna fell back onto the bed in a fit of laughter, leaving her mother to look on in confusion.

"What's so funny?"

"Mommy, do you even know who Chris Brown is?"

"The most popular boy at school, no doubt," Sariah said in a matter-of-fact tone.

"No." The word was almost lost in a new fit of giggles.

"The football team's quarterback?"

Sariah's newest guess didn't help the situation. By now, Giovanna was laughing too hard to give a verbal response. Sariah knew the things her daughter liked. She wouldn't go as far as to define her as "boy-crazy" but Giovanna seemed to be partial to the young men at school who were either into sports or…

"Music!" Sariah blurted the thought that had just entered her brain. "He's on the drum line!"

When Giovanna slid onto the floor, carrying a pillow and a portion of the comforter with her, Sariah surrendered. As much as she fought it, seeing her overdramatic daughter crumpled into a ball, heaving to catch a precious lungful of breath between guffaws, made Sariah laugh, too.

"Nothing in life could really be that funny."

Sariah followed the direction of the bass voice and saw her husband of twenty years standing in the doorway of their bedroom. "That's *your* child," she teased.

Geoffrey Langston was as beautiful a man as Sariah was a woman. His heavy pockets and dashing good looks made him a prime target for women of affluent families. His name had been attached to more than one scandal surrounding infidelity in the first several years of his marriage to Sariah. But somehow, they'd survived the roughest of the rough times. Now, although their marriage wasn't as solid as it appeared to the outside world, there had been no signs of infidelity over the past five years.

Geoffrey looked at his daughter as she lay on the floor looking up at him with a grin. "Pillows don't belong on the floor, Giovanna, and neither do little girls."

It seemed like a simple observation, but Giovanna knew that there was a command hidden in the sentence. Sariah watched as their daughter collected herself and then tried to replace the linen and pillows in the manner they'd been before she disturbed them. When she was satisfied that she'd done a relatively good job, Giovanna sat on the edge of the bed with her father.

"Daddy, do you know who Chris Brown is?"

"I know more than one Chris Brown," Geoffrey said. "Which one would you be referring to?"

"See?" Sariah said, glad that she wasn't the only one who was apparently in the dark. "If you haven't brought him around here, how do you expect us to know him?"

"He's not from my school, Mommy," she whined through an exaggerated sigh. "I can't believe you've never heard of Chris Brown."

Geoffrey slipped his feet from his bedroom slippers and

slid back onto the bed so that his back rested against the headboard. "Are you talking about the singer?"

"See, Mommy?" Giovanna said, standing in excitement. "Daddy knows him. So that makes him the cool parent, right?"

"Haven't I always been?"

At her husband's words, Sariah tossed him an unspoken caution. She probably would have voiced a defense for herself if Geoffrey's words weren't so true. Both her daughters were closer to their father than they'd ever been to her. When they were babies, Geoffrey tended to them more than she did. Even in those years when his faithfulness to Sariah was in question, no one could ever accuse him of not being a good father for his girls.

Sariah tried to be a doting mother when her daughters were infants, but nurturing didn't come naturally for her. Gabrielle and Giovanna were twelve and ten years old, respectively, before they truly formed a bond with Sariah. But even now, they favored their father. Sariah never voiced her true feelings about the matter, but knowing that she could never make up for those years that she'd unknowingly built a wall between her and her daughters was a wound that never completely healed.

"What's this about?" Geoffrey asked. "Why are we talking about Chris Brown?"

Sariah looked at Giovanna and raised her eyebrows in a manner than challenged her to try and talk her father into taking her to Disney World just to see some teen idol perform. The difference in her daughters' personalities amazed Sariah. While she considered both of them to be average teenagers, Gabrielle, her eldest, was far more studious and mature than Giovanna. Even at Giovanna's age, Gabrielle found more pleasure in reading and writing than she did in television and music. There were days when Giovanna seemed younger than her years and days when Gabrielle came across as a girl much older. But despite their differences, most times, both girls were well-mannered and made their parents proud.

"Yeah, Giovanna," Sariah urged in sarcasm while turning back to her vanity to complete the task of pinning up her hair for the night. "Tell your daddy why we're talking about Chris Brown."

"I'm waiting," Geoffrey said when his daughter didn't immediately respond.

"He's going to be performing at Disney World." Giovanna's words were cautious, as though she was second-guessing her own decision to bring up the subject.

"And?" Geoffrey clasped his hands together and placed them behind his head to serve as a cushion between his head and the wooden headboard.

Sariah chuckled knowingly. "Yeah, Giovanna—and?"

Through the reflection in the mirror, Sariah saw her daughter give her a disapproving glance before she turned back to her father. Giovanna's eyes were pleading and Sariah could see her already preparing herself to make a good argument on why she should be allowed to go and see her newest crush. She seemed to have a different one every few months, but for now, it apparently was Chris Brown.

Crawling across the mattress and coming to a stop in a seated position beside her father, Giovanna said, "Remember when you and Mom told me to think about what I wanted to do for my Sweet Sixteen party?"

She's good, Sariah thought. Giovanna knew to start out by reminding them that they were the ones who all but left it up to her to decide how the special day would be spent.

"We said for you to come up with something *within reason.*"

Most times, when one of them had to put their foot down, it was Sariah. She was glad that Geoffrey had chosen today to be one of the rare occasions when he would be the firm one. Whether Chris Brown was a boy at school or a boy on a stage, he was still a boy. His entertainer status just made Sariah's stance even stronger. In her opinion, sixteen was too young for a girl to decide she'd like to spend a birthday with a boy—period. Giovanna was just too young.

"But Daddy, it *is* within reason." Giovanna had already started to whine and Sariah knew that she was only making a worse case for herself. Geoffrey hated it when the girls whined almost as much as she did.

"No, it's not, Giovanna. That's no way to spend your birthday," Sariah chimed in.

"*Please,* Mommy?"

"Giovanna—"

"Please, what?" Geoffrey said. By his tone, he was becoming agitated. "You haven't asked for anything, Giovanna. All you've done is whine. What are you asking? Are you asking us to somehow arrange for Chris to come here and take you out or something? You know that's not happening."

"No, Daddy. I just want to go to Disney World and attend his concert, that's all."

"Giovanna, you've already gotten your answer," Sariah reminded her in a stern voice. "Now think of something else."

"So, all you're asking for is to go to the concert?"

The change in Geoffrey's tone didn't go unnoticed. Sariah placed her hairbrush back in its place and held her breath.

"Yes, Daddy," Giovanna answered. "That's all I'm asking for. You don't have to give me anything else. I just want to go to this concert at Disney World."

In this instance, quietness wasn't a good thing and for a few fleeting moments, it was all that Sariah could hear. She fumbled with her hair products, but what she wanted to do was turn from the mirror and read Geoffrey's face…see why he was delaying the inevitable. The only reason Sariah didn't turn to look was because she knew that Giovanna would blame her when Geoffrey denied her her wish.

"When you put it like that, then I guess it's not unreasonable."

Sariah froze at Geoffrey's response. "What?" She turned from the mirror just in time to see Giovanna throw herself into her father's arms.

"Then I can go? Oh, thank you, Daddy! Thank you, thank you, thank you!" She placed kisses on his cheek between each sentiment, bringing laughter from her father.

"You're welcome, baby. But don't get too happy yet. I need to know all of the details so we can see about getting tickets, flights, whatever else has to be done. Your going is based on us being able to get everything lined up."

"I know." Giovanna placed one last long, loud kiss on her father's cheek. "I'll write everything down and give it to you tomorrow. I love you, Daddy. Good night."

"Excuse me, young lady," Sariah said when her daughter headed for the bedroom door.

"Oh! Good night, Mom."

With that, she disappeared. No "I love you" as she'd told her father. Sariah took note of it and masked the disappointment of it well as she turned her attention to Geoffrey. "You're going to let her go? Just like that?"

"Why not?" he replied. "She'll be sixteen. When Gabrielle turned sixteen, we allowed her to choose her celebration, so it's only fair to do the same for Giovanna." He stood from the bed and closed the bedroom door before peeling off his shirt. "Do you have a problem with it?"

"Does it really matter?" Sariah asked. "You've already told her she could go. You didn't even ask me what I thought before just making a decision. That pretty much cancels out any input that I might have had."

"I don't understand why you'd have an input that wasn't an agreeable one." Geoffrey tossed his shirt in the bin that they would put out for the housekeeper to launder the following day. "It's just Disney World, Sariah. You do know that Disney World is still a part of our world, right? It's not like the girl is asking to go into outer space."

Geoffrey's laughter made Sariah angry. "I'm glad you're being entertained by this," she said as she got up from her chair and headed toward the bathroom.

"What's your problem?" The brief humor of it all had faded from Geoffrey's face. "Every time the girls want to go somewhere, you get your panties in a bunch. They make good grades, they take care of their chores. They deserve to be rewarded every now and then. What's wrong with allowing them to have a little fun?"

Tears burned in Sariah's eyes. "Is that what you were doing all those years?" she demanded. "Is that what you called it? Having a little fun on the weekends because through the week you'd made the grade and taken care of business? Look what it did for you. Look at what it did to us. Do you want that for Giovanna?"

Sariah winced. When she turned to look in the direction of the loud thud she'd just heard, she saw deep frown lines in Geoffrey's forehead. He was visibly fuming, but Sariah was uncertain as to whether the intense grimace was a reflection of his anger or if it was more a reaction to the pain that no doubt radiated through his body from the impact of him banging his fist against the solid cedar wood frame of the bathroom door.

"How many times do we have to go through this?" Geoffrey's voice level was low, probably as an attempt to keep their argument private from the girls downstairs. But his teeth were clenched and his strong jaws were set as he spoke. "What's done is done, Sariah. Get over it, already. You're always dredging up old news when you can't have your way. What happened with me has nothing to do with Giovanna and I'm not going to allow you to try to make her pay for something that doesn't concern her."

Sariah smeared the moisture from her tears with her hands. "Doesn't concern her? You don't think that what you did concerns Giovanna? Well, I have news for you, Geoffrey Langston. What you did then and everything you do from here on out concerns this whole family. Those girls had to find out about your filthy transgressions in tabloids and on the streets. If you don't think that *concerned* them then you're not nearly as smart a man as the world gives you credit for."

"Would it have been any easier had they learned it from me?" Geoffrey challenged.

"Of course it would have been easier."

"Maybe it would have and maybe it wouldn't have." Geoffrey flung his arms into the air and then dropped them by his sides. "The point is that five years later, it's old news and it ain't got one thing to do with our decision to allow Giovanna to go to a concert at Disney World."

"*Your* decision."

"Fine! *My* decision, Sariah. *My* decision. Do you consult me in every conclusion you draw where the girls are concerned?"

"Yes."

"That's a lie and you know it. I see charges on my credit card bill for women's clothes, shoes, jewelry and perfumes that I had no prior knowledge of. Do I make a stink about it? No."

"So because you have a little money in the bank, that gives you a right to sleep with other women?"

"What the—" Geoffrey released an exasperated sigh and turned away from his wife momentarily before looking at her again. "You're impossible, you know that? You're just going to find some way to slip the same old stuff in every argument, aren't you? When we went to counseling, you said you forgave me. I don't think that it's genuine forgiveness when you keep bringing it up—even when it doesn't relate to the discussion at hand. And frankly, I'm getting a bit sick of it, Sariah. I'm not going to keep defending myself for past bad decisions. I admitted my wrongdoing and—"

"You didn't admit anything, Geoffrey!" Sariah's voice rose in agitation and then lowered when she remembered the bedrooms located beneath theirs. "You lied to the press back then and you've been lying to them ever since."

"I admitted it to the people who mattered the most," he defended. "It ain't the press's business what goes on in our marriage."

"You didn't *admit* anything to us, either, if the girls and I are who you are referring to as 'people who mattered the most.' Gabrielle and Giovanna still think you're Mr. Perfect and as far as I'm concerned, well, I had to find out through blackmail photos that were shoved in my face by one of your little whores. You didn't *admit* to anything, Geoffrey, you got caught and then were backed into a corner. There's a difference. Had your girlfriend not told on you, I never would have known."

Laughing with no amusement, Geoffrey shook his head. "And I guess I don't even get brownie points that the reason she told on me was because I ended it with her because I knew what I was doing was wrong, huh? The love I had for you won over the lust I had for her, but I guess that don't mean nothing to you."

"*Won?*" Sariah said the word as though it were laced in toxins. "Oh, I'm a winner because you opted to stay with me? You're a prize now?"

"I am so tired of you finding holes in my words and twisting them to fit your agenda."

"Yeah, well, welcome to the club. 'Cause God knows that I'm tired of finding holes in your character and having to twist my life around to help cover them. How fun do you think it is to have to find your husband's garbage in some-body else's trash can? Do you think I find some kind of joy in having to find out about your sins through a second or third party?"

"So sue me for being imperfect, Sariah."

"Whatever, Geoffrey. Now you're going to try to be the victim here? Is that it?"

"I'm not a victim, Sariah. I'm a human being. I made some mistakes, and okay, those mistakes didn't just affect me."

Sariah turned to face him. "Exactly how many mistakes did you make, Geoffrey?"

"What?"

"You never told me how many there were. I just know about the one who confronted me, but I'm sure there were others. How many? Two? Three?"

"Sariah—"

"Four? Am I even getting warm here?"

"I'm not even going to get into this with you. This is just stupid."

"Fine," Sariah said in a nonchalant tone. "I'm sure I'll find out on the news or in the gossip column of some trashy magazine."

Swearing in anger, Geoffrey walked into the bathroom and grabbed Sariah firmly by the arm, pulling her so close to him that her face was only inches from his chin. She looked up to see eyes that were narrowed in near outrage. Sariah swallowed hard. In all the years they'd been married, Geoffrey had never handled her in such a rigid manner.

"Let me go," she said, failing in her attempt to pull away.

"Are you so perfect, Sariah?" he asked in a voice that was just above a whisper. "When you look in the mirror, do you not see any faults? Have you told me everything—absolutely everything about yourself?"

Sariah gasped. "What?"

"Do you not have any secrets? Anything in your life that you'd rather just not talk about?"

Sariah stood silently, searching her husband's eyes to see if his words were arbitrary or if he knew something that she didn't know that he knew. Tears that she didn't even feel rising were now spilling down her cheeks. Seeing them, Geoffrey immediately loosened his grip. Silence lingered between them for several moments before he stepped away, looking at the hand that had held Sariah so forcefully and then back at his wife. Releasing a lungful of air through his partially open lips, Geoffrey uttered one single word.

"Sorry."

It was so soft that Sariah barely heard it. Once he said it, Geoffrey backed out of the bathroom. Still silent, Sariah watched him pull a clean shirt from the closet and put it on. Then, slipping his bare feet into a pair of Austin-McDonald leather loafers, he grabbed his wallet and keys from the dresser.

"Where are you going?" Sariah asked, regretfully wishing she could turn back the clock and erase the entire conversation that had taken place since Giovanna left them alone.

Placing his hand on the doorknob and not bothering to turn to look in his wife's direction, Geoffrey said, "I just need to get some air. I'll be back later."

Chapter 3

As the drummer at Shabach Worship Center, perspiration dripped down the face of Jaxon Tillman as he and the other musicians provided music for those who had "caught the Spirit" at the close of this Sunday's sermon. Jaxon loved his position as one of the ministers of music at the church that he'd grown up in, but the only reason he hadn't asked for a raise was because the pastor was also his father.

When his dad founded the church thirty years earlier, Jaxon was just four years old. Back then, he had one drumstick and one bass drum that he played, sometimes off-beat, to the congregation that consisted only of his family and several children that lived in a nearby housing project. Their mothers had made them come to church, often dirty and sometimes barefoot, just to get rid of them for a few hours every Sunday. Every now and then the thought of it all amused Jaxon. Those mothers probably had no idea that thirty years later, many of their sons and daughters would grow to be such an intricate part of SWC.

In the place at the front of the church where the full drum set was positioned, enclosed by an acrylic-glass safety shield, Jaxon had a clear view of the congregation. His father had taught him years ago that as a minister of music, Jaxon had to always remain "in the Spirit" during services.

"God has been known to work miracles through music when it is played under the anointing," Newton Tillman told him. "You're not just playing the drums, you're providing spiritual ointment whereby people can be healed, delivered and set free. Demons can be cast out through the music that you provide."

The first time his father had spoken those words, Jaxon reevaluated his love for the drums. He wasn't quite sure that he was ready for that kind of responsibility or if he would ever want it, for that matter. All he'd ever wanted to do was beat a stick against the head of a drum. All that demon talk made him want to hang up the sticks and be an usher like his sister was back then. But he soon discovered that it wasn't his decision to make. God had called him to play the drums and every time he tried to walk away from it, his hands burned for the feel of the sticks. And the more he played, the better he got; and when he played, instead of allowing one of his younger apprentices to do so, the atmosphere in Shabach was on a higher plane. Just like today.

As Jaxon scanned the audience, he spotted LaShun. His wife of five years hadn't been her usual self since this month's *Ebony* hit the stands. On any other Sunday, LaShun would probably be one of those in the aisles, needing the attention of an usher. But today, she wasn't even standing in worship with those around her. Instead, she sat and rocked to the music, cooling herself with the fan she had in her hand. Jaxon closed his eyes to try to block out the thoughts of his wife's dilemma, but doing so blocked out the images of those in praise and allowed him to visualize more clearly the exchange that had taken place in his home over dinner last night. The night had started out well, but the end of it wasn't even close to what Jaxon had in mind.

Saturday night was generally "date night" for the Tillmans and last night, they'd decided to eat in. To surprise his wife, Jaxon volunteered to cook dinner—smothered fried pork chops, yellow rice, collard greens and Mexican corn bread. It was LaShun's favorite meal, although in her quest to lose a few pounds and adopt a healthier lifestyle, she rarely ate it. Her eyes lit up when she lifted the lid of the skillet that contained the simmering meat. Jaxon knew then that he had made a good choice.

"Jaxon, this is goooooood," LaShun sang after the first bite. "You put your foot in this meat."

Jaxon laughed. "It was nothing. Just a little something that I threw together."

"Sometimes I forget how good you can cook," LaShun remarked, taking in another forkful. "I need to let you handle things in the kitchen more often."

"Don't you go getting any crazy ideas, woman."

"Ain't nothing crazy about a man in the kitchen. I think a man in an apron is sexy," she responded with a grin.

"Uh-uh," Jaxon said while shaking his head from side to

side. "I'm not falling for that. You ain't hoodwinking me into cooking. Besides, the kitchen is not my area of expertise. I do my best work in the room down the hall. But I'm all up for taking the apron in there if that's what'll get you going. Don't make me have to give you a demonstration."

"Yeah, like that would take any arm-twisting on my part." LaShun's voice was muffled by the napkin she used to wipe her lips before taking in a drink of water.

"Well, it *is* date night," Jaxon reminded her. "And a brother did just sweat over the stove to please his woman with her favorite meal."

"A minute ago, it was nothing. Now, all of a sudden, this meal required sweat? If anything, instead of rewarding you, I should put you on punishment for cooking this particular meal. You know I've been trying to shy away from fried foods and gravy. I'm trying to be fit and you're trying to make me fat."

Jaxon smiled. "I'm trying to make you fat, all right, but not in this room." Jaxon pointed toward the hall that led to the master bedroom. "I'm trying to make you fat in *that* room."

As soon as he said the words, he knew that he spoiled all chances of them having the romantically playful night that had definitely been in the making prior to his last statement. It had been a five-year-old disagreement that Jaxon thought about quite often, but tried as much as possible to avoid. How he'd let the subject matter slip from his lips at that moment, he still wasn't sure.

"What?" LaShun had heard him, he was sure. Her one-word response sounded more like a threat than a question.

"Nothing, baby," he said, hoping to quickly cover the hole

he'd just dug for himself. But LaShun wouldn't allow him an easy escape.

"You did say something. It ain't nothing new, but since you went there, apparently it's something that I haven't made myself clear enough on. So if you need to talk about it yet again, then let's."

Jaxon stared at the food that still lay on his plate. He was still hungry, but he was almost certain that it would go uneaten. He had stepped into a place of darkness, a road that he knew it was best not to travel with or without LaShun's permission. Her urging for him to talk, as far as Jaxon was concerned, was hypothetical. Her tone said otherwise. She didn't really mean for him to continue this particular conversation. No good would come of it and Jaxon was sure of that. He started his response with a slow shake of his head. "No, baby. Let's not do this tonight, okay? I'm sorry. Let's just leave it alone."

When she obliged with no further comment, Jaxon knew he'd made the right decision. But he also knew that the damage was already done. LaShun immediately excused herself, leaving the table and the remains of her favorite meal. After she showered, she put on the flannel pajamas that she always wore when they had a disagreement. It was her way of letting him know that no intimacy lay in his near future.

The sound of Jaxon's father's voice caused him to open his eyes. Reverend Tillman began singing a song that brought the music's tempo to a pace much slower than it had been. The ushers continued to do their duty, helping people back to their seats and passing out Kleenex tissues to those who were shedding tears as they worshipped. Jaxon had been so caught up in reflections of last night that he bowed his head in silent prayer, thanking God for allowing him to keep the beat of the music even though his mind had wandered from the goings-on in the sanctuary. If his father knew, he wouldn't at all be pleased.

When service finally ended, Jaxon used a nearby towel to dry the lingering perspiration before shaking several hands and heading toward the sanctuary where his wife stood with several of their friends, including Wendell and Carminda. He and LaShun hadn't talked much since last night's episode, but she welcomed his embrace when he greeted her.

"I hear we're going out today instead of to your house for dinner. What's up with that?"

Jaxon was glad that his remark to Carminda brought a smile to LaShun's face. It was the first smile he'd gotten from her all day. She had told him about her verbal exchange with Carminda on Friday and had instructed him to pretend to be a bit disappointed that Carminda had decided not to cook.

"I'm sorry, Jaxon," Carminda said, looking genuinely apologetic. "Pray for me, okay? I just get lazy sometimes."

"Well, we'll let you off the hook this time, but this had better be a good restaurant you're taking us to."

"It is," Wendell chimed in, looking at Jaxon in a manner that told him that while Carminda was fooled by his performance, he wasn't. "We're going to ESPN Zone."

"For real?" Jaxon said through wide eyes as though he didn't already know.

"Yeah," LaShun said. "Carminda thought that this would

be a good way for us to go out and you guys not be in a rush to get home for fear of missing whatever game is on this afternoon."

"Carminda, you are my favorite wife of a best friend."

"I'm sure that makes no sense, Jaxon, but it sounds good, so thank you," Carminda said.

The foursome headed for the exit doors, weaving their way through groups of people who blocked the aisles as they lingered to chat in the sanctuary. When they reached the church foyer, there was an even thicker crowd awaiting them. Some were gathered at the guest services table signing up for various upcoming events and others were waiting in a long line that extended beyond the entranceway of the church's bookstore. The message had been exceptionally stirring today, and on Sundays like this, members of the congregation didn't mind waiting for up to an hour just to get their hands on a fresh copy of the sermon so that they could hear it again in their vehicles during the commute home.

When Wendell and Carminda were called off to the side by one of the deacons, Jaxon seized the opportunity to talk to his wife privately.

"Are we okay?"

This time, LaShun's smile appeared to be forced. "Sure. Why shouldn't we be?"

"I'm sorry, baby. Really, I am. It's just—" Jaxon allowed his voice to trail, not at all certain that he should even try to explain himself. It had never worked in the past and he knew today would be no different. *Beating a dead horse* was what his mother called it.

"It's just what?"

There it was again, just like last night—permission from LaShun for him to continue. This time, though, Jaxon felt the need to say more. He knew the chance of it having much of an effect was slim to none, but he couldn't keep holding in what he knew to be the true reason for LaShun's unwillingness to even consider renegotiating her line of reasoning.

Knowing that their friends would know where to find them, Jaxon slipped his hand in LaShun's and led her into the parking lot. With so many of the church members lingering inside, there was no privacy. Even whispers could be heard if those standing nearby were nosy enough. And Shabach, like most churches, had its share of busybodies. As soon as they came to a stop beside their silver Chevy Tahoe, LaShun picked up the conversation that had been left incomplete.

"It's just what, Jaxon?"

On days like this, Jaxon was glad that he always chose to park in a space far from the church's entrance. Most members competed with one another, seeing who could arrive early enough to get the coveted spots closest to the door. Jaxon never parked in the nearest spots and today made him appreciate that more than normal. There were no vehicles parked near his and he needed the conversation to be kept between him and LaShun only. Jaxon rested his back against the side of his truck, crossed his arms in front of him and thought for a moment before answering.

"It's just that I know you'd be a great mother, LaShun, and I think you're—we're—missing out on something beautiful that can be an added blessing to our marriage."

"You don't think our marriage is good now? You think we need a kid to fill some void?"

"Baby, our marriage is *great*. If we had a bad one, I wouldn't dare think of bringing a child into it. That's just it. We've been together for seven years and married for five. We've always had a very good relationship. About the only time we ever spat is when I bring up the possibility of us having a child."

"Yet you bring it up anyway."

"I try not to, LaShun. And last night—that was almost a joke. I wasn't even really being serious at the time. I wasn't thinking about having a baby, really. I was just thinking about doing all the good stuff that can result in one."

He paused briefly and smiled when LaShun slapped him on the arm. She smiled, too. It was a good sign, and a perfect cue to continue.

"I know you have—"

"Issues?" LaShun offered when he paused to try and find the right word.

"I wasn't going to say that, but since you did, we'll go with it. I know you have issues about being a mother because of your own childhood of being in the system for all of those years—"

"I don't have issues with being in the system, Jaxon. Thousands of kids are in the system. My issue is that I *stayed* in the system. Nobody wanted me. I watched kids get adopted who stayed in the same homes at the same time that I did. The people would adopt them, but just keep me on as a foster kid. Then eventually, I'd get relocated to another home where my foster parents would do the same thing."

"But it all came to an end eventually," Jaxon said. "You got in a stable environment."

"A stable environment is not the same as having a home and a family, Jaxon. Yes, the Williamses were nice. Without them, I never would have found out who my birth mother was, but sometimes I wish I'd never learned the truth," LaShun emphasized. "The fact is, I had a mother who threw me away like common gutter trash. Sariah didn't even give me away like a regular birth mother should if she can't take care of her child. She left me on the porch of some church in the dead of winter. What kind of decent human being does that?"

"I know, I know," Jaxon said, rubbing her arms with his hands in an effort to calm her rising annoyance.

"No, you don't know. Nobody knows unless they've lived the life I've lived. Don't you see? Sariah did the same thing to me that every one of my foster mothers did. She kept the pretty yellow babies and threw away the ugly black one."

"Hold on, now, LaShun," Jaxon said, holding up his hand to stop her. "Now you've crossed the line. Do you look at yourself with the same kind of vision that everybody else does? You might have an extra layer of chocolate on you, but baby, you are a gorgeous black woman who gets second glances from every man who catches a glimpse of you. And I don't know who ever told you that you were fat. You're a size ten, for crying out loud. You got a little more meat in your seat than Carminda and some of your other skinny friends, but ain't *nobody* complaining about that. Believe you me."

LaShun's giggle was reminiscent of a schoolgirl and Jaxon was almost certain that her dark skin flushed. "You're just saying that because you're my husband."

"I'm saying that because it's true. And being your husband doesn't make that comment exclusively mine. Quite a few of the brothers here agree with me."

"Really?" LaShun brightened. "Who?"

"I'm not calling any names. Just know that there are others here who pray to one day have a wife like I have and because I see you for the person that you are, none of that surprises me. Heck, if I wasn't me, I'd be a little bit jealous of me myself."

LaShun's smile faded slowly as she brushed from her face stray strands of hair that the outside breeze had muddled. "That's sweet, but all they see is the outside. They don't know what goes on inside me. The fashion world puts Sariah on a pedestal as though she's some beautiful swan. It's just not fair. I get tired of my friends and even my husband trying to tell me a better way of handling this situation. Why does everybody side with her as though what she did was right?"

"I'm not saying she was right," Jaxon said. "I've never said she was right. Sariah was dead wrong, baby. All I've been trying to tell you for all these years is that at some point, you've got to let that mess go. You can't let it be the path that directs the rest of your life. Because your mom didn't have the capacity to love you, and because none of your foster mothers loved you enough to adopt you, doesn't mean you don't have the capacity to love a child of your own. You are not Sariah, LaShun. Baby, you've let fear keep you from something that I know you really want. I'm not the only one who wants a child, LaShun. You want one, too. I know you do. You just refuse to entertain the thought because of something that Sariah did thirty-two years ago. Don't you see? It's like you're letting her indirectly control your life. Is that the testimony that you want her to live with?"

An invisible wall of silence stood between them for several moments. Jaxon wanted to say more, but felt as if he had already said too much. But he found comfort in the fact that she hadn't interrupted his ramble with declarations of denial as he'd expected her to. LaShun stared at him, saying nothing. Even her eyes were voiceless. On most days, Jaxon could read her eyes even if her lips spoke no words. This time, he had no idea what she was thinking.

"I don't want to talk about this anymore," she finally whispered.

Nodding in agreement, Jaxon reached out to draw her closer to him. LaShun didn't resist. She wasn't crying, but Jaxon could feel her need for his understanding. He couldn't begin to claim to agree with her adamancy not to give them the child they both longed for, but today he found a glimmer of hope, knowing that he'd given her something to think about.

A part of him wanted to feel bad that in a sense, he'd used manipulation. Giving her mother any victory in her life was something that he knew LaShun wouldn't knowingly continue to do. He'd turned the tables from his usual approach. Normally, he would make it an issue that in some ways attacked LaShun, putting her on the defense. Today, he'd laid the blame in a different place, on the lap of the person that it probably legitimately belonged to—Sariah Langston.

Chapter 4

Mondays were considered the busiest day of the week for most corporations, but they were consistently the slowest at LT, Inc., not that any weekday was particularly a thriving one. Although LaShun loved her line of work, her less than impressive income was frustrating, making her decision to waste more than five hundred dollars on copies of a magazine just that much more foolish.

As a full-time publicist and part-time freelance writer, LaShun was able to live out both her dreams. For as long as she could remember, she'd wanted to be a writer. As a child, she wrote short stories that she often read to the people that she knew as her guardians. Some of her foster parents took the time to listen and others didn't. Noah and Eugenia Williams, the parents who took care of her from the time she was twelve until she was eighteen, were the best of all.

Noah would allow her to sit by his feet and read to him

for hours at a time and Eugenia would keep LaShun's supply of pencils and paper stocked. Writing became a form of therapy, helping her, on some level, to cope with her feelings of abandonment. Most of what LaShun wrote, no one ever saw. The notebooks of letters that she'd written to Sariah were never disclosed to her caregivers. Most of them were filled with enraged words and sentences that told her birth mother how angry she was and how much she hated her for making her life so difficult.

When LaShun gave her life to Christ at the age of twenty-four, she gathered all of the notebooks, put them in a plastic bag and prepared to throw them away. But for some reason she couldn't carry out her plan of disposal. So she locked them in a fireproof metal box and stored them away, vowing never again to write another nor look at the ones she'd already written. It hadn't been easy—especially the former—but LaShun had managed to keep both promises.

When she left her job as an assistant in a public relations firm to launch out on her own, LaShun had dreams of making it big. For more than two years now, she'd been struggling to prove her worth to the industry and show the doubters how talented she was in both her professions. But every month, she barely made enough money to keep the roof over her head and to pay Carminda for her three-day-a-week schedule.

"God, this is just crazy." The words burst from LaShun's lips as she looked toward the ceiling for divine direction. "Why am I, a woman who is living a Christian life, struggling like this while *that woman* gets to live lavishly as though she's done *anything at all* according to Your will?"

After a moment, she added, "Lord, You're going to have to help me with this one because I just don't understand it. You know that I'm going to need a *steady* flow of money filtering through this company or else I'm going to have to close the doors. The opportunity to start this business was a direct blessing from You. I know it was. So I know that closing it is not within Your will. I know I *should* be able to go to my rich mother and ask her for assistance, but I can't. I'm the child she gave away and then forgot about. I can't keep going to Jaxon and asking him for money to make up the shortness that I face every month. I know he has a job interview coming up that could result in a higher pay scale and I know he'll continue to help as much as he can, but Jaxon has enough responsibility taking on the mortgage, his car payment and all of the household bills. I need You to hand me a miracle, Lord. Please, God. I don't ask for much, but I'm asking You for this. Please."

LaShun's voice cracked on its last plea. When her eyes dropped, they immediately fell to the stack of bills that Carminda brought to her last week. Thinking about the fact that every single dime that she would collect this month would have to go right back out to pay her overhead nearly brought tears to her eyes. Three months ago, Elder Tillman had done an exhaustive series on faith and putting it into action by believing God, without doubt, to honor all of His promises for the lives of His people. LaShun had attended every service and had taken detailed notes. Every week, she made a special effort to implement those things that she'd learned into her daily schedule. Still, she struggled. And now, in addition to having to deal with the load of her company, *Ebony* had now reminded her of who it was that was really responsible for her struggle.

When the loud ring of LaShun's telephone cut into her private thoughts and the quiet of her office, it startled her. After a quick, calming moment to gather her professional wits, she inhaled and lifted the telephone receiver from its cradle.

"LT, Inc., LaShun Tillman speaking."

"Well heavens to Betsy! You're just the person I wanted to speak to. How are you today, Mrs. Tillman?"

Aw, man! LaShun thought. *It's a white woman—a sure sign of a bill collector. I shouldn't have said my name. If I hadn't given myself away, I could pretend LaShun Tillman wasn't in.*

LaShun knew that lying would have been wrong, but even that possibility wasn't an option now. There was no way to back out of this one. All she could do was hope that she had enough money in her account to pay the minimum amount required to keep the service going.

"I'm doing well, thank you. How are you?"

"I could only be better if I were talking to Oprah," the stranger said just before releasing a lengthy roll of laughter. LaShun didn't find it nearly as funny. She only laughed in hopes that it would work to her advantage in the end. She was willing to do whatever it took to make the bill collector more lenient.

"Who among us wouldn't want to be talking to Oprah?" LaShun remarked. "I know I could use her endorsement right now."

"Tell me about it," the stranger said. "But the way my magazine has sometimes put her weight battles under the microscope, I doubt I could even pay for her endorsement."

Magazine? Now, LaShun was puzzled. "I'm sorry. I didn't get your name."

"Penelope Bion," she announced, "but please call me Penny."

LaShun's heart skipped a beat. Everybody who was anybody in the media knew Penelope Bion. She was the editor of *B.I.O.N. Magazine,* where the letters of her last name turned into an acronym for Believe It or Not. It was one of the hottest celebrity-focused periodicals in the country, and although Ms. Bion had been quoted in many interviews as saying that *B.I.O.N.* was not a tabloid, it came very close to it. LaShun had never had much respect for the publication or its credibility, but she couldn't help but admire the way Penelope had started her company with little and had grown it into the national phenomenon that it was.

After taking a much-needed moment to gather her scattered nerves, LaShun said, "Penny, well, hello. How are you?" She tried to make it sound as though she spoke to important people on a daily basis.

"I'm great, LaShun. I can call you LaShun, can't I?"

"Oh, absolutely. How are things at *B.I.O.N Magazine?*" As she spoke the words, LaShun prayed that Penny was in the market for a publicist. When she thought of the money she could make by being connected to the tail of *B.I.O.N.*'s star, LaShun could see her financial woes quickly becoming an issue of the past.

"Honey, let me tell you," Penny said, sounding like the native New Yorker that she was. "*B.I.O.N.* is going places! In the last three years, our subscriber database has almost tripled. We're up to printing and distributing a half-million copies every month, and by the looks of things, that number can easily double by the time I turn forty."

Penny was thirty-eight and the whole world knew that. Every year, when her birthday rolled around, she made a big ado about it in her magazine. The first issue of *B.I.O.N.* made its debut when Penny was the same age that LaShun was right now. But unlike LT, Inc., by the time *B.I.O.N.* was two years old, it was already a profitable business.

"That's wonderful," LaShun said, feeling somewhat valued by the fact that Penny had started her statement off by referencing her in such a casual "girlfriend" manner. "You are really spreading your wings. It's good to see a woman making it in the industry."

"Well, thank you, LaShun. I'm glad you feel that way because *B.I.O.N.* is having growing pains and this woman needs some help. Would you be interested in being a part of *B.I.O.N.*'s expanding team?"

LaShun's heart felt as though it was going to knock a hole in her chest. *Look at God!* she thought, coming very close to allowing the words to spill out of her mouth. "Sure. My company is actively taking on new clients and I'd love to represent *B.I.O.N.*"

"Oh, no, no, no," Penny quickly said, momentarily draining every ounce of glee from LaShun's body. "We've had a publicist for years and he's done a remarkable job. How do you think we've grown so large in so little time?"

Dummy. For a fleeting moment, LaShun thought Penny had verbalized the one-word insult, but she quickly found that it was her own loud thoughts that had pinned the brand on her own lapel. She should have known better than to think that a woman like Penelope Bion would call Atlanta from New York in hopes of getting a publicist. New York was crawling with outstanding publicists and even if Penelope needed another, she wouldn't have had to go outside of her state.

"What was it that I can do for you then?" LaShun said, taking a sip of water to try to wash down her embarrassment.

"I get several magazines and I happened to run across one in particular that had a great article that you wrote concerning the rise of African-American fiction writers."

"I did," LaShun replied.

"And the following month—last month, actually—you wrote an article for the same magazine wherein you had interviewed some celebrity keynote speakers and wrote an article called 'In Front of the Camera—Behind the Mic.'"

"Yes."

"Well, I was impressed by both of them. You are an outstanding writer, LaShun. I'm surprised that you don't do more of it."

The compliment brought a grin to LaShun's face. "Thank you, Penny."

"Oh, I mean it, honey. You're good. That's why I'm calling you. What I want is for you to write for *B.I.O.N.*," Penny said. "Is that something that would interest you?"

It wasn't the publicity job she assumed the call was concerning, but LaShun sat up straight in her seat. Many times she would write features for national publications and her only compensation would be what seemed to have become the industry standard: exposure in the form of small ad spaces for LT, Inc. or a tagline at the end of her article that identified her as a publicist and writer. Both came with some degree of reward, but money was what she needed most at this stage of her career. And *B.I.O.N.*'s contributing writers not only got paid, but they got paid well. According to their level of experience, Penny was rumored to pay her staff writers almost double the price per word that most publications offered.

Freelance writers vied for the opportunity to be associated with *B.I.O.N.* The only reason that LaShun had never solicited the magazine for writing opportunities was because she'd somewhat viewed the content of the monthly periodical as "inappropriate." She didn't mind having her name linked to secular publications, but with its infamous brash and potentially hurtful articles, LaShun thought it was best to steer clear of *B.I.O.N. Magazine.* But now…

Elder Tillman just spoke about this yesterday, LaShun thought in amazement. *This is I Corinthians 1: 27 fully defined! 'God has chosen the foolish things of the world to confound the wise.' Wow! Thank you, Jesus, for answered prayers!* "What exactly did you have in mind, Penny?"

Chapter 5

Two weeks had passed since the argument that resulted in Geoffrey leaving his family home in the community of Buckhead in the middle of the night. He had no agenda in mind but found himself heading to Sandy Springs, an area north of Buckhead, beyond the Atlanta city limit. He knew he had no business being there. Geoffrey purposefully avoided the area where trouble found him every time he visited.

"Well, Geoffrey Langston," Soy said when she opened her front door to find him standing there. "How long has it been? Three years?"

"Almost five," he mumbled as he stepped into the opening that she provided for him. "How've you been?"

"I've been fine, but I'm even better now that you're here."

"Are you alone?" he asked, looking at her chosen nightwear. "Are you expecting someone?"

Soy laughed. "Yes, I'm alone and no, I'm not expecting anyone. And if I were, he'd be out of luck now."

She said more words, too, but Geoffrey was too preoccupied to hear them. Soy was a beautiful woman made up of the perfect mixture of Asian and African-American. He didn't know her age, but Soy was quite a bit younger than him; perhaps thirty, thirty-five at the most. She had thick, dark, wavy hair that fell beyond her shoulders and a body that God must have designed on the sixth day of creation. Having to mold one such as hers had to be the true reason that He needed to rest on the seventh day. It was the aphorism that Geoffrey used to say quite often during the year that she served as his mistress. Soy wasn't the only "other woman" that he entertained, but she was his favorite. With her, he could be carefree, stress free and just plain *free*. She wasn't demanding and she wasn't argumentative—just accommodating.

When Geoffrey returned from his mental trip to the not-so-distant past, he noticed her walk across the room and come to a seated position on her white leather couch, holding two glasses of champagne in her hands. Soy's home had changed quite a bit since his last visit. All of the furniture was new, the living room walls had been painted with a coat of pale pink and her carpeted floors had been replaced with hardwood ones that glistened as though it had been spit-shined. Geoffrey was all but certain that his generous sum of "hush money" had financed much of the upgrade.

"I never expected to see you again," she said, sipping from one glass and placing the other on a coaster that she had placed on her marble, glass-top coffee table. It was an unspoken invitation for him to sit beside her and Geoffrey accepted with a trace of caution.

"Why?" Geoffrey was fully aware of the answer to his question, but he needed to keep the conversation going.

"Because you said so," she said, affectionately mingling her fingers with his salt-and-pepper hair. "I believe your exact words were, 'I'm sorry but it's time I start doing right by Sariah. You won't see me again, but I hope this cash will be enough to convince you to keep our affair private. If you care for me at all, please grant me that one request.'"

Geoffrey couldn't help but smile a little as he lifted the glass to his lips. "I guess you cared."

"And I would have kept it quiet even without the money you gave me. I cared that much."

"Oh yeah? Then why didn't you give it back?"

"I said I cared. I didn't say I was stupid."

They laughed together.

"So, what sent you back to me all these years later? I know you're still with your wife. I saw her on the front of *Ebony* this month." As Soy talked, she crossed her long legs, allowing her silk robe to fall open just enough to stir Geoffrey's appetite.

He cleared his throat. "We had a fight. I just needed to get away for a while. Needed a little peace, that's all."

"Peace? Is that what I give you?"

Her moves were no longer subtle. When Soy asked the question, she placed her empty glass on the coffee table and with one sweep of her hand she unloosed the belt of her robe. Very little was left to Geoffrey's imagination as he stared at the lingerie that barely covered her body. He swallowed. It had been a long time, but he remembered well what it was like to share a bed with the woman whose first name was all that he ever knew.

When Soy leaned in close to kiss him, Geoffrey didn't resist. It was like old times. From the first time he saw her dancing in one of Buckhead's upscale gentleman's clubs, he wanted her. Nothing had changed. Soy still knew just the right words to say. Geoffrey knew he could ask for anything and she wouldn't deny him. She was still aware of his weaknesses and he was aware of her strengths. But even with her making herself available for his full enjoyment, Geoffrey couldn't go through with it.

"I can't," he said, pulling away and gaining enough control of his buckling knees to stand from the sofa that they'd turned into a makeshift bed.

"What? Why? Geoffrey, what are you doing?"

Geoffrey moved quickly to button buttons and zip zippers that had been loosened during the brief passionate entanglement. "I'm sorry, Soy. I can't. I shouldn't have come here. I'm sorry. Please forgive me. I've got to get out of here."

"No, Geoffrey." Her eyes were pleading. "You don't have to leave. I want you to stay. Please don't leave me like this."

Looking at her and knowing that she wanted him as badly as he wanted her almost made him change his mind, but he couldn't. Geoffrey didn't know why he couldn't just have her one more time. He felt paranoid. As if cameras were hidden around the town house that would forever capture his misconduct. Reminders resurfaced of Yasmin, another unlawful lover who had somehow had incriminating pictures of the two of them taken and then showed them to Sariah. While Geoffrey felt that he knew Soy well enough to be confident that she wouldn't do such a thing, he never would have expected it from Yasmin, either.

* * *

"Mr. Langston?"

The voice that blared through his office's intercom system startled him, causing Geoffrey to wince and turn quickly from the window he'd been staring out of.

"Mr. Langston?" his secretary repeated.

Geoffrey walked to his desk and pressed the button to respond. "Yes, Marla?"

"Your next appointment has arrived."

"Thank you, Marla. Send him in."

Geoffrey wasn't generally the one to do interviews at the companies he owned. As a matter of fact, most times, his was a face that was never seen except by the members of the executive boards. It was only because of Goldstar Pharmaceutical's new shift in power that he was conducting today's interviews. The executive sales manager position was a newly created one that would pay six figures annually. And because of the expectations of the person who would fill it, Geoffrey thought it best that he be the one to meet each prospective hire. So far today, he had interviewed two men and one woman, and although they met the basic qualifications to take the job, Geoffrey hadn't been impressed by any of them.

"Come in," he said, having heard the light knock on his door.

The well-dressed man walked in with a portfolio in one hand and the other outstretched in a warm, friendly gesture. As far as Geoffrey was concerned, he already had an edge over the others, who'd seemed to come to their interviews at a moment's notice. He accepted the gentleman's hand and took note of the firm, confident hand-shake that was delivered.

"Hello, Mr. Edwards. I'm Jaxon Tillman. It's a pleasure to meet you."

"My secretary didn't tell you that Mr. Edwards wasn't the person interviewing you," Geoffrey observed, then watched a look of embarrassment cover Jaxon's face.

"I'm sorry. No, I wasn't made aware."

"No apologies necessary. She'd probably said it so much to others that she just inadvertently overlooked doing the same with you. Please have a seat."

Jaxon obeyed, sitting in a comfortable deep brown suede chair that was situated near the window of the office. Geoffrey sat in a matching one that was near it and browsed through the leather-bound portfolio that he was given.

"You look extremely familiar," Jaxon said. "Have we possibly met?"

Reminded that he never gave his name, Geoffrey laughed out loud. "According to what circles you surround yourself with, it's highly possible. I own this company and several others. But please forgive me for not properly introducing myself. I'm Geoffrey Langston."

He noticed the bewildered expression that engulfed Jaxon's face. "Of Langston Enterprises?"

"That's the one."

"Oh," Jaxon replied, tugging at the sleeves of his suit jacket. "I'm sorry if I seem a bit discombobulated. I wasn't aware that Goldstar Pharmaceuticals was part of your empire."

"Oh?"

"Please don't take that to mean that I came unprepared.

I researched the company quite thoroughly before applying for the position, but I never saw that it was an entity of Langston Enterprises."

Geoffrey smiled. "I believe you." He gestured toward the portfolio that now lay in his lap. "It's obvious that you did your homework. There's a good reason why you didn't see Langston Enterprises' name attached to Goldstar Pharmaceuticals. The buyout was just finalized a few days ago and the press hasn't yet sent out the hounds to sniff out the property."

When Jaxon didn't immediately reply, Geoffrey said, "Let's get to it, shall we?"

"Sure."

"Your résumé says that you've been in sales for quite some time."

"Yes, I have. I've been with the same company for the past ten years. I started out as a sales representative and I recently got my third promotion. I'm now sales manager and have been for the past six months."

"Do you like working there?"

"For the most part, yes. I've learned a lot in the past decade. Prior to taking on the job there, my work history had been in the human resources field. They offered on-the-job training and my experience as a sales rep made me realize how much I enjoyed the aspects of being a salesman. However, I wanted to do more than what my position at that time allowed. Unfortunately, I didn't have the educational qualifications to do so. I rectified that by going back to school and obtained a degree which allowed me to work through the ranks."

"And so you did," Geoffrey said. "But if you are, for the

most part, content in your current position, why do you wish to go elsewhere? One of the most important things in life is to find success in a job that you love. What if you don't have the same degree of appreciation for this job as you have for the one you currently hold?"

Leaning forward in his chair, Jaxon paused, as though trying to search for just the right words to say. "For me, the most important thing in life isn't success on a job, Mr. Langston. What's dearest to my heart is my service to God and my dedication to my family. I have a wife whom I love dearly. She has been blessed with her own business but she's been struggling to get it off the ground. I'm the only family that she has that she can depend on. Quite honestly, Mr. Langston, I want her to know that I'll do whatever it takes to help her live her dream, even if it means filling in for others who *could* help, but won't. Plus, I'm hopeful that we will start a family soon and this job will give her added assurance that an expanded family won't put any further financial strain on us," Jaxon stated.

"I do enjoy my current position, Mr. Langston. But I also enjoy a challenge. And I have no doubt that working for a corporation with Goldstar's proficient reputation and demand for excellence will afford me to be challenged in ways that can only enhance my already commendable skills and will give me opportunities for growth that my current job is not in the position to offer."

When Jaxon was finished, he rested against the back of the chair in a manner that told Geoffrey that he was now free to speak. All of a sudden, Geoffrey wasn't sure whether he liked this candidate or not. Jaxon seemed a bit self-absorbed and egotistical. There was no waver in his voice and when he spoke to Geoffrey, Jaxon never lost eye contact. Quite frankly, Geoffrey wasn't sure how to regard his tone or his body language. All the other candidates seemed a bit unnerved by Geoffrey and in a sense, he appreciated that. It was a show of respect as far as he was concerned. It told him that they knew their place and they esteemed him as the company's new CEO. But Jaxon Tillman showed no intimidation and almost came across as a bit narcissistic. Geoffrey hadn't seen such assertion since…well, since himself at Jaxon's age.

Chapter 6

"Does Jaxon know about this?"

LaShun looked across the table where she sat at Chili's Restaurant and into the frantic eyes of her inquisitive friend. It was Thursday, the one day of the week that she and Carminda always ate lunch outside of the office. It was their way of celebrating the act of making it over the imaginary "hump" that Wednesday represented.

LaShun had held back for three days and during that time, she seriously toyed with the idea of not sharing the news of her latest venture with Carminda. It was a great opportunity, but LaShun wasn't at all certain that her best friend would see it that way. But the secret proved to be stronger than LaShun's self-will. Now, with the reaction that resulted, LaShun was second-guessing her decision.

"He doesn't know, does he?" Carminda said after LaShun didn't immediately answer.

"Yes, Carminda. Of course I told him." The words were mixed in a profound sigh. LaShun could feel a lecture coming on that would include either a heavier accent or those infamous repetitive sentences. She wasn't in the mood for either.

"Are you sure?"

"I just said I did, didn't I?"

Carminda still wasn't convinced. "You mean to tell me that you told Jaxon that you would be composing a continuing article in *B.I.O.N. Magazine* that would be attacking your mother's character and he gave you permission to do it?"

Placing her empty glass on the table, LaShun looked at Carminda through narrowed eyes. "First of all, she's *not* my mother. She just gave birth to me—no more, no less. And secondly, did you just say permission? Excuse me, but since when do I ever need Jaxon's permission to do anything? I'm thirty-two years old. He's my husband, not my daddy. So, no, I didn't get his permission, but I didn't ask for it either."

"You know what I mean."

"Actually, I don't," LaShun said, still annoyed by Carminda's insinuation. "Jaxon knows that Penelope Bion called me and he knows that she offered me a *paying* job with her paper. He also knows that I need an added steady income right now. He had questions and concerns, yes, but I think I calmed most of them."

"What did you tell him about the job?"

"I told him that my assignment was to write about little-known celebrity facts."

"So you lied to him."

"No, I didn't. That is what my assignment is."

Carminda shook her head in disappointment. "I can't believe you, LaShun. I just cannot believe you. How long are you going to hold on to this matter with Sariah? How many more years? This hurt that you've carried around for years is turning into something far more detrimental and that's not good. Do you think God is pleased with what you are doing? Do you think He's pleased?"

"See, that's where you're wrong again. I'm not hurt by what that woman did," LaShun defended. "I was better off without her in my life. I couldn't care less one way or the other about her."

"That's not true."

"How are you going to tell me what's not true? You don't know how I feel."

"If you couldn't care less, why are you doing this article? Of all the things you could have written about, why are you writing about her?"

"Because the public has a right to know," LaShun said. "They have a right to know that her beauty is only skin-deep and they need to know that she threw away a child."

"Why is that the public's business?"

"Because they've been duped by her and it's their dollars that have made her rich. All those years of being the spokeswoman for Beautiful Lady hair products and heading the televised campaign against child abuse when she abused her own child by leaving her out in the elements until someone could find her. I'll bet you that they don't even know that her real name is Sara Faye. I guess she changed it to Sariah Faith because it sounded more polished. Everything about her is fake, Carminda, and she's gotten away with it for long enough. It's time that someone pulled the cover off her and I'm going to be the one to do it."

"But, LaShun, you won't be hurting only her, you'll be hurting her family, as well. Think about her husband and the girls."

"You best believe that Geoffrey Langston already knows he's married to a piece of trash. That's why he messed around on her for all those years. Probably still is. And the kids, well, it's not that I'm going in with the intent to hurt them, but I'm sure the news of finding out that their daddy was hanging his trousers all over town was far more damaging than this would be."

Both the women quieted when the waiter came to refill their glasses and to bring the desserts. Once he was gone, Carminda was the first to speak.

"This isn't right, LaShun. Gabrielle and Giovanna don't deserve this. They're just kids. They aren't responsible for their mother's sins and they shouldn't be made to pay."

"*Gabrielle and Giovanna.* That's another thing. Look at what she named them, versus what she named me. She didn't want to keep me but as a last act of hatred, she named me LaShun and put it in an anonymous letter in my blanket when she left me behind."

"What's wrong with LaShun?" Carminda asked. "I like your name."

"It gives away my race, that's what's wrong with it. Nobody names their kids stuff that starts in 'La' except black folks. Do you know how that could have affected my chances of getting good jobs? A mother should never name her child anything that gives away their ethnicity just by reading the résumé. LaShun. Could she have been any less creative?"

"Now you're grasping for straws," Carminda said. "I don't dislike my parents for what they named me. My father's name is Carmen and my mother's name is Linda. How much thought do you think went into coming up with the name *Carminda*? But it's my name and I embrace it. This isn't about your name, LaShun, this is about a thirty-two-year vendetta that you've had with Sariah and how you've allowed it to balloon into an all-out attack. Your foster mother never should have told you that Sariah was your birth mother. Then we wouldn't be having this problem."

LaShun was tired of having the same discussion over and over again. The subject of her disdain for Sariah was way past old. Nobody could fully comprehend her stance and she could deal with their inability to relate. But she couldn't deal with their tendency to be judgmental, constantly telling her how wrong *she* was for feeling the way she felt.

"Ms. Eugenia didn't tell me about Sariah. She only directed me to people and private organizations that could possibly give me insight on how to find out who my birth mother was. I'm glad she did."

"Why? So you could destroy her?"

"Carminda, when I first began my search for the woman who gave me up for adoption, I wanted to find her to fill the void in my life. I needed to know who she was. I'd watched all of those talk shows on television and had seen the uniting of lost loved ones and I was sure that I was one of those cases. You know, the cases where the moms were poor and desti-tute and gave their children away so that they could have a better life. They thought they had no choice. Then when the kids would find them, they'd also find out that their mothers had been looking for them, as well. I thought that would be my reality, too.

"Then when I finally uncover the identity of my birth mother, I find out that she's the Sariah Faith Langston who had been discovered by the modeling world at fifteen and was world-renowned by the time she was eighteen. She had me when she was seventeen, Carminda. She wasn't poor or destitute. She was just selfish and evil. Probably didn't want me because I didn't match the shoes she'd be wearing in her next photo shoot. I get tired of everybody telling me what I should and should not do. Sariah never considered how her actions would affect my life, so why should I worry about what my column is going to do to hers?"

"Because you know the Lord, LaShun. The difference between you and Sariah is that she needs what you have. And you know what? Because of your knowledge of Christ, He holds you to a higher standard. You can't control what she did to you, but you certainly can control how you react to it and I don't mean to become an overnight preacher, but the truth is, you're not at all portraying Christianity right now, LaShun."

LaShun smirked in Carminda's direction and said, "The Bible did say that in the last day, false prophets would come."

"That's not funny, LaShun. I'm serious."

"So am I," LaShun replied, taking in the last forkful of her brownie. "For your information, I'd just finished praying and asking God for an opportunity for an increase in pay. It wasn't even two minutes later when Penny called. And when I was praying about what my column should be about,

God told me that I should take this opportunity to purge myself of the repressed anger concerning Sariah. He told me to use the gift He gave me to reach all of the men and women out there who are going through what I'm going through and don't know how to work through it. So, check this. I *am* portraying Christianity because I got this straight from the top, Carminda. While you're worried about whether or not I have Jaxon's permission, what you *should* be worried about is whether or not I have God's permission. And I do. So case closed."

Chapter 7

Being on the front of one of the nation's most respected African-American publications had opened new doors for Sariah, offering new life to a career that had been all but laid to rest. April had been a busy month for interviews, commercial tapings and photo sessions, taking her back to the days when she was at the prime of her modeling profession. It had been fun, but Sariah welcomed the month of May, realizing that it would be calmer and less demanding. Sometimes she missed the days when her name was synonymous with glamour and other times she wished she could erase those years from her memory. As much popularity and wealth that her beauty had afforded her, the pain that came along with it sometimes overshadowed everything else. Privately, Sariah hoped that neither of her daughters chose the same path. She was almost sure that Giovanna wouldn't, but as much as she tried not to, Sariah couldn't help but worry about Gabrielle.

While Giovanna had a definite love for the camera, spending endless hours in front of the mirror and taking pictures of herself at every available opportunity, it was all in vain fun. The fifteen-year-old had made it ultimately clear that if she broke into the fashion industry, she would be the one behind the scenes, styling the hair of, designing clothing for and putting makeup on the ones who would be captured on film. In her mind, those who created the beauty were the real celebrities. Models were just billboards that advertised the work of others.

Gabrielle, on the other hand, seemed fascinated with the modeling world. She read more books than she watched television, but *America's Next Top Model* was one of the few shows that she watched religiously. All else in the world came to an abrupt pause when the reality show came on, and until the show ended, nothing else mattered. Aside from that, Gabrielle had already had her first modeling gig. It was for the winter edition of a teen catalog that came out last December and all of the girls chosen were virtual amateurs. But Gabrielle's photos were so appealing that offers for other opportunities were beginning to pour in. Sariah knew that if her daughter found out that she'd been turning them down on her behalf, Gabrielle would never forgive her.

"Coffee ready?"

"Yeah." Sariah had heard her husband descending the staircase and was already reaching into the cabinet to retrieve his favorite mug.

Since their argument that had sent Geoffrey driving into the night, their conversations had be reduced to short sentences that rarely consisted of more than a few words. Sariah tried not to think the worst, but he had been gone an awfully long time that night and when he returned hours later, Geoffrey offered no explanations. After he'd fallen asleep, Sariah pulled his clothing from the hamper and pressed each article to her nose, inhaling deeply. It brought some relief that his scent was the only one that she could identify, but if he had taken off the clothes to do whatever it was that he did in his hours of absence, there would be no other scent on them for her to spot.

"Thanks," Geoffrey mumbled from his place on the bar stool when she handed him his cup. He didn't look at her or bring his eyes from the morning paper at all.

"Busy day today?" she probed.

"Not really." He blew into the cup and took a sip, still scanning the numbers of the stock charts.

"The new hires start today, right?"

"Uh-huh."

Standing at a distance near the refrigerator, Sariah studied Geoffrey's profile. If it weren't for his graying hair, most people would probably never guess that he was nearly fifty-five. Geoffrey's brown skin was the perfect median between his mother's dark complexion and his father's fair, freckled skin. His dark eyebrows and heavy lashes added a softness to his otherwise chiseled facial features. The first time she met him, Sariah was captured. Back then, he didn't seem seriously interested in her—probably because of the nearly five-year age difference. But he had a reputation among many of her industry acquaintances. They raved about his skills, business and otherwise. Every model wanted to walk a runway wearing clothing designed by Eloise Langston. Not so much to be near her, but for a chance to get acquainted with her only son.

"What?"

Only after Geoffrey's one-word question did Sariah realize that he had noticed her stare.

"Huh?"

"Why are you looking at me like that?" he asked.

Sariah opened her mouth to respond but the sounds of her daughters' footsteps against the hardwood floors stopped her. The distraction brought her out of the corner where she'd been standing, but Geoffrey's fixed eyes followed her as if still awaiting her reply. Sariah knew how distant she and Geoffrey had been over the past few days and she knew that both Giovanna and Gabrielle were too smart and observant not to have noticed. But she thought it was best not to reply in their company, especially since she couldn't be sure that an argument wouldn't result.

"Good morning," Sariah said when she saw both girls pass the kitchen and head toward the den without greeting either of their parents.

"Good morning." Both their responses sounded half-hearted.

"You should eat some breakfast before leaving," Sariah advised.

Giovanna had already disappeared around the corner, but Sariah was certain that she'd heard her. Gabrielle, on the other hand, didn't have the luxury of pretending she'd been out of listening range of her mother's suggestion. She was still in Sariah's view when the words were spoken.

"I'm on a diet," Gabrielle said matter-of-factly, stopping by the bar long enough to kiss her father's cheek.

Sariah swallowed back her envy. She couldn't remember the last time her daughters had shown her such affection. She couldn't remember the last time she'd shown it to them, either.

"What do you mean you're on a diet?"

"I'm a senior, Mom. Graduation is coming up soon. I want to lose a few pounds before that time. In case you hadn't noticed, I've put on two pounds since the school term started in August."

Sariah cringed. It was happening. Gabrielle was thinking more and more like a model. Her daughter hadn't been overweight since she was two years old. Back then, she was a pudgy-cheeked toddler, but as her height lengthened, her body slimmed. She was currently wearing a size four. Nothing about Gabrielle's figure hinted the need for weight loss.

"No, I hadn't noticed," Sariah said. "You don't need to lose any weight, Gabrielle. You're thin enough."

"Apparently not. Did you know that both Dena and Tammy got callbacks from that magazine shoot we did last year? They didn't call me back to pose for the new issue. I probably weigh ten pounds more than both of them. I'll bet if I wore a size zero like Dena, I would have gotten called back, too."

Turning her back to her daughter so that the shame on her face would not give her away, Sariah walked to the kitchen counter, picked up a dishcloth and began wiping away an invisible spill. In her effort to protect her child, she was somehow making matters worse. Sariah had turned down several calls that had come in for Gabrielle, hoping no new opportunities would eventually make her lose interest in the business. Now, it was backfiring in an even worse way.

"Your time will come, sweetheart," Geoffrey said, unknowingly rescuing his wife. "I don't want you trying to get down to a size zero for anybody."

"But, Daddy, that's the nature of the business. You know, like long hours and frequent business meetings are the nature of your business. You do what you have to do to succeed."

"All models aren't a size zero, Gabrielle," Geoffrey replied. "Your mother was never a size zero and she was a success."

"Maybe they accepted larger models way back then."

Way back then? Sariah looked at her daughter in disapproval and opened her mouth to defend herself, but never got a chance before Geoffrey spoke up.

"You're beautiful and your body makeup is perfect as it is."

Gabrielle fought not to smile, but the grin broke through and was accompanied by the blushing of her fair skin. "You're just saying that because you're my dad."

"No. I'm saying it because it's true and because I love you."

"But your love isn't going to help me become a fashion model."

"Then maybe you can look into other professions," Sariah chimed in. "You're great in science. Did you ever think of pursuing a career in the medical field?"

Gabrielle's only response was the grimace that loudly proclaimed her objection to her mother's idea.

"What do you mean my love can't help you become a model?" Geoffrey said. "If being a model is what you want to do, I'll arrange for you to become one of the freshest faces of one of our country's top fashion designers."

Gabrielle's eyes enlarged to the size of quarters. "You mean—?"

"Yes. The E.L. Langston line. Your Grandma Eloise would have been proud to have you wear her designs."

Sariah's jaw dropped, but neither of them seemed to notice.

"Really, Daddy?" With her arms tightly locked around his waist and her face pressed into her father's chest, Gabrielle's words were muffled.

"You'll have to work hard like every other model, but if you're willing to do what it takes, I can definitely work out the logistics. You should be able to start as early as when they unveil this winter's line later this year."

As she watched it all unfold, Sariah felt as though her heart would stop beating.

"Thank you, Daddy. I love you so much."

At those words, Sariah used one hand to quickly wipe away a tear that had escaped her right eye. The others, she blinked away, not wanting her family to see her hurt. Not that anyone would have noticed, anyway. Gabrielle and Geoffrey kept talking as though she wasn't even in the same room with them.

"I know you love me, sweetheart," Geoffrey said, returning his daughter's embrace. "As long as what you want to do with your life is something honest and decent, you know I'll support you."

"And you're not just saying this so I won't go on a diet, right?" Gabrielle asked as she took a step backward.

Geoffrey shook his head. "No, but if this will keep you

from trying to become a stick of a human being, then it's definitely a fringe benefit. Besides, if you get too skinny, I'll think you'll break when I do this."

In a sudden swift movement, Geoffrey grabbed his daughter around the waist and pulled her in for a tight hug. Gabrielle giggled as she playfully swatted at him and begged to be released. Her wish was finally granted, but only after Geoffrey had placed a long kiss on her cheek, complete with the loud moaning noise he used to make when the girls were little and he'd tease them in the same manner.

"Here," Geoffrey said, picking up a red apple from the fruit bowl on the bar and placing it in Gabrielle's hand. "Eat this for me, okay? You need brain food for your morning classes."

"It's too late to eat, Daddy. It's time for us to leave."

"You've got time," he said, smoothing down hairs on her head that his embrace had messed up moments earlier. "You can eat it on the way. And take one for your sister, too. You all head to the car and I'll be out in just a second."

"Okay, Daddy," Gabrielle replied, taking the second apple that he offered while biting into the first.

"Good girl," he said with a grin. "Eloise Langston believed in good nourishment, so make breakfast a practice."

"Okay," Gabrielle said and then turned to leave.

"Bye, Gabrielle. Have a good day at school," Sariah called behind her.

She was already out of her mother's sight, but she offered a lackadaisical, "Bye, Mom."

Sariah sighed. She'd wanted a closer relationship with them than she'd had with her mother, but like just about everything else in her life, that mission hadn't turned out as planned, either. She stepped aside and made room for Geoffrey as he placed his empty coffee cup in the dishwasher. After doing so, he turned and looked at her, putting his movements on pause.

"Was there something that you wanted to say earlier before we were interrupted?"

With a thousand thoughts running through her mind, Sariah looked at her husband in silence. He had no idea just how much she wanted to say to him. She wanted to tell him that he looked quite dashing in the gray Georgio Armani suit that he was wearing. She wanted to ask him to be more supportive of her opinions where their daughters were concerned. She wanted to tell him how much she loved him and needed to be held in his arms right now. She wanted to express how regretful she was for bringing up his past the other night and sparking the argument whose aftershock had lasted for days. Sariah wanted to apologize for the secrets and the lies, but of all the things she wanted to say only one word would come from her lips.

"No."

Moving at a snail's pace, as though giving her a chance to reconsider her decision, Geoffrey turned away, picked up his keys from the bar and rounded the corner that would lead to where Gabrielle and Giovanna waited. After hearing the garage door rise and descend and no longer having to be concerned of who would see them, Sariah allowed the tears that she'd been fighting to flow freely down her face.

Chapter 8

"A penny for your thoughts."

Wendell and Carminda had been lying in bed, quietly snuggled in each other's arms, for quite some time when Wendell broke the silence. It was early Friday morning; so early that the sun had not yet broken the darkness of the night before it. For Carminda, the workweek had come to an end as quickly as it had begun. For the past two weeks, LaShun had been in a good mood. And knowing the reason behind LaShun's misguided joy disturbed Carminda. A lot of things weighed on her mind that could cost Wendell more than a few pennies, but she was cautious as to whether she should take her chances and cash in.

"I was thinking about love," she said, running her fingers through the fine hairs on Wendell's chest.

"What about love?"

Carminda repositioned herself so that her elbow rested

on her pillow and her hand was used as a prop for the side of her face. "I don't know. I guess I just look at people who are in love and wonder if love is the same for everybody."

Wendell chuckled. "Well, aren't we being philosophical at four in the morning?"

"I'm serious," Carminda said. "I mean, look at us. How many couples do you know that wake each other up at two in the morning for a lovemaking session?"

This time, Wendell laughed out loud. "First of all, brothas don't usually have these types of discussions with each other, so I wouldn't know what my friends do with their wives in the wee hours of the morning. Secondly, we didn't wake each other up, *you* woke me up."

"Any complaints?" Carminda challenged.

"Not a one."

"I didn't think so."

They shared a laugh as Carminda placed her head back on her husband's chest. For a while, they both lay in silence. Carminda listened to the rhythmic beat of Wendell's heart and enjoyed the slow movement of her head as it rose and fell with his breathing. For a moment, the motion made her think of the gentle waves of water that encircled the cruise ship that they sailed on two years ago in honor of their first wedding anniversary.

Carminda and Wendell's marriage was still relatively young, but it was a solid one, much like their best friends'. LaShun and Jaxon had been married a few years longer and theirs was the union that Carminda secretly used as a model by which to fashion her own. LaShun made Jaxon happy and vice versa. They prayed together regularly, supported one another and respected each other's opinion, even when they didn't see eye-to-eye. They had disagreements like every married couple did, but anger never lingered in their house. That was the kind of marriage Carminda had prayed she would have when she and Wendell began premarital counseling with Elder Tillman and God had granted her the desires of her heart.

But it bothered her that with all the security that LaShun and Jaxon had, LaShun had chosen to withhold from Jaxon the full extent of her relationship with *B.I.O.N.* Carminda didn't care how much her friend tried to explain herself, she was certain that Jaxon didn't know the details about the column that his wife would be contributing to the magazine on a monthly basis.

"Why do I get the feeling that there are more thoughts swimming in your head than one about the stages of love?" When Wendell began talking, Carminda's thoughts were interrupted.

"Probably because you know me well," she said as she sat up in the bed and rested her back against the headboard.

Wendell joined her. "You want to talk about it?"

"I don't know if I should."

Wendell remained quiet, but even in the dim light of the bedroom, which was brightened only by their muted television, Carminda could see the heightened inquisitiveness in his eyes.

"Do you intentionally keep secrets from me?" she asked when he didn't press for more information.

"What? Where did that come from?"

"I'm just asking. My mom always taught me that God didn't find pleasure in secrets within a marriage. She said that His will was that married couples always be open and honest with each other. According to Mama, next to prayer, honesty was the most important key to longevity in a marriage."

"So, you think your folks tell each other everything?"

Carminda took a moment to think and then nodded. "I really do. Growing up, I can remember times that my parents would sit at the dining room table and discuss things as if they were at a board meeting. They even made actual appointments to sit down and talk about whatever was the topic of concern. All of the decisions they made concerning me and my siblings were made together. My mom once told me that when one or the other of them was ready to have another child, they'd sit down and weigh the pros and cons of doing so and they never got pregnant unless they were in agreement."

"So what are you saying? You want to have a baby now?"

"No," Carminda quickly answered. "I'm still down for waiting five years for that. That's not what I'm saying at all. I just want to know what you think of couples keeping secrets from one another."

Wendell shrugged. "I never gave it much thought, I guess. Why? Are you keeping a secret from me that you think I'd want to know?"

"No," Carminda said as she used her fingers as a brush to tame her thick hair. "But I think Shun is keeping something from Jaxon."

"Why would you think that?"

"Well, she told me what the thing was and she says that Jaxon knows, but I honestly think that she only told him a portion of it. When Jaxon finds out the whole truth, I think it could backfire."

Carminda watched a bizarre expression cross her husband's face. It wasn't the look that she expected to get from him and she found it hard to decipher what was going through Wendell's mind. It was almost as if her words had sent him on a mental vacation.

"Did you hear what I said?" she asked.

"Yeah. I heard you." Wendell's answer was accompanied by a slow nod. "What is she keeping from him?"

"Wendell, Shun would kill me if Jaxon finds out."

"He won't find out from me, baby. What's she keeping from him?"

She still second-guessed whether she should reveal her suspicions, but Carminda needed the opinion of someone else and she knew that Wendell would be fair in his assessment. "Shun took a job writing for *B.I.O.N. Magazine*," she started.

"Oh. Jaxon knows about that," Wendell said. "He said he's not thrilled about it, but her feature isn't trashy like some of the other stuff they have in there."

"But it is," Carminda said, her words widening Wendell's eyes and bringing his back to a full erect position. "She's writing sort of a tell-all feature about Sariah Langston."

"What?"

"See, I knew she didn't tell Jaxon the details," Carminda said. The look on Wendell's face was all the confirmation she needed. "Shun told me that she talked to him about it but she kept dancing around the issue when I questioned her about how much she'd told him."

"Oh, man," Wendell said, scratching his head feverishly as though this new revelation had caused an allergic reaction.

"Now do you see why I'm concerned? Do you?" Carminda asked. "If she thought that what she was doing was okay, then why wouldn't she tell Jaxon? Why wouldn't she tell him? And can you believe she had the nerve to tell me that God had given her direction to write the article? Can you believe she'd even shape her mouth to tell me that?"

"Baby, you've got to talk some sense into her," Wendell said.

"Talk some sense into her? Talk some sense into her? Wendell, she's already submitted the first installment and it's supposed to be in this month's issue. You know that magazine comes out the first week of each month. It'll be out any day now."

She watched as Wendell climbed out of bed. She took a moment to enjoy the new scenery before he covered it with his bathrobe. Her eyes remained on him as he paced the floor, mumbling to himself. Carminda had expected the news to shock him, but her husband was a bit more disturbed than she anticipated.

"What is it, Wendell?"

He rounded the bed and came to a seated position on her side, looking Carminda right in the eyes. "She's not the only one keeping secrets," he said. "Jaxon is keeping one, too. You know the new job that he started last week?"

"Yeah. He works for Goldstar Pharmaceuticals now."

"No," Wendell said, whispering as though there were others in the house besides the two of them. "He works *at* Goldstar Pharmaceuticals. He works *for* Geoffrey Langston."

Carminda couldn't believe what she was hearing. How could Jaxon go after a job that was being offered by the man who was married to the woman his wife disdained most?

When Wendell spoke again, his words made it seem as though he'd read Carminda's horrified thoughts. "To be fair to Jaxon, he didn't know that Mr. Langston owned Goldstar Pharmaceuticals."

"Neither did I," Carminda said. "I thought they were a part of—"

"They were. Apparently the company was put on the market and Geoffrey Langston was the highest bidder. That's why they had so many executive positions that were being opened for new hires. He was revamping the whole organization of the company. Jaxon said by the time he found out that Sariah's husband was the company's new CEO, his interview had already started. And when he left the interview, he was so sure that he wouldn't get the job that he didn't even bother to mention it to LaShun. Nobody was more shocked than he was when he got the call the next day that he'd been chosen."

"Why would he have thought he wouldn't get the position?"

"Well, for starters, everybody and their mamas were applying for those positions. So there was a good chance that he wouldn't be the one named executive sales manager. And on top of that, he said that he had a few words with Mr. Langston that could have easily been a deal breaker. When he told me about it, I was sure he wouldn't get the job, either. But he did."

"Why didn't he just turn it down?" Carminda asked.

"Are you kidding? I would have beat his tail myself if he had walked away from this. Jaxon would have been a fool to turn down this job, Carminda. And when it gets right down to it, the truth of the matter is that Mr. Langston didn't wrong LaShun, Sariah did."

"So if I were in Shun's position, would you have taken the job?"

"Yes, I would have. Baby, the problem between LaShun and Sariah isn't Jaxon's dilemma. And it ain't Geoffrey Langston's, either. The only issue I have with this is that Jaxon still hasn't told LaShun. For the past few days he's been trying to figure out a way to let her know who his new boss is without sending her into conniptions. He said he'd give it a week and if he didn't like working with Mr. Langston he'd just quit and no one would be the wiser. But it's been two weeks now and Jaxon loves everything about this job, Carminda. It's challenging, he's got a corner office overlooking Piedmont Avenue, his opinions are encouraged and taken into consideration and the pay and benefits are beyond any job he's ever had. And on top of that, working there is no disrespect to LaShun."

"But that's the way she's going to feel when she finds out," Carminda said.

"I know, I know," Wendell said, once again scratching his head, but with less vigor this time.

"What are we going to do, Wendell? When all of this comes out it's going to be on and popping. This could destroy Jaxon and Shun."

"No, it won't. They're too strong to let that happen." He paused and sighed. "We'll talk about it some more this evening. For now, let's not do anything."

"But I'll be seeing Shun at work in just a few hours. I don't know if I can pretend that I don't know anything about this."

"It's just one day, Carminda," he promised. "We'll talk about it tonight, and by Monday, we'll have figured something out."

Chapter 9

Instead of feeling a sense of satisfaction as she had thought she would, LaShun found herself squirming in her chair as she sat through Sunday morning's sermon. All of the redemption that had her humming as she prepared for church had now leaked from her body, forming beneath her pew an imaginary body of disgustingly dirty water. There was no possible way that her father-in-law knew the details of what she'd done, but as every word of his message slapped her in the face, the sting of it made her feel as though he'd drawn a target on both her cheeks.

Up until Elder Tillman had the congregation repeat the topic of his sermon, LaShun had been proud of the 750-word article that she'd submitted to *B.I.O.N. Magazine*. So proud that she'd purchased several copies of the current issue yesterday, and had even removed the page from one of them and tucked it away in her belongings. Her plan was to present it, as though it was some form of certificate of excellence she'd received, to her husband and their friends over dinner this afternoon. Now, as she slowly and discreetly rubbed her fingers over the slickness of the glossy paper still tucked in the back of her Bible, LaShun couldn't even find the words to describe her emotions.

"Look at somebody on your row and ask them, 'Whose reflection do you see?'" It was at least the third time in the past half hour that Elder Tillman had ordered the congregation to do so.

Most of the people who had packed into the edifice today were on their feet by now and LaShun was glad to be in a seated position. It gave her a good excuse not to have to turn to anyone in obedience to her pastor. If anyone looked into her eyes, they'd be certain to see that the reflection she currently saw was definitely not of God. Elder Tillman's message had hit home in a way that Carminda's lecture hadn't. But now it was too late to do anything about it. The damage was done.

Elder Tillman had stepped down from the elevated platform and was now walking the floor, talking in a raspy, winded voice, as the organist accompanied him, offering a tune by which the pastor could pace himself. "God is a God of forgiveness. I heard a song the other day that said if Jesus could forgive crucifixion then surely we can forgive one another for whatever wrong has been done. But instead of becoming more like Christ, we become more like the people who nailed Him to the cross. We find ourselves trying to destroy somebody, even wishing them death because of one thing or another. Lawd have mercy, somebody!"

The congregation egged him on with encouraging shouts

of "Amen!" and "Tell it, tell it!" Elder Tillman took a moment to wipe beads of perspiration from his brow and then continued. "Jesus was nailed to the cross, not for His sins, but for ours. Those folks didn't even *know* Jesus. They thought He was doing things for one reason when He was actually doing them for another. They saw Him as evil, when in fact, everything He did, He did for our good. Sometimes we hate people and we don't even know them. People do stuff that we don't like, but what we don't realize is that every now and then, even when they don't recognize it, they are doing it for our good."

Elder Tillman paused on that note and ran from one side of the church to the other. His reaction was a trademark one that the members rarely saw. Every time he did it, though, it would be like pouring gasoline on a small fire. Within a matter of seconds, the floor was full of pacing and dancing Sunday worshippers. But their outbursts didn't hamper Elder Tillman's message. With a roll of the keys, the organist took his instrument's chord to a higher note, and Elder Tillman's voice found an octave to match.

"The Bible says that all things— Y'all don't hear me! I said all things work together for the good of them that love the Lord. If your soul is anchored in Jesus, when people do you wrong it won't change your reflection. How many out there have allowed the enemy to change your reflection? How many of you have become the crucifier? When you look into the mirror, do you see the Sanhedrin counsel? Do you see the Romans? Do you see the Jews? I wonder how many out there, when you look in the mirror, see Jesus. Somebody say, 'my reflection is Jesus!'"

While the rest of the congregation sang the words in the same manner as the pastor, LaShun swallowed hard. Her throat was so parched that the attempted gulp was painful. She pretended to struggle to remove a lash from her eye, when it fact, she was ridding herself of a tear that refused to be held back.

As Elder Tillman made his way back to the pulpit, his voice dropped to its normal tone as he made his next challenge. "Are you saying, 'Crucify Him,' or are you saying, 'Father forgive them for they know not what they do?' It takes a mature Christian to truly forgive. Whose reflection do you see?"

The irony of it all was a bit too much. With everyone still standing and the crowd being as thick and as involved as it currently was, it was the perfect time to escape. The sermon was coming to an end and soon Elder Tillman would be offering prayer. The ushers would not allow anyone to walk out during prayer and LaShun knew that if she was going to break free of the smothering sanctuary, now was the time. Grabbing her purse and tucking her Bible close to her chest, she eased from her row and took quick steps toward the closest exit door.

Where is she going? Jaxon looked up from the drum set just in time to see his wife disappear on the other side of the side exit door. As was normal for their order of service, all of the musicians were reclaiming their places as the choir stood to sing and the altar call was being made. He couldn't vacate his duties to go after her now.

The last fifteen minutes of the service seemed to move

slower than all the time before it. As soon as the benediction was given, Jaxon grabbed his belongings. Most Sundays, he would go to his father's office and commend him on another sermon well delivered. But his father would have to wait today.

Once outside, Jaxon scanned his surroundings. Others were emerging from the sanctuary, as well, and if LaShun was upset enough to walk out of the service, he knew he needed to get to her before anyone else did. On most days, his wife was one of the kindest women that a person could meet. But when it came to issues surrounding her birth mother, LaShun could become one to fear.

After several minutes of searching to no avail, Jaxon was beginning to panic. From where he stood, he could see their vehicle still in the space where he parked it upon arrival. LaShun hadn't gotten that much of a head start, but the minutes that lapsed between her exit and the benediction were enough time for her to have walked quite a distance.

"But where would she go?" Jaxon whispered to himself.

Wherever she was headed, he would catch up to her soonest if he drove. Jaxon jogged across the parking lot, hoping to avoid the attention of anyone who wished to fellowship in any manner. He heard Wendell calling for him in the distance, but chose to ignore it as he used the keyless remote to unlock the doors of his truck.

"LaShun!" Jaxon was unprepared to see her sitting in the front passenger seat and the sudden reveal nearly frightened him. "What's the matter, baby? What are you doing sitting in here by yourself?" He climbed in and closed the door behind him.

Tears were pouring down her cheeks. "Let's just go home," she whispered.

"Only if you promise to talk to me once we get there."

"Fine." LaShun had her Bible secure between her chest and her folded arms, holding it close as if she were afraid that someone would snatch it if she loosened her grip.

Jaxon started the engine and was preparing to back out when a pounding on the side of their truck caused him to apply pressure to the brake pedal. Through the tinted windows he saw both Wendell and Carminda.

"Man, where are you going?" Wendell said when Jaxon lowered his window. "We rode with y'all today, remember? Are y'all trying to skip out on taking us to dinner?"

Pushing her husband aside, Carminda stepped forward and added, "I treated you guys to ESPN last Sunday. As hungry as I am right now, I know good and well that y'all ain't trying to get out of treating us."

"I don't feel like going out."

Jaxon knew that LaShun's softly spoken words were meant for his ears only. It was a remote plea for him to do whatever he needed to do to get them excused from spending the afternoon with their friends.

"We'll take the next two Sundays," Jaxon said. "Today's not a good day. LaShun and I—"

"What's the matter with you, Shun?" Carminda said as she looked beyond Jaxon and caught a glimpse of lingering tears. "Are you crying?"

"Carminda—"

Before Jaxon could stop her, Carminda had opened the back door of his vehicle and climbed into the backseat.

"What's the matter?" she repeated. "Are you sick?"

"I'm fine, Carminda."

"Carminda, can we talk about this later?" The words had barely escaped Jaxon's lips when he heard the back door open and close once more. Wendell had joined them. "Guys, can LaShun and I get a little privacy here? She doesn't feel like talking."

"What you want us to do? Walk home?" Wendell said.

"What do you mean she doesn't feel like talking?" Carminda demanded. "What if whatever she has to say, we need to hear? What if because we give up on trying to find out what's wrong, she goes and does something stupid. What if you can't get her to open up? Then what if—"

"Okay, Carminda. Stop it!"

The noises inside of the SUV came to an immediate stillness behind LaShun's outburst. She'd barely beat Jaxon to the punch. Fed up with Carminda's what-ifs, his lips had already parted in preparation to interrupt. Now, his eyes, just like those of Carminda and Wendell, were fixed on LaShun.

"I messed up," she whispered.

Jaxon gave her a moment to say more but when she didn't he asked, "What do you mean, you messed up?"

"I kind of lied to you."

Not knowing if he even wanted to hear the rest, Jaxon's eyes left LaShun and scanned the faces of his friends, who remained silent in the backseat, looking like two children who had been scolded by their parents. They knew something. He could tell that much. But what they knew, Jaxon couldn't decode from their blank, guilt-drenched stares.

"What did you lie to me about?" He watched LaShun's

chest rise and fall, a direct effect of the deep breath she'd just taken. Jaxon couldn't help but breath deeply, too. Trying not to make assumptions that he could live to regret, he kept his voice calm. "LaShun, what did you lie to me about?"

"I write for *B.I.O.N. Magazine* now."

"Sweetheart, you told me that already. You don't remember?"

For the first time, LaShun turned to face him. Her next words were slowed by caution. "I wasn't completely honest with you about the nature of my feature."

Jaxon tilted his head and anticipated her next words. But instead of explaining herself further, LaShun uncrossed her arms and allowed her Bible to slide into the palms of her hands. For several moments, she stared at the leather-grain cover, and just before she slipped her fingers between the pages, Jaxon watched a fresh tear stream down her right cheek. Without an ounce of hurry in her movements, she handed him a neatly folded sheet of paper.

Before taking it, Jaxon glanced into the backseat once more. Wendell and Carminda looked at the paper that was being handed to Jaxon like it was filled with snake's venom. When he finally took it from LaShun's grip, Jaxon turned it over in his hand, inspecting the wording of the full-page ad on the side that was currently visible to him. Not at all sure what to expect, he looked at LaShun for a clue but got none.

Carminda slid forward in her seat and Wendell followed. "Open it, Jaxon," Carminda urged, removing any doubt that she knew what he would find.

At her appeal, Jaxon peeled open the folded paper and with each read word, his eyes widened. "Oh, God," he prayed in a mixture of disbelief and sheer horror, looking toward the ceiling and then back at his wife. "LaShun—please—tell me you didn't."

At first, her response was a slow, silent nod. Then through a burst of tears, LaShun wailed, "I did!"

Chapter 10

Four hours had passed since Geoffrey Langston arrived at work and immediately closed himself inside his office with strict instructions on what was considered an allowed disruption of his privacy. He'd driven through the crowd of news reporters and photographers, nearly running over a stubborn cameraman as he exited his gated property to head to the only place where he felt completely safe. The low-key buyout of Goldstar Pharmaceuticals had been finalized for several days and by some small miracle, the news of it hadn't yet become common knowledge.

Geoffrey banged his fist on his desk when he again thought of the unexpected madness that had met him at the start of his Monday morning. The images of horror on his daughters' faces as he ordered them to lie down in the backseat of his Chrysler New Yorker were still seared in his mind. The windows were tinted, but not opaque. There was no way that he'd allow shadows of his girls' tearstained faces to be smeared on the front of every national gossip magazine. Geoffrey didn't care what those heartless vultures did to him, but he would never let them hurt Giovanna and Gabrielle.

"Mr. Langston." His secretary's sharp, nasal voice reverberated through the speaker on his telephone. "You told me to let you know when attorney Swartz called. He's waiting on line one."

Drinking a mouthful of water to try to cool his anger, Geoffrey thanked her and then wasted little time getting to his point with his attorney. "Elliott, I'm filing for divorce and I need to know what it's going to cost me to make a clean break. How long will it take you to get some legal forms—"

"Whoa, Geoff," Elliott said, his voice putting the image of Bill Clinton in Geoffrey's thoughts. Although the short, balding, sixty-something-year-old attorney looked nothing like the former president of the United States, over the phone, he could easily convince someone that he was one and the same.

Swearing, Geoffrey slammed the palm of his free hand against his desk. "Don't try to convince me otherwise, Elliott. I'm not calling you for a second opinion, nor am I calling you for marital counsel. The decision has already been made. I just need to know how I can get out of this marriage without losing my daughters and the shirt off my back."

"Calm down, Geoff. That's not a problem, don't worry. We can talk about that more in a minute, but let's talk about this first. I was expecting a call from you, but not one demanding divorce papers. Is this about the article that appeared in that rag magazine?"

"See? Even you already know about it."

"I heard the breaking story on the radio en route to work and I understand your plight, Geoff. But you can't just rush into a divorce because of something that a gossip magazine prints about your wife."

"It's not gossip, Elliott, it's true."

A layer of quiet blanketed the phone line and Geoffrey could feel his anger seething again. Picking up the glass of water beside him, he took several swallows. Elliott was the first to break the silence. His voice was calm and cautious, like a sensible man trying to reason with an insane one.

"Come on, Geoff, you're one of the brightest men that I know. You had to realize that a secret like this would be uncovered at some point. I have to admit that I'm a bit thwarted that you didn't fill me in on this so I'd already be prepared should the story ever break. I'm even more surprised that you and Sariah didn't just tell the world yourselves years ago."

"Well, if *Sara* had ever bothered to tell me, maybe we would have!" Geoffrey bellowed.

That reply brought on another eerie silence. But this time it was shorter.

"You didn't know?" Disbelief was the commanding tone in Elliott's voice. "Okay, just for clarification, what didn't you know, Geoff? About her real name being Sara Faye? About this child that she abandoned? What?"

"I didn't know *any* of it, Elliott. Even when I first saw it in the magazine, I didn't believe it. But when I confronted Sariah, she was too blindsided to come up with a plausible lie, so she had no choice but to fess up. She let some dude knock her up as a teenager and now, some crazy, scorned woman whom she gave birth to and threw away wants to even up the score by tearing my life apart. None of what happened is my fault and I won't be disgraced because of it. I have daughters that I had to place into hiding today so that their being at school wouldn't have the building surrounded by cameras and live reporters just waiting for a chance to catch their distress on film. I won't live like this, Elliott. I want a divorce."

Elliott's bewilderment of the whole situation could be heard in his sigh. "Give me twenty-four hours to draw up some paperwork. Under the circumstances, we have the upper hand. I sure do hate to see this happen to you and Sariah, Geoff, but you can be assured that I'll take care of you. I'll call you tomorrow morning."

"Do that." Hanging up the phone, Geoffrey buried his head in his hands. He'd never felt so betrayed in all of his life. Integrity was something that he demanded from all of his business affiliates and he would accept no less from his wife. Sariah had betrayed him in the worst way. How could she not tell him that she'd had a child prior to marrying him?

Geoffrey had been so deep in thought that he didn't immediately detect the verbal argument that was getting nearer to his door with each passing moment. As the volume of the heated exchange increased, Geoffrey sat up and took notice. His body stiffened and he became increasingly aware that Marla was trying to stop someone from entering his office. The thought of having to look blindly into the lights of flashing cameras brought Geoffrey to his feet. He had two choices and little time to make a decision. Either he could pull the handgun from his top drawer and take aim at whomever it was who dared to force their way into his private chamber, or he could get to the door just in time to put on the dead bolt that would keep the uninvited guests out until he could call for the backup of his hired security.

Opting for the latter, Geoffrey circled his desk and dashed toward the only access into his office. He was within a foot of it when the door was suddenly flung open, causing him to jump backward in order not to get hit.

"Jaxon!"

"I told him that you didn't want to be disturbed, Mr. Langston," Marla snarled. "I don't know who he thinks he is to disrespect you in such a blatant manner, but I made your instructions unmistakably clear."

Geoffrey glared at Jaxon. He couldn't believe that the man whose work ethics he'd been so impressed by over the past two weeks could behave so badly. "Jaxon, what is the meaning of this?" Geoffrey's whisper was harsh.

"I'd tried to call you several times this morning, but Marla would not let any of the calls go through. As I told her, I desperately need to speak with you."

Pushing up her glasses on her sharp nose, Marla said, "And as *I* told *you,* Mr. Langston does not want to be disturbed for *any* reason."

"And I understand that, but this cannot wait."

"Any business matters will *have* to wait, Jaxon," Geoffrey said. "I don't care if one of my buildings is on fire. I couldn't care less at this moment. So—"

"It's not business, Mr. Langston. It's personal," Jaxon said.

Geoffrey paused, searching Jaxon's expression for a clearer explanation. "Personal?"

"Yes. And I need to speak to you about it in *private*." Jaxon stressed the last word of his sentence and for even more emphasis he chose to look at Marla when enunciating it.

"I can call security if you'd like to have him removed from your office, or permanently from the entire building." Although her offer was directed toward Geoffrey, the secretary never took her hateful gaze from Jaxon as she spoke.

Ignoring Marla's suggestion, Geoffrey said, "Jaxon, if this is about what was written in that magazine, I don't care to talk about it with you or anyone else."

"It's not about what was written, Mr. Langston. It's about the woman who wrote it."

Geoffrey stared at him in silence. Jaxon had peaked his interest, but Geoffrey was unsure of what good it would do to collect any dirt on the author of the article now. Sariah had already admitted to its accuracy, so it would be no benefit to him or his family for them to try to make this angry, estranged daughter seem like a stalker or an otherwise unstable individual. Slowly, Geoffrey began shaking his head, but before he could refuse any further conversation on the matter, Jaxon spoke.

"Please, Mr. Langston. I have some information that you are entitled to. Information that I should have told you before now."

Jaxon's final plea worked. Marla looked disappointed by the fact that she wouldn't be able to witness Jaxon being dragged from the office in shackles. Heeding her boss's silent instructions that consisted of only eye movement and a slight nod of his head, she walked out and closed the door behind her. But not before giving Jaxon one last look of discontentment.

Once they were alone, Geoffrey released a heavy sigh. He wasn't certain whether it was just another of several that he'd released today as a means for expending built-up frustration, or whether this one was one filled with relief. His pulse had raced at the thought of having to face reporters unprepared. As much as he didn't want to talk to Jaxon, he'd choose him any day over the alternative. When he motioned toward an empty chair, Jaxon sat. Geoffrey, on the other hand, chose to remain standing. As a show of authority, he always stood when speaking to any one of the very few people in the world who made him feel a bit unsure of himself. Something about Jaxon and his level of confidence made Geoffrey feel the need to stand.

"What is this about, Jaxon?" Geoffrey didn't try to mask the impatience in his voice. The whole subject of Sariah and her secret past was still new, but he was already tired of it. Walking the length of the hardwood floor of his office, Geoffrey came to a stop with his back toward Jaxon.

"This lady—this Mrs. T," Jaxon said, referring to the pen name that LaShun had chosen to use. "I know her."

"What do you mean, you know her?"

"She's my wife."

For a moment, Geoffrey felt himself losing all logic. A thousand harsh words, some profane, some not, swarmed through Geoffrey's head but none of them seemed befitting. "Is this some kind of joke, Jaxon?"

"Not at all, Mr. Langston. Believe me when I tell you that

this is no laughing matter to me. All I can do at this point is offer you my sincere regrets. I'm so sorry for this. I really am."

Taking brisk steps, Geoffrey returned to his desk and peered over it at Jaxon. His words were quick and accusing when he said, "You said that this was something you should have told me earlier. Does that mean you're behind all of this? Did you bid for this job just to try to destroy me?"

"No, Mr. Langston. No," Jaxon said. "That's not what I meant at all. I had nothing to do with the article and wasn't even aware of it until I saw it in print yesterday. But what I did know prior to taking this job was that my wife was your wife's biological child. When I applied for the job, I didn't even know you had bought Goldstar, and in all honesty, once I interviewed, I didn't think I'd get the job. When I did, the prestige of working here was so great that I convinced myself that the nonexistent relationship between Sariah, I mean, Mrs. Langston, and my wife wouldn't be an issue.

"I figured that you'd never have to find out, and although my wife eventually would, she'd be too pleased by the amount of money I was bringing home to make any real fuss about it. She always felt that it was unfair that her birth mother had lived such a glamorous life while she'd had to scrap for every dime she made. I thought that this way, in some strange twist of fate, she'd be getting some of the birthright that she felt was due to her. She'd be reaping from her mother's wealth through me—by way of this company, by way of you."

Geoffrey's mouth felt like dried paste. His hand was steady as he swallowed more water, but his insides felt like tree leaves that unsuccessfully fought against the elements on a windy day in Chicago. He emptied the glass in record time. "You, your wife. What do you want from us? What would it take to make her go away? What would it take to make you *all* go away?"

"It's not like that, Mr. Langston. This isn't about money or blackmail of any kind."

"Of course it is," Geoffrey said. "There are too many correlations here. Your coming to work for me, the timing of this article just when Sariah's career resurrected and at the same time that I took over this million-dollar company is just too much of a coincidence. She's an opportunist and an extortionist. Don't play games with me, Jaxon. Just tell me what she wants!"

Geoffrey's eyes bulged when he found himself being manhandled in a way that no one had ever dared to before. Jaxon had grabbed him by the lapel of his designer suit and had jerked him forward. Geoffrey's heart pounded as the younger, stronger man then slammed his back against the wall behind him. Just as quickly as the physical exchange began, it ended. Jaxon released him and with both his hands in a raised position, he began a slow retreat until he was back on the opposite side of the desk.

"I'm sorry," Jaxon said, still clearly trying to gather his emotions. "But don't you ever speak about my wife in that manner. *Nobody* belittles her regardless of how much money they have. Do I make myself clear?"

Still swimming in a sea mixed with shock and fear, Geoffrey didn't know what to say. He slowly straightened out the expensive fabric that Jaxon had muddled, but words would not readily form.

Jaxon spoke again. His voice was low and subdued. "Mr. Langston, I can't make you believe me, but I tell you no lie. My wife and I didn't conspire to force you into a corner. For a long time, for years, my wife has carried deep wounds from knowing that Mrs. Langston gave her away shortly after her birth. She was passed from foster home to foster home and since she was never adopted, she grew up feeling unwanted and unloved. As a young teenager she found out who her birth mother was and she has harbored years of anger and hurt. I think that in some way, she allowed it to fester into something much worse."

Jaxon paused, but Geoffrey still said nothing. His heart had finally stopped pounding against the cavity of his chest but he chose not to interrupt. When Jaxon began talking again, divulging even more information, Geoffrey found himself being drawn into the sordid story that he was never supposed to know about. It was a part of his wife's past that didn't include him, but one that he should have been enlightened on long before now. As much devastation as his family had been forced to suffer over the past several hours, Geoffrey felt empathy for the child that Sariah had tossed aside. A part of him even understood why Sariah's daughter had gone to such lengths to return the hurt that she felt. Still, knowing that what had transpired would have a lifelong effect on his daughters, the punishment, in his eyes, was not a fair one.

"Look, Jaxon. What Sariah did to your wife was cruel, yes. But it was no fault of mine or my girls'. I stand corrected for making your wife sound like some kind of criminal, but she had no right to do what she did. No right."

"I agree," Jaxon quickly said with a nod. "I'm not trying to make excuses for what was done. I'm just attempting to show you the world through L—my wife's eyes. In hindsight, even she knows that what she did was wrong. She's regretful. Last night as we prayed together—"

"It's too late for her to be regretful now, Jaxon. The irreversible damage is done!" Geoffrey's voice rose.

"It might be too late for her to get your forgiveness, Mr. Langston, but it wasn't too late for her to repent to God."

"Repent to God? For what? He's not the one that she hurt."

"Yes, she did. Anytime that we misrepresent God, we hurt Him. As Christians, God requires that our lives reflect who He is. It was a message that our pastor relayed quite well during yesterday's sermon. My wife's actions, the way she handled this whole situation, didn't replicate who God is and that's what made this sin. She wronged her biological mother, yes. And what she did to hurt Mrs. Langston spilled over to affect you and the children that you share together. That's more than unfortunate. But in the full scheme of things, my wife's failure to walk in obedience to God is where she went wrong, Mr. Langston. Had she handled this in a Christian manner, she never would have written that article. And had she never written this article, your family wouldn't be injured, the media wouldn't be blasting your personal lives in the paper and on television and I wouldn't be jacking up my employer for badmouthing my wife."

Geoffrey remained in the same space where he had been temporarily forced to stand. He'd never seen Jaxon read a Bible, never heard him quote a Scripture and had never once heard him declare his Christianity, but hearing it now didn't surprise him. All along, he'd known that there was something different about Jaxon. It wasn't just his poised self-confidence and his driven, assertive nature that had impressed Geoffrey. It was more, but until now, Geoffrey hadn't been able to define it.

It had been years since he'd set foot in a church, so hearing Jaxon speak of yesterday's sermon had a foreign resonance. In the Langston household, Sunday was the day that they did little or nothing. Monday through Friday Geoffrey worked at one or more of his offices while the girls were at school, and Sariah did occasional photo shoots and fulfilled spokesmodel duties. When she wasn't occupied, she had the luxury of staying at home, only cooking or cleaning when she chose to. On Saturdays, the girls had extracurricular activities with friends or at their school, Sariah made sure that the hired help did their weekly duties and Geoffrey made phone calls or had business meetings that would usher him into the upcoming workweek. Sunday, for everybody, was a day of rest. For Geoffrey, it hadn't signified church since before the death of his grandmother.

It had been so long ago that Geoffrey barely recalled the days that his parents allowed his grandmother to take him and his older siblings to church. Although they rarely went themselves, Horace and Eloise Langston knew that they could appease Geoffrey's paternal grandmother, June, if they sent the children. June always said that in the end, loving and serving God was the only thing that meant anything. But within the walls of their house, the Langston children were taught that hard work and success were all that mattered. The last time that Geoffrey could remember sitting through a church service was at the age of ten, forty-five years ago, at his grandmother's funeral. His most memorable moment from that day was hearing his father say, "All Mama ever talked about was God, and what good did that do her? She died with Jesus on her lips and not a dime in her pocket."

Horace swore that his family wouldn't go the same route. They wouldn't be a bunch of poor Christians who never experienced wealth. He promised to take the natural talents and ambitions that he and his wife possessed and turn them into gold. And he did. Horace and Eloise never got along well. Sometimes their disagreements came to physical blows. But they never wanted for anything. Eloise had outlived Horace by seven years, and even their respective funerals were lavish, not easily forgettable like that of Grandmother June. Geoffrey had made the same decree for his family and had rendered the same results: more money and clout than he needed, but a life and a marriage void of true happiness.

"I'm filing for divorce." The words spilled from his lips almost involuntarily.

Jaxon stared straight ahead. "What? No, Mr. Langston, please don't. This has gone way too far already. Two wrongs don't make a right. Your walking out on Mrs. Langston to save your own behind is no more right than my wife writing the article that made your lives an open book."

"You think I knew about this?" Geoffrey narrowed his eyes at Jaxon's implication. "I probably found out about this around the same time you did, Jaxon. I'm not leaving Sariah to save my own behind. I'm leaving her because she lied to me and because of it, everything I've ever worked for could suffer. This is just the final nail in the coffin. Our marriage has been rocky for years and the girls are what have held it together for this long. Well, Gabrielle and Giovanna are old enough now. Besides, I don't know who hates Sariah more right now, me or them."

A look of disbelief covered Jaxon's face just before he said, "The girls are all that have held it together? In all due respect, Mr. Langston, I don't believe the girls were in the picture the first time questions started swirling surrounding your dedication to your marriage."

"Excuse me?" The incredulity in Geoffrey's expression surpassed that of Jaxon's. First he physically attacked him and now he dared to talk about his personal matters? Generally, when an employee crossed the line, Geoffrey only needed to give them a look of disdain and they'd quickly rediscover their rightful place. However, Jaxon proved once again that he was no normal employee.

"I think I was around thirteen or fourteen years old the first time I heard my father call out your family's name during altar call at church. I didn't really know how powerful of a man you were at the time, but I vividly remember my father standing in the gap for you, praying that God would open your eyes to show you the error of your ways. Not only that, but he prayed that Mrs. Langston would find it in her heart to forgive you for your transgressions and that both of you would find Christ."

Geoffrey wanted to yell, swear, even strike Jaxon in the face for his boldness. He could foresee the satisfied grin that would rest on Marla's face if he would just follow up on her offer and have his qualified staff of security personnel take

Jaxon away. Geoffrey thought of several ways that he could have the man beaten and/or banned from his office. With his influence, he could probably ensure that Jaxon wouldn't find another decent job anywhere in the city of Atlanta. But as he continued speaking, all Geoffrey could do was stand and listen.

"You know what else I remember?" At the posing of that question, Geoffrey watched Jaxon sit back down in a relaxed manner, as if he were in the comfort of his own home. "I think it was the third or fourth time that you were in the news, accused of cheating on your wife—probably about five or six years ago. I remember my dad praying a prayer in which he asked God to remove the spirit of lasciviousness from your heart. Told God to create in you a clean heart and a renewed spirit so that even when you were tempted, you would have the strength to refuse."

Remembering what happened with Soy just a few nights ago, Geoffrey shifted his feet. *Is that why I left her? Is that the reason I haven't been able to be with anyone else other than Sariah in the past five years?* Jaxon was still talking when Geoffrey returned from his brief mental retreat.

"I'm not trying to judge you, Mr. Langston. God knows that we all make mistakes and we all fall short of His glory. I'm just saying that as much as Mrs. Langston stood by you over the years when it was you who was lying and scheming, I don't think you should be so quick to bail at the first sign of humanness on her part."

Geoffrey was trembling now. "I didn't ask you for your opinion, Jaxon."

"I know." Jaxon stood and placed the ring that held the

keys to the building and to his office door on Geoffrey's desk. "But I'm already on my way out and this is really the only part of my existence that you have any control over. So I have nothing more to lose."

Chapter 11

From the confinement of her bedroom, Sariah could clearly hear the music that reverberated through the surround sound of the Bose Acoustic Wave music system. It mirrored her emotions. The artist was Sade and although Sariah wasn't familiar with the lyrics that played, Sade's voice was filled with incredible wretchedness as she sang them.

For two consecutive days, Sariah had not done anything constructive. She had barely gotten out of bed at all. The same pajamas that she had on when she saw her husband and children for the last time on Monday morning, she still wore. No makeup had come near her face; nor had soap and water. She refused to turn on the television for fear of what she might see and the radio for fear of what she might hear.

The earsplitting music that played in the five-CD changer had originally served as a means of drowning out the voices of the people who camped outside her gated property, calling tirelessly for her to make a statement regarding the hottest new celebrity news. Whether they were still out there, Sariah didn't know. She hadn't peeked through her security blinds since this time yesterday. And even during the night hours, she never turned on any lights. She didn't want to chance anyone seeing her. She didn't want to chance seeing herself.

"What did I ever do to deserve this?" she said aloud. She was reminded of the answer when she looked at the May issue of *B.I.O.N.* that her husband had tossed on the bed in front of her face as she prepared to get her day started on Sunday.

She'd never seen Geoffrey so livid or her children so torn. They'd all stayed indoors on Sunday as the crowds began to gather outside. Geoffrey and the children camped out in one section of the house and she in another. She felt banished. It was probably the exact sensation that her first-born child wanted her to feel. No doubt, LaShun felt that this was the only way Sariah would even have a clue of what she'd been through. Sariah gasped at the newfound revelation of it all.

The look of revulsion that Geoffrey had given her just before leaving on Monday was bad enough. But it was the deluded looks that her daughters gave her that hurt the most.

Sariah hadn't cracked open the magazine since being forced to read bits and pieces of the devastating article on Sunday. The title of it was still etched in the internal parts of her brain. *The Cracked Mirror.* The words were in bold red letters with what looked like drops of blood oozing from them. They hovered over a picture of Sariah's face that was distorted by jagged lines reminiscent of what a reflection would look like if it were seen through a broken mirror.

The paragraphs that followed the title outlined every detail of how Sariah had abandoned her baby. She was accused of being cold, heartless and cruel. Not only that, but the words indicated that she also had color issues within her own race, fancying men who had lighter-toned skin over dark ones and choosing to keep her fair-skinned children while disowning her darker-complexioned one. The last two lines of the article said, "A cracked mirror gives you a distorted image of who a person really is. Before this revelation, how well did you really know Sariah Langston?"

The feature took up less than two pages of the magazine, but like a short, powerful earthquake, the aftershocks of it had done more damage than could easily be repaired.

As angry as Geoffrey was when he left, Sariah never gave consideration to the fact that he wouldn't return. He'd taken their daughters with him. Surely he wouldn't snatch them from her life without so much as a warning. But he had and she had no one to turn to for help. Almost everything they had was really his to own and hers to borrow. All of their family was Geoffrey's because Sariah had none to speak of. All of their friends were people she'd met through her husband. Even their attorney had been Geoffrey's legal representative before they'd gotten married.

Fighting Geoffrey for anything would be a losing battle. When Sariah married him, she'd been so much in love and so sure that theirs would be a fairytale union, that she'd signed the prenup that Horace and Eloise had insisted that their son present to the fiancée that they never fully embraced. They didn't care if Geoffrey had Sariah for a side dish, but his main course, the woman he was to marry, should be more refined and polished with a family heritage that they'd be proud to include in their own. They'd forgotten their own pasts whose roots were infested with poverty before being fertilized with success.

Even though Sariah's in-laws never gave their son's marriage their full blessing, Sariah loved them and to an extent, won them over. In a sense, Eloise had saved Sariah's life when she took her on as her line's first teenage runway model. And Horace was the first stable male figure in her life. Even with all of their flaws, the Langstons were the closest that Sariah had to real parents. Her mother, Miranda, whom most people knew as Mimi, had always been distant and Sariah never knew her father. It wasn't until she got her first modeling opportunity with the E. L. Langston line that her mother began showing interest in her well-being. Sariah knew that it was her new level of money-making potential that pulled her mother closer to her, but at the time she didn't care. She was just glad to have Mimi play an active role in her life. Then she got pregnant and, although she thought she'd done the right thing in giving up her child, it proved to be the beginning of the end.

Picking up the telephone, Sariah punched in Geoffrey's cell number. She'd called it so much that she was surprised he'd not had it disconnected. In the past, Sariah would hang up at the start of his voice message, but now, she felt desperate.

"Geoffrey, it's Sariah. Please call me. I—I need to know that my children are okay. I need to know that you don't hate me." The tear ducts that she thought she'd drained dry began to replenish and spill over. "I'm sorry, Geoffrey, and I know I don't tell you enough, but I love you. Please call me. Please. I need to talk to you. There's so much more that you don't know that you need to know. I made the mistake of letting you find out all of this other stuff in the streets. I don't want that to happen again. Please call. Please let the girls call. Please, Geoffrey."

Without much hope and with nothing more to say, Sariah hung up the telephone and buried her face in the fibers of her pillow.

Chapter 12

"Carminda, can you please put that away? How many times can you read the same article?" LaShun's eyes were pleading when she looked up and saw her friend examining the contents of the magazine once again.

Snapping the pages shut, Carminda said, "Well, on the bright side, you displayed some great writing skills in it. If it were a fictional tale, I'd give you five stars."

LaShun let out a regretful groan and rubbed her throbbing temples. "How could I have been so stupid?"

"Well, just be glad that, in spite of your lapse in judgment, you kept enough rational thought to use a pseudonym. What if you'd used your real name? What if the words 'Contributed by LaShun Tillman' had been printed? What if they immediately linked it to you? What if they somehow figured out that you were Jaxon Tillman's wife? And what if hearing the name *Tillman* automatically made them think of Elder Newton Tillman and Shabach Worship Center? Oh my goodness, LaShun! What if those folks were gathered outside this business or outside the church like they were standing near the Langstons' home?"

"Okay, Carminda. Okay!" LaShun placed her hands over her ears. As aggravating as Carminda's words were, they forced LaShun to put herself in Sariah's shoes. She couldn't imagine the anguish that her birth mother was going through and she didn't even care to know how much damage the aftermath of the fallout had caused. "I'll admit that I wanted to hurt Sariah, but I didn't think it would get to this point. I've not only hurt her whole family, but I've hurt mine, too. Jaxon had just landed his dream job and now he's lost it all because of what I did. If he doesn't find employment soon, we're going to start feeling it in a major way. The income from this business isn't nearly enough to sustain us. At one time, I was willing to do anything to make Sariah pay for what she did. Now, I'd do just about anything to try to correct my mistake."

"I hope you mean that."

Both women turned as the familiar masculine voice broke into their private conversation. They looked to see Jaxon standing in the doorway of LaShun's office, holding a briefcase as if he had come for a business meeting.

Carminda volunteered to make herself scarce and once the couple was alone, Jaxon said, "Remember the talk that we had with Dad and Mom a couple of nights ago? Well, I have a proposition that just might allow you to put a dent in your quest to right this wrong."

LaShun already didn't like the sound of this. In their hour-long spiritual counseling session with the people who served as both their pastors and their parents, her mother-in-law had told her that if she was going to confirm with God her genuine state of repentance, she'd eventually have to move from her comfort zone and put her words into action.

"You're going to have to talk to Sariah and—"

"No, Jaxon. I can't do that."

"Yes, you can, LaShun, and you have to."

"I was thinking of writing a retraction in next month's edition that outlined my error. Wouldn't that be just as good?"

"No, baby, a retraction is unacceptable. It won't nearly have the effect of the article that preceded it. You have to go to your birth mother and talk to her. It's what you should have done years ago."

"And say what, Jaxon? I'm sorry for what I did, but am I supposed to tell her that? She's never apologized to me for what she did."

"She's probably never known where you were until now. And truthfully, she still doesn't know. She just knows that you're in Atlanta."

LaShun sat back in her chair and crossed her arms in protest. "You really believe that she hasn't apologized in thirty-two years because she didn't know my whereabouts?"

"Frankly, LaShun, I don't care why she hasn't apologized. This isn't about what she owes you. This is about what you owe her. She may have messed up your childhood, LaShun, but if you stop looking behind you and start looking in your present, you'll come to realize that you've got it good, baby. You've got good friends, your own business and a husband who would punch a millionaire in the face if he shaped his mouth to talk about you."

LaShun gasped. "You didn't."

"Not quite, no. But I would. The point I'm trying to make is that your whole past is what brought you to your present. Had you not been given away, you never would have ended up in the care of the Williamses, who brought you to Shabach where you were introduced to Christ and later, introduced to me. I know you had it rough, baby. But isn't all of this worth all of that?"

He was right and LaShun knew it. She'd never quite played it out in her mind in the same manner that Jaxon had expressed it. "Yeah," she whispered, feeling the warmth of his hands covering hers. "It is. I'm sorry."

"You don't owe me any apologies, sweetheart. Me and you, we can survive anything, but every marriage doesn't have God's strength to back it. Everybody can't take what God's people can take."

LaShun watched Jaxon's eyes fall to the desk before he took in a deep breath and spoke again. "Now I have to tell you something that I didn't want to lay on you before now."

"What?"

"Mr. Langston is filing for divorce."

"Divorce? Over this?"

Jaxon nodded. "They're already separated and he took the girls with him. I can imagine that Sariah feels pretty hopeless right now. Her bank account ain't nothing to sneeze at but it's no match for Mr. Langston's, and in the world we live in, money talks louder than people. The break-up is not totally due to the article, so don't think for a moment that you single-handedly ended their marriage. Apparently there were other problems, but according to

Geoffrey Langston, this one was the deciding factor. He learned about everything at the same time the rest of the world did. He never knew about her pregnancy or the child she gave away. He didn't even know that Sariah changed her name for a better chance at stardom. He feels like she betrayed him."

LaShun suddenly felt angry at her birth mother's hypocritical husband. "Yeah, right. Like he's some kind of saint? How can he even shape his mouth to judge her?"

"I know. I reminded him of all of his transgressions but I don't think it did any good."

"What have I done, Jaxon?" LaShun moaned. "You're right, though. I have to try to make this right. I got myself into this and I've got to be woman enough to do what it takes to get myself out."

"You got yourself in this, true enough. But we're gonna get you out." Jaxon stood from his chair in preparation to leave. "By the time you get home this evening, I will have devised a plan."

Chapter 13

When Jaxon took control of a situation, he didn't cut corners and LaShun loved that quality in her husband. She had arrived home from work tired and not at all in the mood for talking about Sariah. When she pulled her car into the garage, LaShun had already planned a speech that began with telling Jaxon that she didn't feel like cooking and ended with telling him that she didn't feel like talking, either. But she never got the opportunity to voice her grievances.

When LaShun walked into her home it was as though her husband had read her thoughts before the sentiments could be expressed. The house smelled heavily of pot roast and the aroma of it drew her directly to the kitchen. Jaxon wasn't there, but the slow cooker that housed the simmering main dish was sitting on the kitchen counter in clear view. LaShun lifted other lids and found side dishes of wild rice, yams and corn on the cob.

It took her a moment to locate Jaxon, but when she did, he had just finished running her bath. The suds that rested atop the steaming water were so thick that she couldn't help wondering if he'd used her whole bottle of bubble bath all at once. It didn't take long for LaShun to realize that Jaxon had more than easing her tension on his agenda.

The feel of the water was heavenly, and the tiredness seemed to escape through the pores of her skin as she sat in the tub that was surrounded by cinnamon-scented candles. Combined with the instrumental music that played softly on the radio, it was almost enough to put LaShun to sleep. By the time she stepped from the water to dry herself with the towel her husband had placed on the counter, the water's temperature had cooled to lukewarm.

She was banished from the kitchen by Jaxon, who was dressed in pair of boxer shorts and an apron, and ordered to bed where her meal was eventually served on a tray with a single, long-stemmed white rose as decoration. The food had only been half-eaten because other appetites had greater demands to be satisfied. The entire evening had been a glorious, much-needed escape from reality. But now, as LaShun lay with her head resting on the fine hairs of Jaxon's chest, she knew that the escape had been temporary.

"I've arranged for us to go and talk to Sariah tomorrow morning."

LaShun quickly rose to a seated position. "Tomorrow? How did you— When did you— What? Tomorrow?"

"Yes, LaShun, tomorrow."

Looking down into his dark eyes, LaShun couldn't believe what she was hearing. "You called her?"

"I'm one of the few people who were privy to Mr. Langston's home number. I called today and made arrangements."

"When? After you left my office?"

"Actually, I called before I came by to see you."

LaShun straightened her back and used her hand to smooth back stray hairs that were dangling in her face. On most days, she liked the fact that her husband was always so confident and sure of himself. But this time he'd taken it too far. "So what are you saying? You promised her I'd come by even before I agreed to do so?" LaShun watched as Jaxon repositioned himself and sat up beside her. She was momentarily distracted as the bed sheets fell below his waist, but she managed to keep her admiration brief and regroup. "How could you do that, Jaxon? How could you tell that woman that I'd be coming to talk to her without allowing me a voice in the matter? Since when did you start making decisions for me?"

When he replied, Jaxon's voice had a rough edge that made LaShun's brazen tone dull in comparison. LaShun had only heard Jaxon take on this pitch a few times in their marriage—those rare times when she overstepped her boundaries to the point that he felt the need to flash his God-given title as head of household like a sheriff's badge.

"First of all, I didn't speak with Sariah, I spoke with her cleaning lady and together, we devised a plan to make this happen. Secondly, I didn't make the decision for you. In fact, I didn't mention you at all. Your name got added to the ticket when you told Carminda that you were willing to do anything to rectify this situation. I just told the woman that I would be there. Whether you'd decided to do the right thing or not was up to you, LaShun. I, on the other hand, was going to do my best to apologize to Sariah whether you accompanied me to the mansion or not. And let's keep the facts straight. *You* created this debacle. Don't try and make it anybody else's invention."

LaShun swallowed back a lump that rose in her throat. Jaxon was right. She'd made a grand mess of things and as wrong as she knew she'd been, she still found herself trying to place blame elsewhere to avoid feeling the pain of the full blow that represented her sin. At that moment, Jaxon's cell phone rang and when he turned to retrieve it from the nightstand, it gave LaShun just enough time to whisk away the tears that had pooled in her eyes.

Although she could only hear one end of the conversation, he identified the caller as his former boss, drawing LaShun's full attention.

"Right now?" she heard Jaxon say just before a pause. "Well, I'd kind of turned in for the evening, so if it can wait—" He paused again. "I thought we'd finished that line of conversation. I said all I needed to say." This time Jaxon was silent for a longer period of time, forcing LaShun to search his face for clues of what was being said on the other end. When he finally spoke again, he said, "Fine, Mr. Langston, but there are some topics that are off-limits and I need you to know that in advance. And I don't think I have to elaborate for you to catch my drift. My coming is contingent on you agreeing to that." Another pause. "Where are you? Uh-huh. Uh-huh. Yeah. I'll meet you there in an hour."

"Where are you going?" LaShun immediately asked when he hung up the telephone. "What does he want?"

"I'm going to Goldstar. Mr. Langston says that he needs to speak to me." LaShun's eyes followed Jaxon as he spoke and gathered fresh clothing at the same time. "I don't know what he wants. I told their maid not to tell either of them that I'd called, but maybe she did and maybe he's not too happy about it. I don't know. I'm going to shower and head out. I'll let you know what's what as soon as I find out something myself."

Chapter 14

The office building was dark when Jaxon drove up to the security gate. Surprisingly, the code he'd been given to get through the metal arm still worked. He could hear the crunch of the gravel under his truck's tires as he maneuvered his way through the maze of turns that would bring him to Goldstar's ground-level parking. Getting out of his vehicle at this time of night felt eerie. The security lights brightened the parking area and no sooner had he stepped from his truck did a guard round the corner of the building with his hands near his holster.

What reason am I going to tell this man for my being here?

"Jaxon Tillman?" the officer said as he approached.

Jaxon felt a pounding in his chest. "Yes."

"Can I see some identification, sir?"

Jaxon relaxed a little, realizing that Geoffrey must have told the security guard that he'd be arriving. He'd turned in his access key when he resigned from his duties and while remembering his personal employee entrance code had gotten him through the gate, Jaxon would have needed a key to let himself into the building.

The guard returned Jaxon's license and then beckoned for him to follow. The two men entered the building and although Jaxon remembered his way to his former boss's office, security continued to guide him until they reached Geoffrey Langston's door.

"Yes?" Geoffrey answered to the gentle knock that the guard had delivered.

"Jaxon Tillman has arrived, Mr. Langston."

The sounds of the locks to the office door disengaging echoed in the otherwise quiet building. In a matter of seconds, the door was open and Jaxon stared into the face of Geoffrey Langston.

"Thank you, Paul," Geoffrey said. "You may leave now."

"Yes, sir," Paul said. And then he was gone.

Geoffrey stepped aside to allow his guest to enter. "Jaxon. Thank you for agreeing to meet me. I know it was an inconvenience."

"You said it wouldn't take long." Jaxon made himself comfortable in a vacant chair without Geoffrey's invitation. He noted a bottle of bourbon sitting beside one empty glass and another that was half-full. Without saying a word, Geoffrey filled the empty glass and slid it toward Jaxon. "No thanks," Jaxon refused, holding up his hand. "You said it was important, Mr. Langston. What was it that you wanted to discuss that couldn't wait?"

Geoffrey took a long sip from his glass that emptied it and

then sat in his chair, rubbing his forehead. "I'm at a cross-road, Jaxon. I don't know where to go or who to turn to. I've got nobody to talk to. Everybody sees the glamour in being Geoffrey Langston, but nobody knows how hard it is to be me. This thing with Sariah—I don't know—I had divorce papers drawn up and I even started signing them, but I couldn't finish. I'm angry, hurt, but we've invested so much into this marriage. You were right, she's been good to me, a good wife on most days, but it feels like it's not enough. Something's missing and I can't put my finger on it."

Geoffrey reached for the bottle and Jaxon snatched it away, removing it from the desk and placing it on the floor beside his chair.

"This is not the answer, Mr. Langston." Geoffrey stared at him, but said nothing. Jaxon continued. "You're asking me for help, right?" Geoffrey's head bobbed a slow nod and Jaxon noted the sadness in his eyes. "Then let me help you."

"I could divorce her and leave her with virtually nothing, you know," Geoffrey said, relaxing his back against the leather of his chair. Jaxon did the same and waited for what he would say next. "My attorney said that the girls are of age where they can talk to the presiding judge and make a request to live with me. They've already said that they'd choose me if they had a choice. I wouldn't have to worry about a long court battle. I can't lose. I'd have to pay spousal support, but nothing I can't handle. This one is a shoo-in."

"Yet you're sitting in a dimly lit room guzzling like a common drunk," Jaxon said. "Why?"

Geoffrey was rubbing his forehead once more. "I don't know." He rose from his chair and stared out his window, whose blinds were partially open. "You said your father prayed for me years ago."

"Yes."

"Women used to make themselves available to me all the time, Jaxon, and I was more than willing to fulfill their desires. Now they present the silver platter and although my appetite is still there, I can't dine. I mean, I *can*," Geoffrey stressed, "but somehow I walk away."

Jaxon smiled. "Daddy always did say that prayer changes things." His smile faded and he sat for a moment and watched the silent struggle that was going on inside Geoffrey. "You love Mrs. Langston, don't you? You thought you wanted to end it with her and you saw her lie as an open door that provided the opportunity for you to walk away, but you can't, can you?"

Geoffrey remained silent.

"I have—my wife and I have an appointment to see her tomorrow," Jaxon began. But his sentence was cut short.

"To see who?" Geoffrey raised his head for the first time in a long while.

"We're going to see Mrs. Langston. We want to apologize for the role we played in this disaster. I'd like you to be there."

Shaking his head, Geoffrey said, "I don't think I want to be there."

"I didn't want to be here, either," Jaxon reminded him. "But you asked me to come and I did. We'll be at the mansion at noon. I hope I can count on you to do the same."

Chapter 15

LaShun fidgeted with the buttons of her leopard-print blouse as the gate in front of her husband's truck slowly opened. As promised, the housekeeper had been watching and waiting for the arrival of the vehicle that Jaxon had described and was allowing them onto the property without Sariah's knowledge.

"Where are you, Geoffrey?" LaShun heard Jaxon whisper as he placed the gear in Park at the highest point of the circular driveway.

Seeing Jaxon reach for his door handle and hoping to buy herself more time, LaShun asked, "Don't you think we should wait for Mr. Langston?"

Jaxon shook his head vigorously. "He might decide not to come. We can't base our duty on his compliance. Let's go."

The front door of the Langston mansion opened before Jaxon could even reach for the doorbell and on the other side of the door stood a woman of short stature who greeted them in her native tongue.

"Hola. Señor Tillman?"

"Sí, señora," Jaxon responded with two of the very few words of Spanish that he knew. "And this is my wife."

The woman looked past Jaxon and replied, "Is it true? Are you really Mrs. Langston's daughter?" Her accent was thick, but her words comprehensible.

LaShun took a step backward. She wanted to turn and run away from the scene, but Jaxon's arm around her waist stopped her.

"Is Mrs. Langston here, ma'am?" he asked.

"Yes." This time as she spoke, her eyes looked beyond both of them and quickly eclipsed with worry. "But so is Mr. Langston. I promise I didn't tell him. I kept my word just like I told you I would. I don't know why he's here. Haven't seen him in days."

From the corner of her eye, LaShun could see Jaxon turn to look over his shoulder but she couldn't bring herself to do the same. A suffocating sensation tightened her throat. LaShun had known that he would join them but now that he'd arrived, her mouth felt like old paper, dry and dusty.

"It's okay, Ms. Remírez," Jaxon said in a calming voice that LaShun knew was more for her benefit than the house-keeper's. "I asked him to join us."

Relieved and nodding, the woman stepped aside to allow them to enter and directed them to the Victorian-style den. The home looked immaculate, barely lived in.

"Teresa, are you out there?" a voice called from some-where nearby where the threesome stood. "I thought I heard someone—"

When the owner of the voice rounded the corner, LaShun

swallowed the unanticipated sob that rose in her throat. She couldn't believe her own emotions. Aside from photos in magazines and images on television, she had never seen her birth mother. Carminda was right. Sariah was breathtaking for a woman of her maturity. Even void of cosmetics, she was beautiful. LaShun wanted to turn away, but she couldn't peel her eyes from the woman she'd hated for so many years.

"I'm sorry," Sariah said, visibly unprepared for the strangers that she saw in her home. She used her hands to pull the fabric of her flowing silk kimono closer to her body and looked at her housekeeper for an explanation. Teresa remained silent.

LaShun bit her bottom lip, not sure if she was more hurt or insulted by Sariah's reaction. Portions of her father-in-law's Sunday-morning sermon replayed themselves in her head. *Whose reflection do you see?* It was all that stopped her from unleashing reheated angry words at the woman who birthed her. Releasing those words would be far from Christ-like, but they begged to be set free from her innermost thoughts anyway. Here they were, she and her mother in the same space, and Sariah had looked directly at her but had no clue of her identity.

"Mrs. Langston, please forgive us for interrupting your afternoon." Jaxon stepped forward and extended his hand. "I'm Jaxon Tillman and this is my wife. We were hoping for a moment to speak with you."

Sariah's fair skin paled. She looked at Jaxon's extended hand but instead of accepting it, she moved her eyes to the woman who stood less than ten feet from her. "Teresa, what is the meaning of this? You've allowed reporters into my home?"

It was then that the tears LaShun had previously been victorious in withholding spilled down her cheeks. Over the years LaShun had convinced herself that she didn't care that her mother hadn't gotten to know her, but now, a raw and primitive grief overwhelmed her, seeing firsthand Sariah's unawareness of her identity. Through vision blurred by tears, LaShun saw Sariah's lips part to speak, but before she could, the front door opened.

Chapter 16

Sariah wanted to run to him, but her ostrich-plumed slippers seemed glued to the floor. She stared in silence as her husband strode into the den, placing his keys on the mantel of the fireplace before returning her gaze. Sariah watched as his eyes left her face and traveled the length of her body before returning to their original focal point. She was sure that somewhere in the mixture of disappointment and remnant resentment, something intense flared through his entrancement. The elongated silence in the room was thick like cane syrup.

"Before we begin, can we pray?"

Sariah turned her attention toward Jaxon, her face filled with perplexity. *Begin what? Who is this man?* As soon as the thoughts exited her mind, Sariah remembered where she'd heard the name before. Upon Jaxon's introduction of himself, the name rang familiar, but only now did she remember why. Jaxon Tillman was one of the executive staff

Kendra Norman-Bellamy

members that Geoffrey mentioned having hired a few weeks ago. *What is he doing here? Why did his wife burst into tears? What's going on?*

Not knowing how to respond to Jaxon's request or his outstretched hands, Sariah looked at Geoffrey for direction. He paused for several moments, during which time, he and Jaxon seemed to communicate to one another without speaking a word. After a short while, Geoffrey moved so that he stood between Teresa and Jaxon, taking one of their hands in each of his. Sariah knew right away that he'd purposefully repositioned himself so that he would not have to touch her.

Sariah took Teresa's unoccupied hand and then looked across the room at the woman who hadn't spoken one word since she'd walked in to find them in her den. One of the stranger's hands was locked securely to her husband's but the other dangled free. Sariah observed with growing suspicion as Jaxon nudged his wife just before she looked up at him with pleading eyes. She didn't want to hold Sariah's hand and Sariah didn't know why. Although Jaxon said nothing verbally, his eyes' unyielding fixation spoke volumes. With delayed footsteps, his wife inched toward Sariah until she was just close enough for their outstretched hands to meet.

All eyes around her were closed and each head was lowered, Sariah observed. The left hand that she held in her right was still moist with the tears that it had been used to wipe away just a few minutes earlier, and Sariah could feel it trembling. Her eyes left the hand of the woman beside her and came to rest on her husband. Aside from the times that tradition had called for it, Sariah had never seen Geoffrey's head bowed in prayer. Yet, today, he did it so naturally, as if it was something he'd done before in recent days.

Jaxon's ongoing words suddenly captured Sariah's attention. "And, Lord, we ask that You let Your peace that surpasses all understanding rest upon this home and all who have gathered here. Our wrongdoing toward one another has been great, but none have been greater than the sins that we've committed against You since the beginning of mankind. Yet, somehow You loved us so much that You sent Your Son to die for the forgiveness of our sins. Give us a heart of forgiveness, Lord, and help us to realize that none of us are perfect and none of our mirrors are without cracks. We ask for Your healing so that we can truly reflect Your unflawed image. We pray these and other blessings in Your name. Amen."

She was in her own home but to Sariah, nothing going on at the moment was familiar. Following everyone else's lead, Sariah sat, all the while wondering if this dream would ever end.

Still the voice of command, Jaxon asked Teresa to bring a supply of water and as soon as she left the room, he looked at his silent wife and then at Sariah. "Mrs. Langston, I know we've blindsided you with our invasion of your time, but we—my wife and I—wanted to speak with you. I asked Mr. Langston to join us."

"What is this about?" Her voice was almost a murmur.

Jaxon looked again at the woman beside him and then back at Sariah. "Please allow me to speak on behalf of both of us," he said. "This concerns the article that was written in *B.I.O.N. Magazine*."

It was the last thing that Sariah wanted to discuss. Especially not in front of Geoffrey. Jaxon must have known that a protest was on its way because he held up his hand to stop her from speaking.

"Please, Mrs. Langston. Let me finish. I want to apologize for the article and the hurt that it brought upon you and your family."

Sariah's confusion continued to mount. "Why are you apologizing?"

During the short silence that followed, Jaxon's eyes were downcast. It was the woman beside him who finally spoke.

"I wrote it."

Sariah's back stiffened. "What?"

The woman stood from her seat and as she approached, Sariah instinctively coiled closer to the back of her chair. Jaxon stood, too, and Sariah wasn't sure whether it was in support or out of concern for what his wife might do.

"You don't even have a clue of who I am, do you?" the woman asked. "I'm LaShun. That's my name. You should remember that since it's the only thing in life that you ever gave me."

Hearing it caused Sariah to release a heavy gasp. She saw Geoffrey suddenly lift his head and turn to her, but she couldn't look directly at him. Sariah's hands crossed one another as she placed them against her chest. A mixture of emotions assaulted her body, causing her teeth to chatter and her body to tremble.

LaShun continued with damp, glistening eyes. "I'm sorry for what I did. I was wrong and I admit it. As angry as I was, as angry as I have been for years, I'm disappointed that I wasn't able to be a better woman than you. It shouldn't have been that hard to do."

Sariah stared at the daughter she hadn't seen since tearfully leaving her behind for strangers to care for. She had grown into a beautiful woman. Sariah wanted to touch her, hold her and tell LaShun all the things she'd never known, but she didn't even know where to begin. And judging from her harsh words, Sariah knew that much of it would be too little too late. The depth of her firstborn daughter's agony was painfully obvious.

"I'm sorry" was all that Sariah could muster through tearful intakes of breath. "I thought you'd be better off with someone else."

"Why? Because you couldn't stand looking in my black face?" LaShun yelled. Jaxon attempted to calm her, but it did no good. "I spent my whole life in foster care and watched the girls whose flesh looked taupe and tawny get adopted while my raven skin got passed over and passed along. I shouldn't have expected any more of them when my own birth mother did the same thing."

"What? N-no."

"Oh, really? Look at the girls you kept, the only daughters that you have ever claimed giving birth to, Sariah. What color are they? I know I was wrong for writing that article and trying to inflict on you the hurt that I thought God should have delivered a long time ago. But I just got so tired of the world thinking you were some kind of role model when I have lived my whole childhood living the results of your prejudices and self-hatred."

Sariah shook her head. "No, LaShun, it was nothing like that. You don't understand. It had nothing to do with your skin. I thought I was doing the right thing for everybody. You—me—Geoffrey—"

No sooner had she uttered his name than Geoffrey was on his feet. "The right thing for me?" he demanded. "How? By keeping it from me all these years? How right do you think it was for you to be throwing my past in my face all while you were hiding lies of your own? You didn't think you were doing the right thing, Sariah. Just tell the truth. You were selfish. Everything you did, you did for yourself."

"No!" Sariah screamed. "I wasn't being selfish! I did it for all of us. Especially you, Geoffrey."

"Oh, cut the crap, Sariah! Don't you dare try to place any blame my way. You didn't give that child away for my sake. We didn't get together until years later. How in the world could what you did to your daughter have anything to do with me?"

"Because she's your daughter, too!"

Sariah's last words brought all the yelling and accusations to a complete silence. The glasses that Teresa had been balancing on the tray in the hallway behind them fell to the floor, sending shattered pieces dancing across the hardwood. No one flinched. Sariah's hands were cupped over her mouth where they'd tried unsuccessfully to catch the words before they spilled from her lips.

"What did you say?" Geoffrey whispered, his face a gamut of perplexing emotions.

Sariah sank onto the cushions of the love seat where she sat alone and wept aloud, rocking back and forth. For the time that she cried into her hands, it seemed that no one else in the room so much as breathed. When she finally looked back up into their faces, they displayed the same stunned looks they'd had when she first blurted the words.

Calming herself as best she could, Sariah turned to her husband. "We didn't become a couple until years later, but we did get together, Geoffrey. Remember?" Her bottom lip quivered as she brought the night back to his recollection. "I knew that if I told my mother the truth of my baby's paternity, she'd use it to blackmail your family. I was only sixteen, Geoffrey, and you were twenty-one. If she could have used statutory rape to bilk your family out of millions, she would have."

"I didn't rape you." Geoffrey's voice remained at a low volume.

"I know. But that wouldn't have stopped Mama. She was so angry when she found out about my pregnancy. She wanted me to terminate it, but I refused and that made her even madder. By then, I was entering my second trimester and had just gotten that permanent job with the E. L. Langston line and I had to make up an excuse to take some time off so that I wouldn't lose the job forever while I had the baby. Mama told Ms. Eloise that she was dying and had only a year to live. She told your mother that she needed me to care for her for a while."

Geoffrey's head began a slow nod and Sariah knew that he remembered the turn of events. How could any of them forget? Eloise Langston was disappointed that her first teen model needed to take a leave so soon, but to grant Sariah's mother her "dying wish," Eloise promised she would keep the job secure. When Sariah returned to work ten months later, Eloise and Horace Langston bought the story that a rare transfusion had saved her mother's life.

Sariah felt a shudder of humiliation. "I had to go along

with it. I loved you too much to let your family's name be destroyed. I knew you didn't love me at the time, but I loved you. I still do, Geoffrey, and I'm so sorry for constantly putting your past under a magnifying glass in an effort to minimize my own." She turned her eyes to LaShun. "And I loved you, too. I wanted to keep you but I knew I didn't have what it took to be a good mother and I would have died before I would have allowed my mother to be your guardian. I thought if I took you to the church, God would watch over you and make sure you were taken care of."

For the first time, Sariah saw softness in her daughter's eyes. The tears were still streaming, but the glossed-over anger had dissolved. When silence lingered, Sariah continued. "It had nothing to do with your complexion. Your paternal grandmother had raven skin, too. That's where you got it from. When I looked at you moments after giving birth, Ms. Eloise was all I could think of."

"That's why you named her LaShun," Geoffrey thought aloud. From the manner that he stood looking at his eldest daughter, Sariah knew that he could see the resemblance as well.

"What's the reason she was named LaShun?" Jaxon said, looking for clarification.

Geoffrey said, "My mother's maiden name was spelled L-A-S-H-O-N-N. It's the *L* in *E. L. Langston*."

For several moments all that could be heard were the sounds of scraping glass as Teresa used a broom to sweep up the spill that hearing the news had caused.

"I'm sorry," Sariah whispered as she watched LaShun tearfully bury her face in her husband's chest. "I'm so sorry."

Chapter 17

On Sunday morning, LaShun sat on the side of the bed taking deep breaths, trying to put to rest the butterflies that fluttered in the pit of her stomach.

"Everything is going to be fine, sweetheart," Jaxon said, planting a kiss on her forehead as he passed her spot on the bed.

LaShun hoped he was right. She hadn't seen her biological parents since she left their home three days ago. The blaming, the screaming, the crying and most of all, the praying, had all served as a source of therapy. LaShun never thought the day would come when she no longer hated her birth mother and the name that Sariah had given her, but it had. Forgiveness was a powerful thing.

Jaxon crossed in front of her again, headed in the opposite direction. "So, when you spoke to your parents last night, how did it feel?"

My parents. The thought of it brought an unrehearsed smile to LaShun's face. "Bizarre, I guess. It's going to be even stranger to have them sitting in church with us. Not to mention that I'll meet their daughters for the first time."

"Not just their daughters," Jaxon corrected. "Your sisters. You have a bigger family now, LaShun. Get used to it. And get used to them worshipping with you, too. I have the feeling that getting my job back was just the first of many things that God is going to use to strengthen our ties to the Langstons."

"I think so, too," she agreed. "It's a little bit scary for me, though. I'm almost ashamed to say it, but after all of this, I'm still struggling with everything. It all happened so fast."

"No need to be ashamed, baby. If it's how you feel, confess it. The Bible says the truth shall make you free. All this coming clean has been liberating for us all." Jaxon's voice dropped to a level that made it seem as though he was talking to himself. "Wonder if I should go ahead and tell Carminda that her food is nasty. Wonder if that would free us from having to eat what she cooks today."

LaShun laughed out loud. "You'd better not."

"I'm just saying," Jaxon replied on his way out of the bedroom.

Walking into the bathroom, LaShun touched up her makeup. She'd have to control her emotions today or all the time she'd spent in front of the mirror this morning would go to waste. The mirror, she thought. It was such a deceptive device. All the while that she had been finding the fractures in the one that Sariah looked into, she'd not been able to see the rupture that had begun in hers as an infant and, in thirty-two years, had enlarged to the size of a tunnel.

"Forgive me, Lord, and allow me from this point on to see my own shortcomings before seeing the flaws of others. Let my image always reflect You." It was the same prayer that she'd whispered to herself more times that she could count in recent days.

"Ready, baby?" she heard Jaxon call from the living room.

Grabbing her Bible, LaShun took one last deep breath. "As ready as I'll ever be," she whispered.

* * * * *

HONOR THY HEART

Honor your father and your mother, that your days may be prolonged in the land which the Lord your God gives you.
—*Exodus 20:12*

Chapter 1

Gritting her pretty white teeth, Sienna St. James had just thought of all the inane things said to her at one time or another by her mother and a host of others regarding her pageant career. Trying her best not to scream at the top of her lungs, she stared into the mirror, scrubbing her face clean with an Olay moisturizing wipe.

Looking back at Sienna from the gold-gilded two-way glass on the wall was a shadow of a twenty-one-year-old woman, one who appeared sad and terribly lonely. Her thick mass of long, light brown hair was pulled straight back and wrapped in a delicate band. Her full lips trembled as glistening tears flooded her green eyes. Raw emotions were running rampant.

Would the excruciating pain ever go away? Would she ever be free from bondage?

Sienna had to wonder, as she had done practically every day of her adult life.

Upon Sienna hearing her mother's high-heeled footsteps clicking against the marble floor, she rapidly reached behind her and locked the bathroom door. She sucked in a deep breath and held it in until the footsteps moved on down the corridor, though she knew they would eventually return. Her private bathroom inside her suite of rooms was one of only two places where she could be alone with her thoughts. The other place was when she was tucked into her king-size bed, but only after the lights went out in her parents' room.

Well, she thought, the lights in her mother's bedroom.

Sable and Duquesne St. James had no idea that their daughter was aware they hadn't shared the same bed for a long time. Putting up such a front was more than likely her mother's idea. It was a huge six-bedroom, eight-bathroom house; 6,500 square feet of well-appointed space. It was very easy to lose oneself in it. Her mother would die of embarrassment if their living arrangements were ever exposed. Sable St. James was very much into appearances.

On the other hand, there was nothing pretentious about Sienna's father, yet he often went along with Sable's agenda. It was probably easier than suffering the living hell she was capable of putting him through. He had tried to move heaven and earth to spare his daughter any amount of pain, only to fail miserably at it. Duquesne had no clue how badly his young adult daughter was hurting because Sienna had stopped complaining to him a long time ago.

Sienna's handsome father was fondly referred to as Duke by his family members, close friends and colleagues, but in the courtroom he was respectfully known as Duquesne, one of the most brilliant African-American prosecutors in

Houston, Texas. Sienna was his one and only baby, the brightest light in his world, a daddy's girl in every sense of the word. Duquesne could do no wrong in his daughter's sight. Sienna adored him just as much as he cherished her.

Father and daughter had been constantly separated over the years because Sable had entered Sienna in every beauty pageant in the country by the time she was a year old. Although Duquesne had vehemently objected to his wife's putting his daughter through the grueling, meaningless contests, his remarks had always fallen on deaf ears. He hated the lipstick, the eye shadow and the revealing costumes that turned his child into something unnatural. His heart broke every time Sable packed Sienna up and carted her off to only God knew where.

Duquesne actually hated everything to do with pageantry, but he was powerless against his wife's determination and strong will. His voice still went unheard. Nothing he had ever said had made a bit of difference to Sable. His feelings were never considered, not in the least. It was his best guess that Sable had been and was still living vicariously through his precious angel.

Sienna was everything Sable desired but had failed to become.

Sable rarely listened to anyone, including her daughter. Around the age of six, Sienna had begun to loudly express her dislike of being put on public display. Her little temper tantrums and falling-outs had only kept her in hot water and had done nothing at all to quell Sable's desire to have her daughter crowned as the most beautiful child in the world, her very own little beauty queen.

Sable was currently propelling her daughter toward the Miss Texas pageant.

Sienna held her breath when the loud clicking of heels ceased. That meant her mother was about to enter her bedroom. As though Sienna were still a little child, Sable made it a point to check on her daughter every night, making sure she had cleansed her skin properly and had given her hair a hundred brisk strokes with the specially made brushes she kept in ample supply.

How pathetic was that? As if Sable could actually tell how many times Sienna had pulled the brush through her hair. Sienna chuckled inwardly at that one, fearful of laughing out loud.

For all of Sienna's truculent thoughts about her mother, she would never think of voicing them aloud. Verbally disrespecting either of her parents would come hard for her. However, if she wasn't able to mentally tell Sable what she thought of her and the sick world of beauty pageants and such, Sienna knew she would have gone stark raving mad long before now.

"Honor thy father and thy mother" was one commandment Sienna feared breaking, yet she knew God would also hold her accountable for her undesirable thoughts. Still, it was better to think them than to say them aloud.

Sable, dressed in silk lounging attire, entered Sienna's room without knocking, which wasn't anything out of the ordinary, since she only did it every single night. "Sienna, what is taking you so long? You should have been in bed an hour ago. You have an eight o'clock class. Come out of that bathroom this minute."

Wishing she had the nerve to outright defy her mother,

Sienna entwined her fingers as she said a silent prayer to ask God for strength. After taking a last-minute glance in the mirror, hoping every hair on her head was in place, she slowly opened the bathroom door.

"It's about darn time." Sable walked over to the mahogany four-poster bed and pulled back the beige satin comforter and top sheet. She plumped the pillows before gesturing to Sienna to climb in. "Did you moisturize your skin thoroughly?"

"Yes, ma'am."

"What about your hair? One hundred brisk strokes?"

"Yes, ma'am."

"Good. Get into bed now. You need your beauty rest. I'll see you at breakfast. Don't be late." Sable then stuck out her cheek for Sienna to kiss. Once she received the gentle peck of affection from her daughter, she turned and walked out of the room without bothering to return the favor.

Wishing that her father were home to give her a hug, Sienna climbed into bed. Duquesne was out of town on business, but he had been expected home earlier in the evening. She had kept an ear tuned in to the garage door opening up all during dinner, but to no avail. It wasn't like him to not come home when he was supposed to so she figured something had gone awry. Perhaps he had missed his flight. She hoped that he was okay and that nothing bad had occurred.

If Sable thought Sienna was going to be the lead model in the agency she was in the process of opening, she had another think coming. She had been banking the success of her modeling agency on the constant demand for her daughter in the world of high fashion and the performing arts. Countless magazines had already put in their bids for Sienna to grace their front covers and inside layouts. In Sienna's opinion, she had already been used enough.

Graduation from college was only a couple of months away. It was hard enough to get a decent job with a good education, but it was definitely more difficult without one. Sienna wanted a good education and she planned to attend postgraduate school, as well. When she did go out into the world alone, she would be extremely well prepared. She had no intentions of continuing to use her face and body to make a living. Those days were almost over. Armed with a degree in psychology, she planned to make her own mark on the world.

Sienna had also stayed in her parents' home past eighteen for one other reason besides her educational goals. She was due to inherit a good sum of money from her paternal grandparents once she graduated college. She was also to receive the monies she had won in the pageants.

If Sienna had dared to try and leave home before graduation, Sable would have found a way to stop her inheritance, though state law wouldn't allow her to control the pageant monies. The inheritance money was a much larger sum. Her mother's hold on her was soon to be broken. If she had to end up fighting her in a court of law to get what was rightfully hers, Sienna had already made up her mind to do so, tooth and nail.

Sable was about to find out how much control she didn't have over Sienna St. James.

Sienna was half-asleep when she heard the garage door open. Worried about her father, she hadn't been able to fall into a deep slumber. After climbing out of bed, she slipped into her robe and headed for the double doors. Before stepping out into the hallway, she listened for any and all sounds. Instead of using the front stairs, she decided to use the back staircase, which was the one her father always used to reach the second floor; it also led upward from the door leading to the garage. Sienna still wasn't sure which room her father slept in, but she knew it wasn't the master suite.

Glad that she didn't have to go past Sable's bedroom door, Sienna quickly made her way down the stairs. Just as she reached the bottom landing, she saw her father heading toward the kitchen. "Daddy," she whispered, hoping he could hear her. The last thing she wanted to do was awaken her mother. Duquesne turned around upon hearing Sienna call out to him.

Sienna ran across the foyer and flung herself into Duquesne's arms. "Oh, Daddy, I've been so worried. Is everything okay?"

Duquesne gently pressed his lips against Sienna's right temple. "Everything is fine, sweetheart. Sorry I'm so late. Did I wake you?"

"Not really. I wasn't fully asleep. I had been listening for the garage door to go up."

"Come with me." Duquesne took Sienna by the hand and led her into the kitchen, where he pulled out a chair from the table. "How about joining me for a cup of tea?"

Sienna looked anxiously toward the staircase. "Is that wise? I don't know—"

Duquesne waved off Sienna's concern. "Nothing to do with this household is wise. Afraid of waking your mother, aren't you?"

Sienna nodded. "You know how she is. You'd think I was still a two-year-old."

"Don't worry about Sable." He gestured for Sienna to be seated. "If she comes down, I'll handle it. Lemon or orange spice?"

"Earl Grey works better for me." As Sienna sat down, she bit down on her lip. "Why are you so late, anyway? Mom said you'd be home by dinnertime."

"To be honest with you, sweetheart, I had no desire to come home, period." Duquesne sighed hard. "If it weren't for you, I'd never step foot in this house again."

Sienna looked shocked. "That hurts me to hear you say that."

"Please don't take it personally, Sienna." He moved away from the table long enough to turn on the gas under the teakettle. Duquesne took the seat opposite Sienna. "My feeling that way has nothing to do with you, my precious." He looked down at the floor and then back up at his daughter, hating to see the obvious pain in her pretty eyes.

"Daddy, what is it? What's going on with you?"

Duquesne rubbed his forehead with the heel of his hand. "You're an adult now, Sienna, though God knows you haven't been treated like one. You'll just have to handle the truth no matter how much it may hurt. I've been toying with the idea of leaving your mother. No, that's not altogether true. I just came home to get a few of my things together. I'm moving out of here tonight. I have forgotten how long it's been since I've been sleeping apart from your mother. I've already reserved a hotel suite near the office."

Sienna didn't know what to say, but she wasn't surprised

that he wanted to leave home. She wanted to leave, too. But she hated that her father wanted to move away from her. "I don't think I can bear to live here without you. I'm living like a little girl. Daddy, please don't leave me here alone with her." Sienna's tears began to fall. "Please, can't you wait until I graduate?"

Duquesne reached over and put his arm around Sienna's shoulder. "Please don't cry, sweetheart. Your tears are something I can't bear. Aren't you going to ask me *why* I want to leave your mother?"

"I don't have to. If I was married to her, I'd leave her, too."

Duquesne chuckled at the way Sienna had said that. "I know this isn't a laughing matter, but I have to do something to keep from breaking down. I never dreamed I'd be this unhappy."

That makes two of us. Sienna hadn't voiced her thoughts because she didn't want to add to her father's sorrow. He looked sad enough. It wasn't in her to hurt him, though she thought he could have prevented a lot of the pain she had endured at her mother's hands by standing firmer. "I'm here for you, Daddy. Always."

"Thank you, baby." Duquesne removed a handkerchief from his breast pocket and wiped the tears from her eyes and then his. "I'm sorry I haven't been here for you."

Sienna couldn't stand to see her father hurting so badly. She could have lashed out at him in her anger, but he was already in enough pain. "Oh, but you have been."

"Not really. I gave up on being an active parent a long time ago. I accepted too easily that I had no say in your upbringing. If I had, you wouldn't have ever gone to those horrible pageants. You wouldn't have had to wear that war paint, either. I failed you in so many ways."

Sienna honestly didn't blame her father for any of the bad stuff that had occurred in her life. He had fought—and he had fought hard for her right to be a child. Deep in her heart she knew he was also a victim of Sable.

"Don't do this now. I'm so close…"

"Close to what?"

"Graduating." *So close to getting out of prison* was what had been on the tip of Sienna's tongue. Happy that she had been able to bite back her acid response, she sighed inwardly. Sienna would do anything to spare her father any more undue pain. She loved him as much as life itself.

Sienna wasn't sure her father really knew how unhappy she was living at home. She had wanted to live on campus when she had first entered college, but her mother wouldn't hear of it back then. Buying her daughter the new Toyota convertible to get back and forth to school had been Sable's way of maintaining control of Sienna.

At least, that was what Sable believed. Sienna had worked hard for the Solara and everything else she had in her possession, all of which could be taken away from her by her mother without a moment's notice. There were two things that Sable couldn't and wouldn't take away from her daughter.

Sienna's iron-strong will and her endless determination.

For Sienna to live her life exactly the way she saw fit was going to happen come hell or high water. Her inheritance would help her do as she pleased, when she pleased. Sable had no idea how strong her daughter's will was, but Sable wasn't too far away from finding out.

Sienna couldn't remember not being on a schedule of some sort. Ballet, voice, piano, aerobics, several foreign languages and the countless modeling and grooming sessions were all the things Sienna had been forced into by her mother. As far back as she could remember, every waking hour of her day had been designated for one thing or another. Then there was the eight hours of beauty sleep, an absolute must for a beauty queen.

Sienna covered Duquesne's hand with her own. "If you can't stay until I graduate, I'll understand. But how will I get to see you if you move out? You may not be welcome here."

"How well do I know that!" Duquesne shook his head. "I won't run out on you, Sienna. For once in my sorry life I'm going to stand up and fight for you and for me. I'll stay—"

"Stay where?" Sable stood in the doorway with both hands on her hips.

Sable cut her frosty eyes at Sienna. "What are you doing up at this hour, pray tell?"

The thundering of Sable's voice and the sudden shrill whistle of the kettle had Sienna feeling as if her heart was leaping out of her chest. At the anger in Sable's voice, Sienna knew that her deep-seated fears had just arrived in a beautiful lacy nightgown and matching robe.

Duquesne rushed to his feet and scurried across the room to tend to the kettle.

Sienna cowered in fear, nearly crumbling in her seat. "I came down to talk with Daddy. I was really worried about him when he didn't come home for dinner."

"I'm glad you two have had your little chat, but it's time for you to get back to bed." When it looked as if Sienna might challenge her, Sable clapped her hands. "Move it, girl!"

Sienna had just gotten to her feet when Duquesne stepped in front of her, reaching back for her hand, as if he might find strength there. "My daughter and I have not had our tea yet, nor are we finished with our conversation. I know, Sienna needs her beauty rest," he mocked. "There's no such thing as designer eye bags, which is exactly what your eyes will be wearing in the morning if you continue to rant and rave like a maniac. Your ugliness is showing—and you are the one that could use an overdose of beauty rest. Good night, Sable."

Sable was obviously taken aback by her husband's tone of voice, not to mention the authority in it. Duquesne hadn't challenged her in this way in years. The look on his face would brook no argument from the average person. Sable was anything but average.

To try to achieve some semblance of peace, Sienna tried to let go of her father's hand so she could comply with her mother's wishes, but he only held it tighter. "Stay right here, Sienna. I've got this one."

Sable glared at her husband. That he would dare to challenge her authority in front of their daughter had her beyond incensed. "Can I speak to you in private, Duke?"

"Sure thing, Sable." He looked down at his watch. "Later on this morning, after Sienna has left for school. Not a minute before."

Unable to believe her ears, Sable jerked her head back. "Excuse me!"

Duquesne nodded. "I can do that with ease. You are excused, Sable."

Sable raised her fist and pounded the air. "If you were so

eager to spend time with your daughter, why weren't you here on time for dinner?" Her eyes challenged him to a duel.

Determined not to have this conversation any sooner than the time he'd given Sable, he glared back at his wife. If it was a battle she wanted, he was ready for her to bring it on.

A stare-down ensued between Duquesne and Sable for a couple of minutes. Sable withdrew her gaze first. After mumbling a few expletives, she turned on her heel and left the room. She wasn't through with her husband yet. "How soon we forget," she said to herself.

Duquesne knew what he was in for when he and Sable *did* talk, but it wasn't anything he hadn't already faced with his wife. She was a mean-spirited woman, but he would stick to his guns this time and he planned to continue on in that mode. Enough was enough. He would no longer allow her to belittle him in front of his daughter or otherwise. Divorcing Sable was second on his list of things to do. Reconnecting with his daughter and protecting her was his top priority.

Duquesne had never asked Sienna why she had stayed at home past the age of eighteen. He already knew the answer. She wasn't about to leave without staking claim on her inheritance. Neither would he have left all that money behind. He was sure that that was his daughter's main reason for asking him to stay on until after graduation. As difficult a task as staying until then would be, he wasn't going to abandon Sienna yet again. The next couple of months couldn't be any more unpleasant than all the previous years he had been married to Sable. Duquesne squared his shoulders, vowing to let the chips fall where they may.

* * *

The lack of sleep was beginning to affect Sienna badly. Her Spanish III class would be over in a few minutes and she could hardly wait for it to end. She loved this particular foreign-language class, especially because Mr. Lopez made it so interesting, but it was difficult for her to concentrate on anything after what had occurred with her parents last evening.

What was going on at home had Sienna worried sick. Her father had probably been blasted out of his shoes by now, maybe even thrown out of the house. If her mother hadn't put him out—and he felt he really needed to go—she wouldn't think of holding him to his promise of staying on until after she graduated. Everyone didn't have to be miserable. Should her dad leave, she would not let her mother keep her from visiting with him.

When Sienna looked down at her watch, she realized she had enough time to grab a cup of hot tea before heading to her modeling session. As she made her way through the throng of students crowded into the hallway, she suddenly began to feel overheated. A bout of nausea followed. She tried to shake off the bad feelings, but to no avail. She couldn't afford to come down with the flu or any other kind of illness for that matter. A cup of tea would surely help, but the heat she felt had now grown more intense. Something hot to drink might not be the right thing to do for what ailed her so she decided to purchase something cold instead.

After fumbling around in her purse for a few seconds, Sienna pulled out a handful of change, more than enough to purchase a can of 7-Up from the vending machine, thinking it might help to settle her stomach. As she inserted the first coin into the slot, another bout of nausea caused her to double up. She closed her eyes, hoping the nauseous feelings would go away.

A minute or so later, feeling a tad better, Sienna was able to complete her purchase. After retrieving the soda from the lower bin, she immediately popped the top and took a long swallow.

On her way to the parking lot, just before she stepped outside the exit door, she felt horribly sick again. Her vision began to blur and her eyes burned. As she went down to her knees, she felt her eyes rolling to the back of her head.

"Clear the way. Give her room to breathe," Dr. Erique Prescott shouted to the crowed quickly forming around Sienna.

Chapter 2

Sienna tried to sit up on the examining table inside the infirmary, but a pair of gentle hands stayed her. Her head ached something awful and her stomach still felt queasy.

With grave concern, Dr. Prescott looked down on the beautiful woman who possessed the creamiest olive complexion. "When was the last time you ate something, young lady?"

The voice was strong and soothing to Sienna's ears. Her almond-shaped eyes burned and she had to strain to see the face belonging to the voice. As she thought about the question asked of her, she recalled picking at her food during dinner and she had also skipped the lunch break earlier. The absence of her father at the dinner table had made it impossible for her to take in a reasonable amount of food. Besides that, the scale in her bathroom had shown that she had gained nearly half a pound. Her mother would have been furious over the added weight, which had caused her to tamper with the numbers on the scale, setting it back a full pound. Sienna closed her eyes when another wave of nausea struck.

Dr. Prescott reiterated his question to Sienna.

"At dinnertime last evening," Sienna finally managed to respond.

"Dieting?"

"No. I just wasn't all that hungry."

"Not hungry or terribly upset by something?"

Sienna looked up at the tall stranger, immediately noticing how handsome he was. His eyes were an odd shade of amber, yet they were beautiful and piercing. His physique was pretty hot-looking, too, but that was the last thing she needed to have on her mind with all the bad stuff going on in her life. Sable would have a fit if she even thought of getting involved in a love affair. She could imagine the angry tirade her mother would fly into.

"Is it possible that you might be pregnant?"

Sienna had a hard time not laughing at that silly question. "Sure, it's possible. That is, if an immaculate conception were possible."

"So you're a virgin?"

Sienna felt her olive complexion color significantly. "Who are you, anyway?"

Erique extended his hand to Sienna. "Dr. Erique Prescott. Pleased to meet you, though I wish it were under more pleasant circumstances."

Sienna had realized when she first opened her eyes that she was in Texas University's infirmary because she had been there before. The guy looked too young to be a doctor, but who was she to question his legitimacy? Age wasn't always determined by how a person looked, anyway. Some folks looked a lot older than their actual age and sometimes much younger.

"I'm okay now. I really have to be going." Sienna tried to sit up again, only to lay her head back down rather quickly. "Oh God," she moaned, "what *is* wrong with me?"

"Well, for sure we know you're not pregnant. *That* you should be thankful for."

Dr. Prescott was really starting to get on Sienna's nerves. "Thanks, I guess. In your very best medical opinion what do you think is going on?"

"A flu bug perhaps. Or maybe you just need to eat properly."

"Is that your official diagnosis, Doctor?"

"Pretty much. Let me help you sit up." He put his hand behind her neck and lifted her head gently, keeping a close eye on her at the same time. "How do you feel now?"

"Like crap."

"Hmm. Interesting choice of words."

Sienna rolled her luminous green eyes at Dr. Prescott. "Why's that?"

"I hate to be the bearer of bad news, but you look just like you feel."

"Gee, thanks a lot. Are you sure you're a doctor? If so, your bedside manner leaves a lot to be desired."

Dr. Prescott shrugged his broad shoulders. "I just call it like I see it. Mind if I take your temperature, Miss St. James? Maybe that will tell us something."

"Do I have a choice?"

"Of course you do. But it would behoove you to try and

help me get to the bottom of your illness. We *did* just pick you up off the floor."

"*We?* Who are *we?*"

"A couple of students and myself. Do you by chance know a young lady by the name of Ginger Phillips?"

"Ginger. She's my friend."

Sienna didn't really have any close friends, but she and Ginger took a lot of classes together and they had somehow developed a great rapport with each other, though neither of them had visited each other's homes. Ginger was also very popular around campus, especially with the opposite sex. However, she was very much into her boyfriend, Randall Hastings, paying very little attention to other males. Randall was a star athlete, playing the position of center for the Texas Gamblers basketball team.

"You should thank Ginger when you see her again. She's the one who came and got me and brought me to where you lay flat on your back. She also told me your name." He held up the digital thermometer for Sienna to see before inserting it into her mouth.

Sienna fought the urge to smile. Dr. Prescott was pleasing to look at and very interesting. She stole another glance at his eyes, deciding they were quite dreamy despite the strange coloring. His lashes were longer and thicker than hers. He also had great teeth and a heartwarming smile. He appeared to be six feet tall or possibly a bit more. Nice body, she thought, smiling inwardly, thinking it would be fun to spot for him on the weights.

"Your temp is normal. Who is your primary physician?"

"Dr. Samantha Meyers."

"I suggest you see her as soon as possible. She might want to run some laboratory tests to rule out a few things. Something caused you to black out, though I still suspect your poor eating habits as the culprit. Is there someone I can call on to take you home?"

"My car is in the parking lot."

Dr. Prescott shook his head from side to side. "I don't recommend your getting behind the wheel of a car. If you were to go out like a light again— Well, we don't have to go there. I think you get the picture."

"I get it, but I have another class to get to, off campus. I can't miss it."

"What type of class is there that you can afford to put your life at risk for?"

"It's a modeling session."

Dr. Prescott raised both eyebrows. "Oh, one of those types. That explains everything."

Sienna bit down on her lower lip to keep from retorting. She rolled her eyes instead, making sure he got the message of how annoyed she was with his remark.

Erique laughed, taking notice of how even more beautiful Sienna was when agitated. He stepped away for a second to pick up a clipboard, which he then handed to her. "Are you feeling up to filling out this form? Or do you want me to do it for you?"

Sienna practically snatched the clipboard from the doctor's hand. She instantly regretted acting so childish, but she didn't apologize. The minute she finished filling out the short questionnaire, she slowly got to her feet. "There should already be one of these on file. I was in here a month or so ago."

"Same symptoms?"

"Just a bad headache."

"I see."

"Thanks a lot for helping me out. I have to run now."

Dr. Prescott looked at the wall clock. "Since you're determined to drive, I'm going to follow you to your destination to make sure you stay safe. I'm officially off duty now."

"You following me won't help any if I crash my car."

"I can call 911 immediately, but I've decided to take you to your class and bring you back for your car. Come on. Let's go. I have no intentions of letting you out of my sight for the next couple of hours." Nor was he about to let her risk her life on some stupid modeling class. Sienna was one beautiful woman, but he didn't think she had an ounce of common sense. Still, he desired to be in her company a while longer. As for *how* long, he wasn't sure about that.

"That's a little extreme, don't you think?"

The defiant set of Erique's jaw wasn't lost on Sienna. He meant business, so she decided not to fight him on the issue. Admitting that she was very attracted to him came easy enough for her, though she knew nothing could ever come of it. Sable St. James wouldn't have any of it.

Sienna kept her eyes trained on Erique as he locked up the infirmary. She couldn't help wishing that her circumstances were very different from the reality of how she was forced to lead her life. The thought of graduation being just around the corner caused her to light up like a lantern. Another day until her prison break would soon be marked off on her calendar.

* * *

Sienna felt better this evening than she had all day long. *Was Dr. Prescott the reason for her upbeat mood?* She had to wonder. He had shown her such genuine care, something she knew very little about. Her mother had used her and abused her emotionally. Her father loved her, but in a strange kind of way. Duquesne didn't have a clue how to keep her safe from the woman who had birthed her. Sienna wasn't even sure if she loved her own mother. After a few quiet moments of deliberation, she decided she *did* love Sable McNair-St. James, very much so. The woman had given her life. If for no other reason, Sienna had to love her mother for that.

Hatred wasn't inside of Sienna. Yet her anger toward her mother was so strong that it often scared her silly. Because she had dammed up her rage for so many years she feared what would happen it she were to ever release it.

Sienna lay still for the next hour or so just pondering her situation. As she sorted out the things that had gone wrong in her life, she realized she was as much to blame for her pain as anyone. The money from her inheritance had somehow become more important to her than just walking away from the life she positively loathed. She had failed to try and make a go of things without the creature comforts a large bank account would afford her.

Sienna wondered what had really kept her from getting a normal job. She wasn't too good to work as a cashier or a waitress while working her way through school, though Sable had pounded into her head that she was much better than that. Her mother had placed such a high value on Sienna's stunning looks, so much so that it made her feel ugly inside and out.

All Sienna could do was stare at her cell phone since it rarely rang. When it did, she could easily figure out who was on the other end. Her parents and Ginger were the only ones with the number. Now that Dr. Prescott had it she wasn't all that sure who was calling. It actually felt good not knowing. Before she answered the phone, she prayed that it was the handsome doctor. She liked the way he made her feel. Protected. As if she were something very special.

"How are you feeling now, Sienna?"

Sienna's heart pounded hard, making it difficult for her to think clearly. "Much—better, thank you. It's so nice of you to call and ask."

"Why do you think I *really* asked for your number?"

Sienna stifled a giggle. "I guess I didn't think about it," she lied. That's all she had been able to think about since they had parted in the university parking lot.

"You're a very interesting person, lady. Did you know that?"

"I do now. What do you find so interesting, Dr. Prescott?"

"Everything. The way you walk and talk and I love your beautiful smile. You can be mean as a snake one minute and then turn gentle as a lamb in the next. I guess I'm a bit out of line, huh? But I'm just being honest, Sienna. When can I see you again?"

Sienna's breath caught. This was like a dream she had suddenly walked into. How could such an educated man find her so interesting? He was handsome, too, extremely. What an incredible combination, lethal looks and brains to boot. Reality checked in on Sienna all too soon. Her mother would never allow her to date Erique Prescott, despite his pedigree. Sienna would always be reminded that her career goals came first, though modeling was not her choice.

Erique came from a long lineage of medical doctors. The man had told her so much about himself during their rides back and forth to the parking lot. It had been as if he had wanted desperately to let her know he was an upstanding gentleman and a solid citizen. She didn't get the idea that he had been trying to impress her, though. As he liked to say, he was just being honest. She liked that about him. He knew exactly who he was and he was very comfortable in his own skin. Erique had claimed the Prescotts to be a prestigious yet down-to-earth family.

Besides Sienna's career, Sable had always said that an older man was a more suitable partner for her daughter even though Duquesne was only a couple of years older than her. Older gentlemen were more mature and stable in Sable's high-handed opinion.

"Are you still present and accounted for, Sienna? I guess I've scared you off, huh?"

"No, no. That's not it. I have so much on my mind. I was thinking about your question, but I just don't know where I'd find the time for social stuff. I'm extremely busy with school and my modeling and other classes. Everyone is dedicated to something or other."

Erique could hardly believe his own ears. This striking young woman sounded as if she hadn't ever dated anyone. *How could that be? Was anyone that dedicated to anything?* He had a minute of thought about his own profession. It hadn't stopped him from dating, but he had been awfully dedicated to his studies. He wouldn't have made it this far along otherwise. Erique had had only one serious relationship all through college and medical school, which had ended badly. Adrianna Caine had accused him of being married to his career goals. *How ironic was that?* It seemed as if Sienna was also married to her ambitions.

"What about sharing lunch with me tomorrow? We can meet in the cafeteria. You do take a lunch break, don't you?"

Scared of what this all meant, Sienna sucked in a deep breath to try and calm down her escalating heart rate. She really didn't know how to respond to Erique's request, but she *did* want to see him again. School was a safe place for meeting him. Her mother rarely came there, unless a special event of some kind was taking place. *How could a twenty-one-year-old woman be this terrified of accepting a simple luncheon date?* Knowing how Sable would react to it was definitely just cause. "Okay." Sienna knew if she gave it another thought she would chicken out. "I normally take lunch at twelve-fifteen. I'll see you in the cafeteria."

Erique was totally surprised by her response. The fear he heard in her voice had him believing she wouldn't accept his offer. He was so eager to learn what had her so frightened and seemingly uncertain of herself. It wasn't quite adding up for him. "It's a date. I'll see you then."

Sienna sobered rather quickly at the mention of it being an actual date. "Will seeing me socially put your job in jeopardy?"

"Hardly, since I volunteer my time. The university doesn't pay a dime for my services. At any rate, I'm not on duty tomorrow. I'm only there two days a week, four hours each day. Are we still on?"

"Twelve-fifteen. Have a good evening, Erique."

"You do the same, Sienna."

The call hadn't ended a second too soon. Sable came through Sienna's bedroom door just as she was disconnecting.

Beautifully dressed in designer attire, as she always was, Sable swept across the room as if she was on the high-fashion runway. The silk rustled slightly as she quickly pivoted. "Why were you late for your modeling session, young lady?"

Did nothing get past this woman? Sienna cringed inwardly, hoping she wasn't about to be raked across the carpet. Wishful thinking on her part. She tried to avoid direct eye contact with her mother. "I wasn't feeling well so I stopped by the infirmary. And I wasn't all that late."

"A second late is still late. You were fifteen minutes late to be exact. Pierre called here to see if you were okay. I guess you wouldn't have mentioned it if I hadn't brought it up."

Pierre Conti was Sienna's modeling coach and owner of one of the largest modeling agencies in Texas. He was also the biggest gossip Sienna had ever met. He had the tendency to go on and on about anything and everything. The man didn't know how to be quiet.

As Sable dropped down on the pure white two-cushioned damask sofa, she finally had the good grace to look concerned for her daughter. "What was bothering you enough to cause you to seek medical attention?"

"I felt nauseated and dizzy." She didn't dare tell Sable she had blacked out. It would be off to the emergency room immediately.

Sable got up from the sofa gracefully and walked over to

the bed and peered right into Sienna's face. "Please don't tell me you've been fooling around with some no-account boy at school. Have you? Is it possible that you're pregnant?" Sable instantly paled at the thought.

The question caused Sienna to think of Erique. He had asked her the same thing. How Sable could ask her something like that was beyond her. Her mother knew her every move, even her bathroom habits. She had just proven that by questioning about her lateness for class. "Impossible, Mother."

Sable looked relieved. "That is something I won't tolerate from you. Be downstairs in a half hour. Dinner is ready and we don't want the food to get cold."

Once the door closed behind Sable, Sienna grabbed her cell phone and took it into the bathroom with her. She had been dying to talk to Ginger to find out what she knew about the good Dr. Prescott, although their conversation would have to be short and sweet.

Sienna also wanted to find out how unladylike she may have looked sprawled out all over the hallway floor since she had worn a dress to classes that day. Just the thought of her clothing rising to the degree of indecent exposure caused her to cringe.

What were all the parts of her anatomy Erique had gotten a glimpse of?

Seeing Duquesne already seated at the dinner table made Sienna happy. That told her he hadn't been kicked out of the house, at least not yet. She couldn't wait to talk to him once dinner was over to find out the outcome of the showdown between him and her mother. She could bet that it hadn't been a pleasant event. It never was when Sable was on the warpath.

Sienna also wanted to talk to her father about Erique. He knew most of the prominent families around town so she figured he knew the Prescotts or knew of them.

The meal was eaten pretty much in silence. Just as Sienna had suspected, she hated the food. Eggplant Parmesan was disgusting. Sable knew that her daughter couldn't stand the purple stuff. That had just been another of her ways of taunting Sienna. Practically everything on the table was vegetarian. Meat was only served three times a week in their house—and sometimes just once or twice. It depended on Sable's mood that day.

Sable looked across the table at Sienna. "Now that you've finished your dinner, darling, can you allow your father and I to have some time alone for a short while?"

Darling, indeed! Sienna looked thoroughly distressed by Sable's request.

Duquesne could not stand to see the look of utter disappointment on Sienna's face. He had ignored her pain far too long. "Sable, you and I can talk later. I have somewhere I want to take Sienna. We won't be gone long." He got up from the table and walked to where his daughter was seated and then pulled out her chair. "Come with me, sweetheart."

Sable had fixed her mouth to protest, but there was something about her husband's demeanor that caused her to have second thoughts. He had changed somehow, but she didn't know if she liked the seemingly new him or not. He had gotten much too vocal for her liking.

Though surprised by yet another intervention on her

behalf from her father, Sienna wasted no time in getting to her feet. Any amount of time she got to spend with Duquesne was invaluable to her. That Sable wasn't loudly protesting against the idea of them going off somewhere together was just as surprising to Sienna.

Sienna was surprised yet again when her father ushered her out the front door rather than going into the garage where the car was parked. When he had said he wanted to take her somewhere, she had assumed they would take one of his three cars. The Jaguar was a favorite.

Duquesne took Sienna by the hand. "Let's just you and me walk around the property. We haven't done that in such a long time."

Sienna loved the idea. Their home was situated on two acres of land so they had a lot of area they could cover. Her favorite place was the grove of trees on the back side of the property.

Out there nestled among the trees were a few marble stone benches cemented into the ground. The cabana and pool area was also a beautiful spot to hang out in, with lots of choices in seating. The sun was about to go down and that made their time together even more special for Sienna. She couldn't recall the last time she had watched the sun go down with her father at her side. They had walked a lot when she was younger and she really didn't know why he had stopped suggesting taking long treks around the property with her. She hadn't suggested it, either.

Much busier schedules, Sienna guessed, wishing they could get back all the lost time.

Chapter 3

For the first ten minutes or so Sienna and Duquesne walked in total silence, each enjoying being in the presence of the other. Sienna felt at peace for the first time in a long while.

Once they reached the grove area, Duquesne summoned Sienna to have a seat on one of the benches. He then seated himself right beside her. "How were your classes today?"

Sienna responded to Duquesne's question first and then she shared with him the story of her bout of illness. Her eyes sparkled with light as she told him a bit about Erique Prescott.

Duquesne looked pleased by the expression on Sienna's face. "I know the Prescott family very well. But before we get into the story of the young doctor you seem so smitten with, how are you feeling, sweetheart? Is it something we should be truly worried about?"

Sienna shook her head in the negative. "I'm much better. Whatever it was it passed rather quickly. No need for anyone to worry. How well do you know the Prescott family?"

Duquesne shared the story with Sienna of how the family had needed his legal services when the elder Prescott, which would have been Erique's grandfather, had gotten a DUI, driving under the influence. Once the young, fiery lawyer had looked into the matter, he had found out this infraction was only one of many. Dr. A. C. Prescott had a history of getting tickets while driving intoxicated yet he was one of the most brilliant heart surgeons in the state. Being the fine lawyer that he was, Duquesne had been able to get the latest charges reduced.

Getting Dr. Prescott off scot-free wasn't something Duquesne had wanted to do because he knew that one day Dr. Prescott just might kill someone in that fancy car of his, an old, beautifully restored Bentley. Even though it had been frowned upon by the senior partners in his law firm, Duquesne had insisted that Dr. Prescott quietly enter a rehab program. After much ado and haranguing over his inflammatory suggestion, he had finally persuaded his firm to go along with the idea. It had really been in the best interest of everyone, especially the doctor himself.

"I'm sure the headline news about a local child being killed by a drunk driver around that same time frame was what had persuaded the others to see it my way. His wife and two brothers, all of whom were also physicians, looked quite favorably upon the fact that I had the guts to even talk to Dr. Prescott about going into a rehab program. They had later admitted to me that it wasn't a subject any one of them would have dared to broach with the good doctor."

Sienna looked at Duquesne with admiration. "That *was*

pretty gutsy. I imagine the family wielded a lot of power around the city because of their prestigious standing in their profession."

"Oh, yes, quite a bit of power. His wife was the driving force behind the final decision. She had threatened to leave him if he didn't get help. Back then, separation or divorce was as scandalous as the drunk-driving charges."

"I guess Erique would be pretty embarrassed if he knew I was aware of this story."

"It has probably remained a family secret from everyone other than the people I've mentioned. I don't imagine you're going to ever confront him with it."

"Of course not, Daddy."

"Good. Attorney-client privilege should be strictly adhered to even if you are my daughter. Everything I tell you should be held in the strictest of confidence."

Sienna looked dismayed by her father's last comment. "You don't have to tell me that. When is everyone going to stop treating me like a child, like a little girl who has nothing but air in her brain? It's maddening."

Duquesne regretted saying something to draw his daughter's wrath. "Please forgive me. You are one of the brightest young women I know. I didn't mean to insult you."

"Well, you did!"

"Okay, I'm sorry."

Duquesne tried to think of something to say to pull Sienna up out of her funk. She wasn't the least bit pleased with him, which was unusual for him to see. She was always in such adoration of him, her eyes never failing to convey her love for him. Whether he had let her know it or not, Sienna was the main reason that he hadn't walked out on Sable years ago. Although the time had come for him to do just that, until Sienna was out on her own, he'd stay right there.

"I see that you're on a first-name basis with the young man. How did that come about?" Duquesne felt triumphant when Sienna smiled brilliantly. It looked to him as if she also had love in her eyes for another man. Just the mention of Erique's name had caused her dark mood to lift.

"It's quite a story. Do you have time to listen?"

"I promise to make time for anything you ever want to tell me." Duquesne softly kissed his daughter's forehead.

It took Duquesne very little time to figure out that young Erique Prescott had impressed the heck out of Sienna on their very first meeting. He had never heard her mention any man, let alone be this excited about one. She was bubbling over with enthusiasm. He loved it.

As Sienna's eyes sparkled like tiny flecks of precious jewels, Duquesne suddenly felt like crying. He hated that he had let Sable run his daughter's life. Was he too late in trying to make it all up to Sienna?

The loud arguing had Sienna wanting to cover her ears. Sable was the person she heard shouting the loudest, but Duquesne wasn't shying away from the confrontation. There was much heat in his voice, as well. Sienna hated that her mother was putting him on the carpet simply because he had dared to go off with his own daughter, choosing time with her over discussing the important issues his wife had been interested in tabling.

"You seem to have forgotten a thing or two, Duke. You

need to understand that I'm not going to stand by and let you undermine me in front of my daughter—"

"*Our* daughter," he interrupted.

Sienna was proud of Duquesne for not allowing Sable to discount his rightful position in his daughter's life. She thought she should go back into her bedroom and close the door, but something was telling her to continue listening to what was going on. She still feared that Sable might throw Duquesne out of the house. Not that she could remove him physically. Because he already had a desire to get out, Sienna didn't think Sable would have to do a lot to get him to go through with his original plans of moving out.

"Whatever! If *your* daughter knew what kind of man you really were, do you think she would be proud of you? I can answer that for you. She would lose all respect for you, in a heartbeat. Don't push the issue, Duke. I'm sure you wouldn't want me to have a little heart-to-heart conversation with *your* daughter about *your* indiscretions."

Sienna's ears perked up at the caustic sound of that remark, causing her to move to a position that would allow her to hear things even clearer. The loud shouting was what had made it easy for her to make out everything being said, but Sable's voice was now calmer and lower.

"That's the threat you've repeatedly held over my head for years now, Sable. No matter what I've done to try and make things up to you, you never let me forget the biggest mistake of my life. I actually think you get sick pleasure out of bringing it up to me. But I always notice that you only make this threat when things aren't going your way. Well, things aren't going to go your way this time. Let's just call

Sienna down here and tell her the truth right now. No longer is this threat going to work in your favor."

Sienna didn't know what to make of what her father had just said, but she would sure like to see the look on her mother's face. It had sounded as if he was calling her bluff. That had to be a first. Just in case he really planned to call her downstairs, she hurried the short distance down the hallway until she reached her bedroom. Before going inside, she listened for any sounds of her father approaching the stairs. When nothing but silence greeted her, she turned the doorknob and walked into her room.

Indiscretion? What kind of indiscretion? As Sienna thought about the heated discussion between her parents, she dropped down on the sofa and put her feet up. She could only guess at what her mother had been referring to, yet she had a pretty good idea about the nature of Duquesne's indiscretion. He was an extremely handsome man, a brilliant attorney, he had lots of money—and he was a very unhappy, dissatisfied husband.

All those ingredients made up the perfect recipe for adultery.

Tears threatened but Sienna held them back simply because she didn't know whom she should be crying for. If her father had cheated on her mother, her tears shouldn't be for him. No matter how she looked at it in regard to her mother, Sable certainly didn't deserve her tears.

Crying for herself would be more appropriate since she had been the one most hurt by her parents' unhappy union. *Why had they ever gotten married in the first place?*

Once Sienna was old enough to define the word *happy,*

she couldn't recall their marriage ever being in a state of euphoria. There had been bitter arguments between them as far back as she could remember. A lot of the fighting had occurred over the beauty contests and pageants, but Sienna now knew that there was a lot more than that to the constant battles.

Sienna had to wonder if it had been the *indiscretions* her mother had referred to.

When adultery occurred in a marriage, it happened to the entire family, from the children to the in-laws, because it eventually affected everyone's happiness one way or another. As despicable as Sable could be, Sienna didn't think any woman deserved to be devastated like that, including her mother. The bedroom door opened before Sienna could figure out how she would actually feel about her father if he had cheated on his wife and family.

Duquesne had tears in his eyes. He looked downright miserable as he approached the sofa where his daughter was seated. The look on Sienna's face was disheartening to him, as if she knew something awful was about to occur. *It was.* He had to tell her the truth about so many things. He wasn't sure of how his daughter would react to everything he needed to say, but he knew she would more than likely be deeply hurt.

"We have to talk, Sienna. May I sit down with you?"

Looking like a frightened rabbit, Sienna moved to the very corner of the sofa. After picking up a pillow, she pressed it against her abdomen. Her eyes never left her father's face. As he sat down right next to her and took hold of her hand, Sienna thought she could feel the blood coursing through Duquesne's hand.

Duquesne let go of Sienna's hand long enough to run his through his hair. He then took hold of it again, kissing the back of her hand before entwining their fingers. "There's something I have to tell you, Sienna. I hope it doesn't make you hate me…"

Sienna gently shook her head. "No, please don't. I think I know what you have to say. If I'm right, I know I can't handle it. Can we have this conversation another time, when I'm strong enough to deal with it?"

"Are you sure?" Duquesne's heart was breaking because he knew he had let his daughter down. He didn't know how she knew, but he somehow felt that she had already figured out the truth.

"I'll come to you when I'm able to handle hearing what you might have to say. Okay?"

"Okay, Sienna." Duquesne pressed his lips into her forehead. "I'll let you rest now."

"Thanks, Daddy. I do need to lie down, but I'm going to read awhile after I shower." She laid her head upon his shoulder. "Are you staying in tonight or going out?"

"Staying in. I think I'll read a little, too. It just might help me relax."

It took Sienna only a minute to locate Erique after she stepped into the cafeteria. She couldn't help smiling when she saw him. He looked so good in designer jeans and a Dallas Cowboy sweatshirt, which he had a lot of nerve wearing in Houston. He was so young-looking that he could've easily been mistaken for one of the college students. Watching Sienna intently as she slowly approached the table, Erique got to his feet. It appeared to him that she was forcing her small feet to move forward. He wondered if she was suddenly having second thoughts about being there. The smile she had cast his way was gone, now replaced with a slight frown. Erique noticed that Sienna also looked scared.

Sienna stopped at the table, shuffling her feet nervously. "Afternoon, Dr. Prescott," she greeted, deepening her southern accent so he wouldn't hear the edginess in her voice.

"Pretty nervous, huh? You don't need to be, Sienna. Go ahead and have a seat. What kind of drink and food do you want?"

"Unsweetened iced tea with lemon will be fine. I don't think I'm ready to eat yet. I always have to wind down after classes." Sienna took Erique up on his suggestion by dropping down on the bench-style seating.

Erique raised his right eyebrow. "That's interesting. I'll get the drinks. We can decide on the food later. But I actually thought we were having lunch together."

Sienna quickly decided not to respond. Erique had sounded a little agitated, but she hadn't come there to fight with him. If he knew that she had changed her mind a dozen or so times, he might not be so quick to spar with her. The things she had heard her parents talking about had caused her to rethink their date. Her strong desire to see him had won out in the end.

Ten minutes later, Erique came back to the table carting two iced teas. "Since it is so nice outside, would you like to take a walk around campus? Maybe that'll spark your appetite."

"Good idea." Sienna jumped to her feet, taking the offered cup from Erique's hand. "Thanks for the tea."

Erique smiled broadly at Sienna. "You're welcome."

* * *

The massive university campus, inundated with beautiful evergreen trees and other plants and shrubbery, was bustling with lots of activity.

Erique looked at Sienna with concern. "How are you feeling today?"

"All is well."

"No more dizziness?"

"None whatsoever, Erique."

"Glad to hear it. Are you going to take my advice about seeing your personal doctor?"

"Eventually. I'm also going to take your advice about eating properly."

"You could've fooled me. Did you or did you not just turn down the offer of food?"

"Only temporarily, Erique. I plan to eat once we finish our walk."

"Good. Sorry for being so cynical."

"You, cynical? No, not you." Sienna laughed to show Erique she was only joking.

Sienna and Erique walked a solid half hour before going back inside, where she directed him toward the cafeteria line. After she ordered a chicken-salad sandwich, garden salad and steamed mixed vegetables, he placed his order for a tuna sandwich and garden salad. Refills on their drinks were also ordered. Once they were given their food, Sienna and Erique went back to the same table where they had been seated earlier.

After the couple settled in, they began to eat their meals. Erique was pleased to see that Sienna had a good appetite. She was eating with gusto. Because he was still suspicious of her poor eating habits, he had halfway expected her to poke and prod at her food and then end up eating very little of it. He had so many preconceived notions about her and he was eager to learn which ones he was right about. He had also gotten the distinct impression that Sienna was a very unhappy young woman. Erique actually hoped he was dead wrong about that one.

Sienna looked up from her plate. "Besides having a long line of doctors in your family, what made you want to become one?"

There were so many reasons why Erique had wanted to become a physician, but none was as important as his desire to help lower-income families who were without medical insurance. Seeing to it that little children and the elderly received proper medical care was also on his list of reasons for becoming a physician. In fact, he had given lots of thought to going into either pediatric or geriatric medicine, but he was currently doing his residency in general surgery.

"My desire to serve the medical needs of others less fortunate than myself is the best reason I can give you, Sienna. Why do you want to become a model?"

"Your best reason is a wonderful one. Since you work at the university for free, I guess I don't have to ask if you do pro bono medicine." She broke eye contact with him, hoping he wouldn't notice that she hadn't answered his question.

"I work at several free clinics, many of which were started by my family. The Prescotts are champions of the uninsured. It's so sad that we live in the greatest country in the world, yet its citizens are without medical insurance and affordable medical care. It stinks to high heaven."

Sienna had never been able to understand why some folks had so much while others had barely enough to keep them going. Like Erique, she had been born into a life of privilege, but that alone didn't always make you special. Money wasn't always a blessing, either—and the love of it was at the very root of all evil. In many instances, privilege and wealth could be a curse.

What one did with privilege and money was the most important issue. Sienna hadn't been poor a day in her life, but that hadn't made her merciless. It wasn't love for money that kept her heeding her mother's demands. All the things she would be able to do with her inheritance money was the real reason she had endured the life she led. Helping others was always in her thoughts, but she couldn't help make a difference in the lives of others without the mean green.

Sienna's comments sounded every bit as fiery to Erique as his remarks had to her. As well as in her voice, passion was in her eyes. He saw the passion burning brightly there. That she would be someone to be reckoned with someday was also one of his preconceived ideas. "Why do you think we keep putting some of these jerks in office?"

"Fear."

After Erique put his hands on top of his head, he linked together his fingers. Sienna had his undivided attention. That she would have such a keen interest in politics *wasn't* one of the things he had predetermined. He was very intrigued by what she had said. "Do you vote?"

"Every year since I turned eighteen."

Not only did Sienna vote, once she moved out of her

parents' home she planned to get involved in getting folks registered to vote. There were many students right on this campus who had never voted in any election and she hoped to help change that someday. There shouldn't be a person in the world who didn't vote if allowed, especially African-Americans.

It seemed to Sienna that the civil rights movement had somehow gotten lost somewhere down through the generations. The younger folks just didn't seem to understand all the bloodshed that had occurred for their right to cast their ballot. After Sienna told Erique her contentious thoughts on the absence of the black vote, both his eyebrows lifted sharply.

Leaning forward, Erique stared right into Sienna's eyes. "I never thought I'd hear someone as young as you say something so provocative. I am so impressed."

"There are many who think I only have air on the brain. When I come into my own, this world had better look out. You could be looking at the first African-American female president."

Erique chuckled. "I never would've guessed that to be one of your ambitions. If you believe you can become president someday, why do you want to become a model?" *Maybe she'll answer this time.* Erique was sure Sienna had purposely ignored his question before.

Crossing her arms over her chest, Sienna sighed, jutting her chin out with an air of insolence. She hated that Erique had asked her that dreaded question again. "I don't want to become a model. I've never had any desire to be one."

Erique now looked totally perplexed. He scratched his head. "I'm confused over here. Just yesterday you risked your health to get to a modeling class—and now you're saying you don't want to be a model. Please help me understand that one, Sienna."

Frustration was steadily mounting in Sienna. She wished she hadn't blurted out her true feelings even if she had spoken the honest-to-goodness truth. This situation was much too complicated for her to try and explain. "It's a long story and we're out of time." With that said, she got to her feet. "Thanks for lunch. I've got to run now."

Sienna was halfway out the door by the time Erique began to recover from the shock. He took out a five-dollar bill and put it on the table, forgetting that he was in the university cafeteria versus a restaurant. He was nearly out of the exit when he turned back to retrieve his money. It was then that he realized how shook up he was over Sienna walking out on him like she had. Erique knew he would have to run to catch up to her, but he was determined to make it happen.

"Hold up, Sienna," Erique yelled out to her.

Sienna turned to face the direction Erique was coming from. He was quite the sprinter. His long legs had carried him much faster than hers had and she had had a decent head start. Her heart was thumping hard against her breastbone. Just watching his fluid movements was like watching poetry in motion. Sienna knew she should just hop into her car and speed off, but her heart wasn't in it. Erique was such a fascinating male subject, one she enjoyed studying.

All Erique could do was stop and stare at Sienna when he reached her. He wasn't out of breath, because he was in great physical shape from running five miles every single day. It was the enchanted look on her face that had taken his breath away. Her eyes had grown large and appeared quite luminous. She looked both mystified and enraptured, as if the wait for her Prince Charming was finally over. "Why did you run off like that, Sienna?"

Sienna sucked in a deep breath. "Nerves, I guess."

Chapter 4

Sienna's heart wanted to reveal all of its secrets to Erique, but her mind thought she would be crazy to do so. He seemed trustworthy enough to her; she simply didn't trust herself. She didn't even know what it meant to be in a romantic relationship, let alone maintain one. Although she wanted to experience the joy of male companionship and the wonders of true love, her fears were greater than her desire. Besides that, if her parents' relationship was the blueprint for marriage, she wasn't interested in getting involved in something so emotionally unhappy.

In Sienna's mind, she thought that the prestigious Dr. Prescott would probably find her innocence boring and pathetic. At this very moment she hated what she had allowed herself to become. She blamed herself for allowing her mother to mold and shape her into a ball of beautiful nothingness. There wasn't a single benefit in all that she had been put through just to show the world how beautiful she was. Sienna just didn't see beauty as a profession.

"We need to talk, Sienna. You are wound up tighter than a drum. It might help if you could talk about what's going on inside you. You can trust me with anything. I will never betray that trust. Do you think you can confide in me?"

As though Sienna were having an out-of-body experience, she reached for Erique's hand. "I think I can. But I can't tell everything all at once. We'll need to spend lots of time together."

The babylike softness of Sienna's hand felt so nice to Erique. His heart rejoiced at her last remark. "You can have as much of my time as you need. I can promise you that much."

Sienna looked down at her watch. She already knew she was going to be late for her dance class, but she no longer cared. "Can you give me a little more of your time today?"

"As much of it as you desire. Do you want to go back inside?"

"Let's just walk. Okay?"

"Okay." Erique squeezed Sienna's fingers as he began walking alongside her.

There were so many things Sienna wanted to tell Erique, but she didn't know where to begin. She didn't know what she should share with him nor did she know the things that she shouldn't reveal. For him to get the full picture, she had to give him quite a few vivid frames of her life. Starting with her childhood seemed appropriate.

"According to my parents, especially my mother, I was the most beautiful child in the world. My so-called beauty has been nothing but a curse to me. However, my looks are what led me onto the path of beauty pageants and numerous competitions. My mother repeatedly flaunted me in front of strangers. Is that one of the reasons why I'm wound up so tight? I think so."

"You *are* beautiful, Sienna, but I don't think you see it. Is it because of the pageants? Please tell me why you feel the way you do."

The lowering of Sienna's eyelashes often occurred when she was pondering a serious matter. Once she got her thoughts in order, her lashes slowly lifted. She then began to respond to Erique's query the best she could.

Was it the pageants? No, it wasn't. It was mostly a parent's obsession with pageantry.

Sienna explained to Erique that it was all the people behind the pageants and all of those deeply involved in them. The parents and the contest officials had a lot to do with how pageants were viewed by both participants and observers. Sienna went on to say that the pageants had begun to receive so much bad publicity via the media because what was going on behind the scenes was troubling. Pageants could also be extremely damaging to the contestants' self-esteem.

The older Sienna got, the more intense were the competitors and the pageants. The amount of money spent on costumes was downright obscene in her estimation. All the mothers tried to outdo each other, especially when it came down to what their child wore. It was nothing for her mother to pay fifteen-hundred dollars and upward for one of her glitzy costumes. All of her outfits were custom-made. Sienna didn't have one retail-store-purchased costume.

"Win at all costs" was the message the participants received. *Win* was the one directive that Sable constantly pounded into her daughter's head. To lose a competition was the biggest humiliation contestants could suffer, at least in the eyes of many parents.

Erique stared at Sienna, trying hard to see past her beauty, asking himself if he would have been this attracted to her had she not been so easy on the eyes. In just a short time of being in her company he already knew there was more to her than just a beautiful face and stunning figure. Her passion for politics had come through loud and clear earlier. No one would have guessed that about her just by looking at her. Erique felt that he would truly be interested in her if he had actually had a conversation with her without seeing her. She had a lot to say. She was also compassionate, intelligent and witty, a combination that he found very attractive in a woman.

There was definitely more to Sienna St. James than what met with the naked eye.

Erique whistled. "It sounds to me like you hate what you do. If so, why do you continue to do it?" Sable sounded like a mean ogre to him, but of course he wouldn't say that to Sienna.

"I have good reasons, believe me. Maybe I will share them with you someday. When I was younger, I didn't have much choice in the matter. This was something my mother wanted for me and she didn't care who objected to it, including my father. I'm afraid we're all paying a high price for my mother's dreams, but I don't think she sees it yet. Unfortunately, she will, but it may already be too late."

"Do you get the sense that your mother is living vicariously through you?"

"All the time. Sable St. James is a very beautiful woman in her own right. I don't know why she didn't pursue her beauty pageant dreams or even a modeling career. I've asked her that, but she remains tight-lipped about it. Daddy says he doesn't know the answer, either." Sienna hunched her shoulders. "Maybe it's one of her deep, dark secrets. I don't know."

"What beauty-industry goal are you working on now?"

"Let me put it like this. My mother has her eye on Miss Texas for me. But it won't end at that. Trust me. As long as there is a higher pinnacle to reach in this treacherous business, she'll want me to continue competing. Miss Universe and Miss World are waiting in the wings."

"What do *you* want for you, Sienna? What are some of your personal goals?"

"I want all this to end, more than I can say. I have so many personal goals to achieve and I intend to reach every single one of them. That will all come in due time." The psychology degree Sienna was seeking was every bit as much for her health as it was for others.

"And in the meantime?"

"I'll remain the ever-dutiful daughter. There's a lot at stake, Erique, things that I'm not ready to speak on." She looked down at her watch again. "Gosh, the time has really gotten away from me. I've missed out on my dance class, but that's the least of my concerns."

"Why is it the least of your concerns?"

"Because of what my mother will have to say about it. There'll be hell for me to pay."

Erique appeared upset by Sienna's statement. "Is your mother abusive?"

"Only verbally and emotionally. To physically scar my body would keep me out of pageantry, but there are times when she would like nothing better than to knock my head off. I'm used to it. I've actually learned to tune her out in most cases. She can't hurt me anymore. I have grown a very thick layer of protective skin. Well, enough about that. I do have to go. It's been nice talking to you, Erique. Thanks for letting me bend your ear."

Erique didn't want Sienna to leave. He wanted to take her in his arms and keep her there until her heart healed. He couldn't protect her when she was away from him and he believed she needed protecting. He had to wonder if her mother had a clue as to what she was doing to her daughter emotionally. All he knew was that Sienna didn't deserve to be abused in any form. That an adult woman would stay and take that kind of abuse had him stumped. She had said she had her reasons, but he didn't think there was any reason good enough for her to endure verbal and emotional abuse.

Erique slipped his arm around Sienna's shoulder. "I know you have to go." He paused for a moment and then looked deeply into her eyes. "Are we going to see each other again?"

Sienna smiled beautifully. "That would be a safe bet for you to make."

Eric appeared pleased with Sienna's response. She had no way of knowing how much he desperately wanted to spend more time with her. "Do you think I'll ever meet your parents?"

Sienna frowned slightly. "I'm afraid I can't answer that one. I'd like to think so." She wanted to tell him that her father knew his family, but then she thought better of it.

"Do you think your mother will object to us dating?"

"Without a doubt! We can pretty much count on it."

"Does she have that much influence over you?"

"She does. But not for much longer." Sienna bit down on her lower lip to keep from saying more. She had probably said too much already.

"How's that?"

"That's just something else I'm not ready to talk about. Can you bear with me?"

"I can. So when are we going to get together again? I'm off this weekend."

"I need to go home and look at the calendar. There is always something for me to do. It's maddening. That's why I can't keep up with it all. Can you give me a call later this evening?"

"You got it. Where's your cell phone?"

Sienna lifted her jersey and removed the cell phone on her belt.

Erique took the instrument from Sienna's hand and began to punch in his numbers. He recorded into her phone every number where she could reach him. "I'm on call for you 24/7."

Sienna blushed. "Thanks. I wish I could return the favor."

"Don't worry about it. I've got a pretty good idea of the kind of pressure you live under. Just remember that I'm here for you. Don't despair. Call me whenever you want. If I don't answer one number, try the next. Leave me a message if all else fails. I *will* call back."

"That means a lot to me, Erique. You're the only person I've ever really confided in."

"I got that impression. I have your back, Sienna."

"My life isn't an easy one by any stretch of the imagination, but I've learned to cope over the years. Don't worry. I'll be fine. Talk to you tonight." Sienna stood on her tiptoes and tenderly kissed Erique's cheek, surprising him and herself in the process.

Erique fought his desire to take Sienna into his arms. Instead, he opened the car door for her and then closed it securely. He watched after her until she had buckled her seat belt and drove off. His heart skipped a beat when she honked her horn in a farewell gesture. He was as perplexed as ever by her and the things she had confided in him. He was also worried about Sienna, worried about how much influence her mother actually had over her.

Sienna's behavior seemed unnatural for a woman her age, but Erique wasn't about to judge her. One moment she seemed frightened and unsure of herself and even child-like. Then she would suddenly surprise him by showing a mature attitude and come on strong with her intelligent conversations. Apparently she had good reasons to stay in a situation that she could walk away from simply because she *was* an adult.

Would Sienna eventually exercise her right to walk away? Erique could only wonder.

For whatever reason, Erique didn't think Sienna was strong enough to stand up to her mother. That alone made their chances of seeing each other again a risky proposition. He didn't know Sable St. James, but he felt certain that she would be totally against them dating. He didn't want Sienna to go against her mother's wishes, yet he hoped she wouldn't let anyone keep her from following her own heart. Erique could only hope that Sienna wanted to see him again, as much as he wanted the same. There were way too many things that he didn't know about her.

It was highly unusual for no one to be at home in the St. James household. Sienna had called out to both her mother and father after she had come through the garage door, but neither of them had responded. Marjorie, the family's cook, wasn't there, either, another unusual occurrence. She was normally in the house until after the evening meal was served and the kitchen had been cleaned and put back in its original state.

Sienna hurriedly climbed the staircase and went straight to her suite of rooms, where she unloaded her leather, shoulder-style briefcase and laid it at the base of her computer desk in the good-sized alcove that served as her office. Thinking that a shower would help her relax, she went into the bathroom and turned on the water and removed a white fluffy bath sheet from the linen closet. Once Sienna retrieved her robe and slippers and a shower cap, she disrobed, covered her hair and quickly stepped into the pulsating spray of hot water.

Twenty minutes later, feeling relaxed and rejuvenated, Sienna thoroughly dried off her body and then slipped into a pair of loose-fitting pajamas. Turning on her computer came next. She didn't know why she even bothered to check her e-mail because there was hardly ever anything there but spam. She hadn't ever shared her e-mail address with anyone outside of the family and Ginger because she didn't want to correspond with most of the people she knew.

The majority of people Sienna came into contact with

outside of her college classes were the folks in her modeling and dance classes. Most of the young women were self-absorbed and she had no desire to hang with any of them outside the sessions. Sable often reminded Sienna that these other women were her competitors and to never mix business with pleasure. Although she no longer bought into her mother's garbage, Sienna still preferred to stay on her own.

On occasion there would be an e-mail from Sienna's father. He preferred sending her little love notes and funny greeting cards via the Internet. Sable also sent her messages from time to time, but she dreaded getting them. The e-mails from her mother were more like orders and constant reminders of what she had to do to prepare for upcoming engagements.

That last thought reminded Sienna to look at her calendar to see what was up for the weekend. She didn't think for a second that she was free, but if there was a way to see Erique for just an hour or two on Saturday or Sunday she would be tickled pink. As well as the calendar on her office wall, she also posted her engagement dates and scheduled classes on her AOL calendar. Since she was already on the Internet, she decided to look at that calendar first.

Much to Sienna's surprise, both Saturday and Sunday evenings were open on her schedule. She had a dance recital early Saturday afternoon. A piano recital was scheduled for Sunday, right after the morning church service. Both recitals only lasted an hour. Friday evening was open also, but that was when she normally did her course work so she wouldn't have to slave over it during the weekend.

Rarely was anything slated for Sienna on Fridays, but it

hadn't always been that way. She had had to tell her mother that she had to have time to work on her studies or she wasn't going to get through college. Sable wasn't keen on cutting back her schedule in the beginning, but Sienna was finally able to convince her that she had to study. Because Saturdays were normally chock-full she was genuinely shocked to see only the one event on the calendar.

Sienna removed her cell phone from the nightstand so she could call Erique and ask him which one of her free evenings would work best for him. She located the numbers he had logged in. Then she recalled he had said he would call her. As impatient as she was to talk with him, she thought it best for her to wait. She didn't want to come off as desperate.

Thinking she might be acting too bold, not to mention way out of character, Sienna gave more thought to having a real date with Erique. She didn't like sneaking around to see him. She hadn't made a promise to him, but she had told him he could make a safe bet on them getting together again. Of course she didn't want to renege on her word. And she quickly decided that she wouldn't.

The last thing Sienna wanted to do was irritate her mother. Sable *would* go off on her in a heartbeat. But if she was going to start living her life the way she wanted to, there was no better time than the present. Dating Erique would be met with severe opposition from Sable, but Sienna thought she should just go ahead and tell her mother about him. *What harm would it do?*

Plenty of harm, Sienna thought, rapidly reassessing her idea to expose her relationship to Sable's microscopic scrutiny. She had to admit that it was kind of exciting to secretly see Erique. Their top-secret rendezvous were kind of special. She thought of the number of times he had made her laugh in the short time they had spent together. His sharp wit and unending charm were a huge part of his personality. In being honest with herself, she could hardly wait to see him again. Sienna was more than ready for the excitement Erique would bring to her otherwise dull life.

What Sable didn't know in this instance wouldn't hurt anyone, Sienna decided.

The sound of footsteps out in the hallway caused Sienna to look toward the entry. Sable, no doubt, she thought. In a couple of seconds her bedroom door would open and her mother would step inside. Sienna wasn't looking forward to the visit. Her absence in dance class would more than likely be the hot topic of conversation. Sable would be none too happy with her.

Just as Sienna had predicted, Sable came through the door. Sienna instantly knew that something was wrong. Her mother's clothing looked rather disheveled and her hair stood out all over her head. "What is it, Mom? What's wrong?"

Sable hardly blinked as she walked over to the sofa and took a seat. She then made direct eye contact with her daughter. "I'm afraid it's your father. He's in the hospital…"

"In the hospital!" Looking fearful, Sienna leaped off the bed. "What happened to him?"

Sable pressed her lips together. "We don't have a definitive diagnosis yet. He was having chest pains so I called 911. The paramedics came to the house. After checking him out, they felt he needed to be transported to the E.R. I just came from there. He wants to see you."

"Did he or didn't he have a heart attack?" The irritation in Sienna's voice was easy to detect. The expression on her face also showed how impatient she was for direct answers.

"Sienna, calm down right now! Falling apart is not going to help matters. Get your purse so we can be on our way to the hospital. The doctors should have answers for us pretty soon."

Sable wasn't acting quite right, as far as Sienna was concerned. She seemed very nervous and high-strung. She suspected her mother of withholding vital information from her. "What was going on when Daddy began having chest pains? Were you two arguing again?" The look on Sable's face gave Sienna the answer. They *had been* fighting. Why wasn't Sienna the least bit surprised? It sure explained her mother's strange behavior.

Without further ado, Sienna grabbed her purse off the bed and began walking toward the door. She felt sick inside, but she knew she had to hold it together. Her father needed her to be strong. Hearing Sable calling out her name caused Sienna to come to an abrupt halt. She then turned to face her mother. "Yes."

"I need you to keep yourself together. Your father doesn't need any more drama in his life right now. Do you think you can remain in control of your emotions?"

You are the one with all the drama. Sienna looked right at her mother but didn't respond. The question was offensive and it had struck a bad nerve. She turned away and walked toward the entry, anxious to get to the hospital to see how her father was doing for herself.

"Sienna St. James, I asked you a question and you darn well better answer it. Turn around and look at me this minute."

Sienna kept walking.

"Young lady, you are out of control! I'm not going to repeat myself again. Turn around and face me or face the consequences of your actions."

Sienna finally turned and cast her eyes on Sable. *You're the one who is out of control. Why do you think it is okay for you to speak to me so rudely, so often? Why do you continue to badger me, especially at a time like this?* Those were only some of the things Sienna wanted to say to Sable but she didn't dare to. It was really hard for her to show any kind of disrespect for her mother, but her patience had grown thin. She didn't know how much longer she could keep ignoring the disrespectful way in which her mother spoke to her. Sable's tone was sharp enough to cut Sienna to the bone. "I heard you, Mom. You have made yourself very clear."

"Glad to hear you say that. Don't you dare challenge me ever again."

"Yes, Mom."

Sienna had a mind to get into her own car and drive herself to the hospital. Riding in the car with her mother would be a very unpleasant ordeal. Listening to her putting down her father was always difficult for Sienna. Maybe she wouldn't do that under the circumstances. Sienna hoped her mother would show some compassion for her husband. He certainly didn't need her to treat him badly at a time like this.

It was difficult for Sienna to see Duquesne looking so pale. She kissed both of his cheeks and gently rubbed his forehead, whispering into his ear how much she loved him. She had expected to see him looking much worse than he did, so she felt much better than she had during the drive up to see him. She didn't like the fact that he was hooked up to so many machines and had so much tubing running from here and there on his body, but she knew that all the equipment was necessary for assessing his medical condition. Sienna prayed to God that his ailment wasn't life-threatening. She couldn't stand the thought of losing her father now or ever.

Duquesne looked so happy to see his daughter and he also appeared relieved. He was glad that he didn't have to be alone in the room with Sable. The woman made him downright crazy. The vicious verbal attack Sable had leveled against him was what had gotten him so upset earlier. He didn't know if it was the reason for the onslaught of chest pains, but they had come right in the middle of their heated battle. He had nearly passed out, but had managed to hold on. Duquesne had been terribly relieved when the paramedics had finally arrived.

Several men and one woman stepped into the E.R. cubicle. One of the men introduced the entire medical team. They were all physicians. One man was a cardiologist and the woman was an internist. The other doctor was a general practitioner.

"Sienna, while we talk with the doctors, I'd like for you to go down to the cafeteria and get yourself a cup of tea," Sable said. "Go on now."

Sienna didn't know why she couldn't be present to hear what the doctors had to say about her father's condition, but she knew it wouldn't do any good to protest. Besides that, her father didn't need to deal with any more stress. The slight nod from Duquesne's head and the look in his eyes had let Sienna know he wanted her to do as her mother had asked just to keep the peace. She gave her father another kiss before leaving the room. Sienna didn't even look at Sable.

"What are you doing here, Sienna? You're not sick again, are you?"

Sienna knew that deep voice. She then looked up at the handsome face that made her heart do crazy things. "Gee, I never expected to see you here. Are you on duty, Erique?"

"I just finished my evening rounds. In fact, I was getting myself in gear to phone you. Mind if I sit down with you?"

"Please do. I'm here to see about my father. He's being admitted. Chest pains. He's still in the E.R. The doctors are speaking with him and my mother right now."

"Let me guess. Your mother didn't want you to hear what was said?"

Sienna smiled weakly. "You guessed right. I left the room because it was for the best and it was also what my father wanted me to do. He knew she might cause a major scene otherwise."

"That's unfortunate. I'm just glad to know that you're not ill. Did you have a chance to look at your calendar when you got home?"

Sienna nodded. "I'm free both Saturday and Sunday evenings." She went on to tell him about the recitals she had during the day hours. "With my father being in the hospital, I may not be able to see you over the weekend. Before I can commit to anything, I need to know what's going on with him medically."

"I understand perfectly. Do you think they'll come clean with you about his condition?"

"My father will. He'll tell me everything, but he'll also tell me not to let my mother know he told me. That is, if she doesn't want me to know the truth. Weird, huh?"

Erique chuckled softly. "Very weird. Sounds like your family keep lots of secrets."

"Right again. Are you off duty now?"

"Just saw my last patient ten minutes ago. I have to tell you how pleased I am to run into you like this. You're the last person I expected to see here in the hospital. Can you hang around a while longer? I had dropped in here to get myself a cup of coffee to help me stay alert."

"I'll be here for at least another twenty minutes. I don't want to go back to the E.R. too soon. I'm sure my mother has a million and one questions to ask the doctors, questions that she won't want me to hear the answers to."

Keeping his eyes fastened on Sienna's lovely face, Erique lifted her hand and pressed a soft kiss into the palm. "I'll be right back."

"I'll be waiting for your return." Eagerly so, she added in her thoughts.

Chapter 5

As if Erique thought Sienna might up and disappear, he kept looking back at her to make sure she was still seated right where he had left her. Smiling sweetly, Sienna waved at Erique the last time he looked back at her. It felt good being in his company, but she had to wonder how long it would be before her mother found out about him and set out to destroy what they had.

Realizing he was wasting precious time, since Sienna couldn't stay long in the cafeteria, Erique propelled himself to hurry up and get his coffee, something he badly needed. He had stayed up half the night thinking of her and the sad situation she was in with her mother. He now felt extremely fatigued due to the lack of proper rest, but he planned to sleep well tonight.

So many thoughts passed through Sienna's mind in Erique's absence. Concern for her father's health had occupied the majority of her thinking. She once again prayed that it wasn't something serious. Chest pains were a result of many things, including indigestion. As much as she wanted his ailment to be nothing more than a case of simple indigestion, she knew her father had been under a tremendous amount of stress lately.

After Erique slid back into his seat, he took the lid off his coffee cup and poured the small container of cream into it. He didn't take sugar. "Did you miss me?"

Sienna smiled broadly. "Miss you? Did you go somewhere?"

"Okay, okay. I get it." He smiled. "I felt your absence even if you didn't feel mine."

"Just joking, Erique. I felt your absence, too. You mentioned needing to be alert. I guess that means you're tired. What's on your agenda after you leave the hospital?"

"Getting plenty of sleep. I was up half the night. I had a lot on my mind."

"Anything you care to share with me?"

Erique looked closely at Sienna, wondering if she could even appreciate what he wanted to say. He didn't want to say anything that might cause her to run scared. She was the most fragile soul he had ever come into contact with. The fear in her eyes was solid, as if it was firmly set in place. However, when she gave him one of her dazzling smiles his world suddenly seemed much brighter. Shards of brilliant light shone on her face when she found enough courage to laugh without constraint. As far as he was concerned, her laughter didn't happen enough.

"I was up all night thinking of you, Sienna. Is that too much information?"

"That depends on whether or not your thoughts of me were good or bad."

"Can you deal with a mixed bag of reviews?"

"You don't mince words, do you? I like your honesty. I don't deal well with lies."

"Neither do I. There is no reason for anyone to lie, though there are many people who would not agree with that statement."

The corners of Sienna's mouth curved into a cynical smile. "I believe I know some of those people."

"Most of my thoughts of you were favorable. But I still can't figure out why you would stay in an abusive situation now that you're grown. Is there some sort of payoff for you to stay? In other words, what are you getting out of remaining in your present situation?" Looking thoughtful, Erique stroked his chin. "I'd also like for you to tell me exactly what it was like being in beauty pageants as a small child. About how many contests did you do in a single month?"

"I'm afraid we don't have enough time to get into all that. Since you were going to call me later on this evening, why don't you still do that? Maybe we could get into all of that then."

"That's fine with me. I'd love to talk with you again later on." Erique knew he was going to have to get some sleep at some point, but he would stay up all night talking with her if that was what she needed from him. If only he knew how to heal her tortured soul.

Sienna was thrilled that she would speak with Erique again later. After recapping the plastic cup, she stood up and then threw it into the trash bin directly behind her. "I need

to go now. I'm anxious to learn about my father's health."
She sucked in her lower lip. "Can you do a favor for me?
Could you please keep a close eye on my father while he's
admitted here? I wasn't even aware that you also worked at
this hospital so I really see it as a blessing."

"I'd be happy to do that for you. No problem, Sienna. Is
it okay for me to introduce myself to him? That is, when your
mother isn't in the room."

"Wow. You've really caught on, haven't you?" Sienna
laughed. "I've already told him that I met you. In fact, he
knows your family."

Erique looked very curious. "What's your father's name
again?"

"I'm not sure I ever told you his name. Duquesne St. James."

Recognition of the interesting first name flared brightly
in Erique's eyes. "Of course! A good while back, he defended
my grandfather on a DUI. He *is* an attorney, right?"

"That he is. A darn good attorney if I may say so myself."
Sienna was surprised that Erique would speak on DUI
charges filed against a close family member. He didn't seem
the least bit embarrassed by it, either. She gave him lots of
credit for how he chose to deal with it.

"I've only heard of how good an attorney he is. My father
once told me that your dad helped save his father's life and
his medical career by talking him into rehab. My grandmother was very pleased with your dad's recommendations.
That's highly commendable."

That was what Sienna had said to her father when he had
shared with her the elder Dr. Prescott's story. Of course she
couldn't tell Erique that she had heard the story before.

Her father had already reminded her of attorney-client privileges.

"Come on, Sienna. I'll walk you back to the E.R."

Sienna didn't think that was such a good idea in case her mother happened to be out in the hallway, but she wasn't going to turn down Erique's kind offer. She was in no doubt that her mother would find out about Erique one way or the other, but she couldn't say she was looking forward to the unpleasant occurrence. "Thanks."

"Don't worry. I'll practice discretion. No one will suspect a thing. Actually, there is nothing for anyone to be suspicious about. We're just friends, right?" He looked over at her as if he wanted her to put a name to what they had going on.

"Right." That Erique had so easily picked up on her reluctance for them to be seen together astounded Sienna.

Sienna didn't think Erique had sounded too sure of his statement about them being just friends. She wondered if he had said that because he wanted more than a friendship with her or had he said it to let her know he wanted nothing more than that? Until he clarified his position one way or the other, *mum* was the word for her. At any rate, Sienna didn't know how they could ever be anything more than close friends despite her desire for much, much more.

Just before Sienna and Erique turned the corner that led up to the E.R. reception desk, he looked all around the area to see if anyone was standing nearby. The coast was clear. It was highly unusual, but the normally extremely busy corridor was totally empty. Even the desk clerk was absent from her post. Erique knew the area wouldn't remain that way for long. He smiled gently at Sienna, quickly sidling up next to her. "We'll talk later," he whispered softly. "Have a good visit with your dad. I'll check on him often—and I will keep you posted on his condition."

"I thank you for that. Later, Erique."

That Duquesne was to be moved to the cardiac care unit (CCU) within the next few minutes had Sienna thoroughly upset. According to what Sable had been told by the cardiologist, his heart needed to be constantly monitored for at least the next thirty-six hours. He had already been given nitroglycerin. Sienna felt scared. Losing her father was more than she could ever bear. Although she was very fearful for him, she was grateful he been brought to the E.R. before his health had worsened. Sienna had to close her eyes and thank God for sparing her father's life.

"Sable, I'd like to talk to Sienna alone. Would you please excuse us?"

As if Sable couldn't believe her ears, she looked back and forth between her daughter and husband. This was the third time in less than a week that Duquesne had asked to spend time alone with Sienna. Sable didn't think she was jealous over it, but she didn't understand his sudden desire to be with his daughter without her present. For sure she knew she didn't like it.

Deciding to respect her husband's wishes, Sable slowly got to her feet. She suddenly felt very weary, knowing she needed a good night's rest. "How much time do you need, Duke?"

"Sienna will come out and get you when we're through talking. Why don't you go to the cafeteria and get something to eat and drink. You haven't eaten all day." He looked down at all the tubes he was hooked up to. "As you can see for yourself, I'm not going anywhere."

Sable managed a small smile at Duquesne's remark.

Once her mother cleared the room, Sienna walked over to her father and bent over his bed, lovingly pushing her hands through his naturally wavy hair. "You're mighty pale, Daddy. Please tell me the doctors said everything will be okay."

Duquesne wrung his hands together. "I wish I could tell you that. We have to wait until after all the tests are run. They suspect I may have a blocked artery or two. It can be fixed once we have the diagnosis. I don't want you to worry, Sienna. There are a couple of things I want you to do for me while I'm in here." He put his hand on the back of her head and gently pulled it down to him. He began to whisper into his daughter's ear.

Now that Sable had left Sienna's bedroom, it gave Sienna the opportunity to lie still and think of some of the things her father had told her during Sable's absence. He had confided a lot in her, even telling her the things she had told him she wasn't ready to hear. He thought it was high time that she know everything there was to know about him, the good and the bad.

Sienna wasn't the least bit surprised to learn about Duquesne's affair with another woman, someone named Marianne. He had known her before he married Sable, but she was totally stunned out of her mind to learn that he had been deeply in love. Although they hadn't been together in years, he revealed to Sienna that he would always have feelings for her. The other woman had been there when he had desperately needed someone to care about him.

With Sable on the beauty-pageant road all the time, Duquesne had often felt lonely and full of despair. When she was at home, she was totally occupied with getting ready for the next road trip. He couldn't begin to recall how many nights she had turned him away, making him feel less than a man in the process. Getting her to attend any sort of social function with him was absolutely out of the question. His work could only fill so many of his hours and it was his downtime that had eventually allowed him to stray into forbidden waters. The other woman had been right there for Duquesne, all too willing to help ease the aching loneliness.

Duquesne had also told Sienna that he didn't know when Sable had stopped loving him, but he was sure that she no longer did. The disconnection between them had occurred suddenly and without any warning. He hadn't done anything to try and reconnect them, because he hadn't known what to do or even how to do it. That was only one of his deepest regrets.

Duquesne had ended his lengthy speech by also confessing to Sienna that he was afraid he might die without ever again experiencing the joy of true love. He also said that he would like nothing better than to keep his family together, but he didn't see that happening. It was too late for him and Sable to reconcile their numerous differences. If he came through this health crisis, divorce was the only way out for him. At that point, his tears had begun to fall.

Minutes later Duquesne had been whisked away to the CCU by an attendant.

Sienna and Sable had stayed in the CCU room with Duquesne until he had drifted off to sleep. He had looked so tired lying there so still, which had caused Sienna much grief. She was also a bit concerned about her mother. Sable had been oddly quiet during the drive back home. The music playing on the radio had kept total silence at bay.

When Sable had come in to say good-night to Sienna, she hadn't been her usual bossy self. She had appeared somewhat subdued. She hadn't asked her daughter if she had done her nightly routine nor had she barked out any new instructions for Sienna to follow. The strangest thing of all for Sienna was when Sable had bent over and kissed her on the forehead. Her good-night bidding had been spoken softly as a whisper. Sienna couldn't even remember the last time her mother had kissed or hugged her, yet she knew that it had been a very long time ago.

Sienna couldn't help wondering if her father's illness was somehow adversely affecting Sable. Was her mother regretting the way she had treated Duquesne all these years? Did she possibly fear that her husband might pass away before she could make amends?

Hoping Erique was on the other end of her musical cell-phone ringer, Sienna reached over to the nightstand and grabbed hold of her purse. She had forgotten to take the phone out of her bag to put it on the charger. If she didn't have enough power to complete the call, she would call him back on the private landline in her room. That is, if it was Erique calling.

The smile on Sienna's face showed her joy at hearing Erique's voice. "Hey, you sound drowsy. I guess the coffee didn't help any."

"It never does when I'm beyond tired. I don't know why I bothered to drink the last cup. But I'm not as sleepy as I am bone tired. Are you in bed already?"

"All tucked in, but I'm not ready to fall off to sleep. Once again, I have a lot on my mind. I can't stop thinking about my dad. I keep praying that he's going to be okay."

"It seems that I need to teach you how to be still. I'm not just talking about stilling your body movements, either. You have to still your mind and your spirit, completely. Let all your troubles float into nothingness. There is such serenity to be found in quiet time. I want you to start taking time out just for you. A little me-time if you will. You have to stop taking on the burdens of the world. They are not yours to lug around. Are you willing to learn how to be still?"

The engaging idea of Erique teaching her to be still was appealing to Sienna. If he could teach her that, she would be forever grateful. Nothing about her was still. Her body was always in perpetual motion and her mind and heart raced all the time, even in sleep. "I believe I could benefit from learning to be still. When do the lessons begin?"

"We'll get right on it before we hang up. I'm eager to talk about what I had asked you earlier. How was it for you being involved in this beauty junket as a small child?"

Sienna sighed hard. There was so much to be said on this particular subject. "Well, it's a long story, so I'll only give you a small dose of it this time. By the time I was three years old,

I had been entered into over one hundred pageants, winning all of them in at least one category or more."

"Three years old and one hundred pageants! Oh my God. I can't even imagine a three-year-old having such a grueling schedule. How many categories are there in these beauty contests?"

"Numerous. There are trophies awarded for best fashion, prettiest eyes, best costume, best swim or casual wear, best makeup, best dance moves—just to name a few. I never went home without a win in at least three or four categories."

Erique whistled. "This sounds crazy to me. What are these parents thinking?"

"Unfortunately, they're not. It's mostly the mothers. Like my dad, many of the fathers are not keen on the idea of their daughters being exposed to a bunch of strangers. Some of the mothers are both obsessed with and addicted to pageantry. My mother is past addicted and obsessed. She has spent my entire life preparing me for these superficial competitions. It can get pretty sick in the world of beauty pageants."

"Are these pageants very expensive? If so, do both of your parents agree on the financial end of it?" Enrique said.

"Pageants are horrifically expensive. The costumes alone could cost a small fortune, starting at around one hundred and fifty per outfit. Numerous custom-made costumes could be needed based on the number of fashion categories a contestant was entered into," Sienna remarked.

Duquesne made extremely good money as a successful attorney and he considered himself to be a great family provider. He objected more to the loss of Sienna's childhood and her right to lead a normal life than anything to do with the money portion of it. Her right to run and play and romp with other children had been snatched right out from under her. He wanted his daughter to have beautiful things, desired her to have the best of everything, but he objected to the revealing clothing she was often forced to wear. He didn't like his daughter's midriff bared, period. His baby girl dressed in skimpy bikinis and other sexy attire made him physically sick. The facial makeup, false hair and nails were as appalling to him as the sexy clothing.

Duquesne thought these innocent little girls were a pedophile's dream—and he had often voiced that very sentiment to Sable, only to have it fall on deaf ears. He could be all right with some parts of the world of pageantry if he thought his daughter was a happy participant. She had never been happy with these contests or the lifestyle that came with it—and he knew it.

"Mothers actually make their kids wear false hair and nails?"

"Absolutely, but that's not the half of it. I remember when I lost my two front teeth at the age of five, my mother took me to the dentist and had me fitted for a flipper, a plastic and wire dental fixture with teeth on it. I wore false teeth when competing, up until my adult teeth came in. Using flippers for missing front teeth is a common practice in the world I grew up in."

"Unbelievable! False teeth. That's taking this beauty thing too far. I'd never allow that to happen with one of my kids."

Sienna blinked hard. "Do you have kids?"

Erique had to take a second to think back on what he had just said. "Maybe I should have said I would never allow that to happen if I had kids. I don't have any children, Sienna.

I don't even have a cute little puppy or a big friendly dog to keep me company."

"Me, neither." Sienna laughed. "I always wanted a puppy, a cocker spaniel, but my mother would constantly say we don't have time to take care of a dog. Then she would say, 'We're too busy making sure your beauty mark will always be visible to the eyes of the world.'"

The sadness and disappointment in Sienna's voice came through clearly to Erique. The average person wouldn't have been able to endure half of what she'd gone through. That she was still standing at all was a miracle. He had many more questions he wanted to ask her about the business she was in, but he thought she'd had enough for tonight.

"Put your pillow behind your head, Sienna—"

"What?"

"It's time for you to be still, Sienna. First off, do you have any type of meditation tapes? If so, put one on. I'll wait for you."

Sienna kept a "sound of the sea and surf" CD in her night-stand drawer. After inserting the hands-free device into her cell phone, she placed the earpiece into her ear. Once she retrieved the meditation CD, she popped it into the player and pushed Play. "I'm ready, Erique."

"We're going to try to achieve stillness together, Sienna. Don't worry if it doesn't work for you the first time. We just have to keep at it. Make yourself as comfortable in bed as you can. Now try to shut down your mind completely. I know that's hard to do, but try anyway."

"Okay." The soothing sound of Erique's voice was already pretty relaxing to Sienna.

"To help you relax as much as possible, I want you to start

inhaling and exhaling, very slowly. Close your eyes and breathe in and breathe out at a normal pace. Lift yourself way above your troubling circumstances. Continue to breathe in and breathe out. Keep inhaling and exhaling steadily. Let the healing sounds of the surf take you away. Allow the serenity in and let it slowly seep into your soul. Keep your eyes closed and keep inhaling and exhaling. We'll talk tomorrow. Sweet dreams. Now lay your head back on the pillow and hang up the phone."

Chapter 6

The breakfast foods looked and smelled very appetizing, but Sienna didn't have an appetite. Marjorie had prepared soft scrambled eggs, thick slices of turkey ham, grits and buttermilk biscuits. She had also squeezed fresh orange juice and had made pots of coffee and herbal tea.

Sable wasn't a big eater, but she had done quite a bit of justice to the food. She had eaten everything that had been prepared and had gone back for seconds. Sable rarely ate starchy foods, but she had eaten two good-sized helpings of the grits. For a woman who was maniacal about watching her weight and her daughter's, she had eaten more than her fair share of food. She had also downed two tall glasses of orange juice and was now on her second cup of black coffee.

Sienna was surprised by the amount of food Sable had eaten and how quickly she had gobbled it down. She had never before seen her mother eat like this. Nor had she ever seen her mother acting as nervous as she was this morning. Her behavior was as odd as it had been the previous night. It seemed to Sienna that Sable had lost her tight control.

Sienna looked at her mother with genuine concern. "Are you okay? You seem out of sorts this morning."

Sable waved off her daughter's concern. "It's nothing." She then slammed her fist down hard on the table, scaring the daylights out of Sienna. "Your father must've talked someone into letting him use a computer. I can see him charming one of the nurses now. That charming devil has such a way with the women."

"Daddy's in CCU. He wouldn't be able to use a computer. What are you talking about, Mom?"

"Either he had access to a computer or he gave his Wells Fargo password to someone. There is two hundred and fifty thousand dollars missing out of one of his bank accounts and another fifty thousand has been withdrawn from one of the others."

"How do you know that?"

"I know everything. My name isn't on any of his three business accounts, but I learned how to gain access to them a long time ago. Duquesne always did leave his wallet lying around. Someday the wrong person is going to get hold of it."

Seems like the wrong party already has, Sienna thought, eyeing her mother with deep curiosity. "Why are you looking up information on his bank accounts, anyway?"

"Why wouldn't I? If he were to die, I'd need to know about all of his assets."

Perhaps you need to know because he's been threatening to divorce you. Sienna hoped that wasn't the case. Her mother was cold-blooded, but was she cold enough to start looking into her husband's finances because she thought he might die? Had the doctor told them something they hadn't shared with her?

None of this was possible, Sienna told herself quietly. Her father had confessed so much to her last evening. She was sure he had been honest with her about everything he had told her. If he were dying, wouldn't he have told her that, too? He had mentioned the possibility of a couple of blocked arteries, but he had said they could be easily repaired. She didn't think he would lie to her about something so serious. After she thought about what he had asked her to do, she had to quickly reassess things. She knew she had to get up to the hospital as soon as possible, without her mother. She needed some answers.

Sienna excused herself from the table. Before she could get to her feet, her mother asked, "What's going on? Where are you off to in such a big hurry?"

"Class. Where else?"

"I don't know, Sienna. Maybe you should tell me?"

Sienna sucked her teeth impatiently. "Could you please spell things out for me?"

"I'd be happy to. Why weren't you in dance class yesterday?"

Sienna's heart sank down to her feet. "Maybe you should tell me. You seem to already know everything else that goes on with me."

"I've warned you about your insolent mouth before, young lady. I don't want to have to keep warning you. You are getting very bold lately. Is that Ginger person responsible for your insolence? I don't like you hanging out with her."

"Ginger and I only take classes together. We don't hang out."

"Her number is certainly on the cell phone bill numerous times, which is evidence that you talk to her outside of class. I want it stopped immediately. She does not fit in with your career goals. You have to be very careful about whom you socialize with. You weren't raised to hang out with trailer trash. Protecting your proud heritage is a must."

Sienna was terribly hurt by Sable's insensitive remarks about Ginger, but she remained quiet. Her mother's comments had proved that she knew nothing at all about Ginger. Her parents were both college professors at prestigious Texas colleges. Arguing with her mother would only delay her getting out of the house so she said nothing.

Sable had to answer to a power greater than any man. God couldn't possibly be happy with how she chose to conduct her life. Her deeds would not go unpunished. And to think she had thought that her mother might be changing for the better. Fat chance!

"You can go now. I don't want to hear that you've missed another class, Sienna. If you continue down this errant path, I will personally accompany you to class to make sure you go. I'm sure you don't want that. I have a doctor's appointment this morning. After that, I'll be on my way to see your father. Come right home from ballet class so you can go to the hospital with me for the evening visiting hours. I know you hate all my rules, but everything I do for you is for your own good. One day you will thank me."

Sienna sighed heavily. "Goodbye, Mom. I'll see you later on."

* * *

Panic quickly set in on Sienna when Duquesne wasn't in his room. An inquiry to the nurse at the nurses' station let her know that he was just downstairs for special testing. Even though she wasn't sure how long she could wait for him to get back, Sienna took a seat, her mother's earlier warning ringing loudly in her ear.

As Sienna fumbled around in her school bag for a notepad to write on, her cell phone rang. Upon seeing that the number was one of Erique's, her spirits lifted. "Good morning. How are you?"

"I'm great. What about you?"

"Same here. Your teaching methods really worked wonders for me. I can't believe how relaxed I was last night. Not long after you hung up I went right off to sleep. How is that for being still?"

"I'm really glad to hear that. Where are you?"

"At the hospital, in my father's room in the CCU. I'm waiting for him to come back. He's downstairs having some tests done."

"Have you seen him at all?"

"He wasn't in the room when I got here. I don't know how much longer I can wait. I have to get to class pretty soon. Where are you?"

"Turn around."

Erique smiled brightly at Sienna from the doorway of her father's room. The shocked look on her face had him cracking up. "I'm not psychic. I saw you come into the hospital. I phoned you just as I stepped off the elevator."

Sienna smiled brightly. "Very clever of you! I'm glad to see you, Dr. Prescott."

"Not half as happy as I am to see you. Have you had breakfast?"

"Yeah, but I didn't eat that much. My appetite is pretty poor when I'm worried."

"We're going to have to do something about that, too. Did you know that worrying is a sin?"

"It is?"

"It is if you believe in God. *Do* you believe in Him?"

"Of course I do."

"Then you have to show Him that. When we turn something over to God, we have to leave it with Him. He can't fix it for us if we don't get out of the way." Erique walked over to Sienna and pulled her to her feet. He then gave her a warm hug. "Good morning."

"Good morning again. Seeing you here this morning is a real treat for me."

"That makes two of us. Want to get a cup of coffee or tea?"

Sienna slapped her palms together. "It is always about time with us. I seem to never have enough of it when we see each other. I've got to be leaving shortly."

"I think we do okay."

"I agree. Are you on duty?"

"I just finished making my morning rounds. I have a superheavy schedule today. There are all sorts of things going on. Do you have any outside classes today?"

"You already know the answer to that. I have one class or another every single day, Monday through Friday. I caught heck from my mother today because I missed my dance class yesterday."

"You caught the blues already this morning, Sienna, this early?"

"Mom doesn't have any set time to rip into me. Rarely does she give notice before one of her tirades comes on. It just happens."

"Does she ever apologize for going off on you?"

"If she has, I've never heard her say it. People only apologize when they're sorry about something. Mom doesn't know what the word *sorry* means."

Erique scratched his head. Sienna was living in a weird situation, one she really didn't seem to want out of. No one in their right mind allowed themselves to be abused like this. Maybe what she hadn't told him might explain it, but right now he just didn't see how it could justify what she was basically putting herself through. Perhaps she was a glutton for punishment. Some people were addicted to pain and suffering. He had seen a little bit and a whole lot of everything in his profession, especially when he had worked in the E.R. while doing his rotation in emergency medicine.

"I don't understand the relationship you have with your mom. Until you're able to share with me why you stay in an abusive environment, I guess I won't know. At any rate, I thought about all the things you told me last night and I'm still flabbergasted."

"Does that mean you weren't still after we got off the phone? We were supposed to be still together."

"We were. I thought about all of that when I woke up this morning and then again on my way into work. I went out like a light right after we hung up."

Sienna had no control over the huge smile taking over

her lips. "You keep your word, don't you? That's another thing I like about you."

Erique put his forefinger up to his right temple. "Let me see. You like my honesty and the fact that I keep my word. Do I have any more endearing qualities you would like to mention? I'd love to hear them."

Sienna grinned. "In need of having your horn tooted?"

"Yeah, I guess you could say that." Erique chuckled at his own response.

"You've come to the right place." Sienna made a tooting noise with her mouth, causing Erique to laugh. "Besides the two things I've already mentioned about you, you are highly intelligent and extremely sensitive for a man. You are also compassionate. So that your head doesn't swell right out of that surgical cap, I'm going to stop filling it up."

Erique folded his hands together and made a pleading gesture. "Please don't stop. I love hearing what you think of me. I don't get kind compliments very often."

"You'll get to hear more of it, Erique. I can promise you that."

"I'm going to hold you to that, Sienna."

"You won't have to. I am a woman of my word also."

"I believe that about you, Sienna. You're compassionate, too."

The conversation between Sienna and Erique came to an abrupt halt as Duquesne's bed was wheeled back into the room by one of the hospital attendants. His eyes were closed so he didn't see his daughter standing there. Sienna didn't know if he was asleep or not, but she hoped he wasn't. She really needed to know how he was feeling before she left for class. Since her father was probably fatigued from all the medical tests and procedures he had endured, Sienna decided to save her tough questions for later.

Smiling gently, Sienna looked over at Erique and shrugged. In return, his eyes held her in a warm embrace, causing fiery heat to spread deep down inside her soul.

"Sienna, what are you doing here so early?"

Sienna drew in a few calming breaths and then practically flew over to Duquesne's bedside, where she leaned over and kissed him in the center of his forehead. "So you *are* awake. I came to see you. Why else would I be here? How're you doing?"

"I'm really tired, but I'm not hurting anywhere. The chest pains are gone. By the way, aren't you going to be late for class?"

"Not to worry, Daddy. It's cool. I always get my course work done." Sienna summoned Erique by crooking her finger. "Daddy, I want you to meet someone."

Erique stepped into Duquesne's line of vision. "Good morning, Mr. St. James."

Duquesne tilted his head slightly to get a closer look at the person speaking to him. Then a bright smile lit up his eyes. "You have to be young Dr. Prescott. I definitely see the family resemblance." Duquesne extended his hand to Erique. "Nice to meet you."

Erique gave Duquesne a firm handshake. "The pleasure is all mine, sir. Your daughter has asked me to keep a close eye on you for her. Any objections?"

"None whatsoever, son. What my daughter wants is what she gets. Well, mostly everything," he joked. "Anything that will keep Sienna from worrying."

"She does a lot of that. We're actually going to work on that. She's too young to have so many things to worry about."

Duquesne raised an eyebrow at that. "I like you already, son. It seems to me that you'll be very good for my precious angel."

Sienna blushed, wishing they weren't talking about her as if she wasn't even there.

"And I'll be good to her. From what I know about her so far, she seems like a great girl."

"She *is* a great girl. She is as smart and pretty as they come."

Wishing her father hadn't gone there, Sienna groaned. "Okay, guys. I'm standing right here. I know it may seem like it at times, but I'm not invisible, you know."

Erique leveled a curious eye on Sienna, feeling a sudden bout of empathy for her. He was sure she had no idea how much her last comments had revealed to him. He wasn't at all surprised that there were times when she felt invisible. He figured that she probably really felt as if no one could see her in the presence of her mother. It seemed to him that Sable St. James overshadowed her daughter in many ways. It wouldn't surprise him in the least to learn that her mother was more than likely fostering a strong rivalry with Sienna. Could Sable be jealous of her own daughter, her only child?

If that just happened to be the case, Erique thought it made perfect sense.

Erique's pager went off, causing him to excuse himself. He quickly stepped out into the hallway, leaving Sienna and her father alone.

Sienna ran her index finger down the side of Duquesne's face. "I guess you know I have to get going, but I'll be back to see you this evening."

"You're not going to ask me what I think of your young man?"

Sienna bucked her eyes. "He's not *my* young man. Daddy, come on, you know how it is. Mom would never let us have a real relationship. I know I'm just spinning my wheels when it comes to Erique and me. There can be no *us.*"

"Do you want the two of you to become an *us?*"

Sienna blushed again. "What do you think? I love having him around."

"Then I think you should go for what you want. I'll talk to your mother about it. You can trust me to handle her. I'm not letting her get away with anything anymore."

Looking terribly fearful, Sienna shook her head. "Oh, no, please don't do that. She will kill this relationship just like she has tried to kill my spirit all these years. I know you mean well, but nothing good will come from it. Just let me get through graduation. Everything else will eventually fall right into place."

"Don't you dare put your happiness on hold, not for anyone, Sienna! I've been guilty of doing that very thing for a long time now. Whatever you do, please don't follow my lead in the area of personal relationships. If you want that young man in your life, fight to have him right at your side. Fight even harder to keep him there."

Sienna inhaled deeply, doing her best to suck up the unyielding pain. She knew her father was right, but she also knew what havoc her mother would heap onto her relation-ship with Erique if she found out about it, even more so if she thought her father was all for it. Duquesne could say something was white and Sable would say it was black, just for the sake of argument. "I've got to go, Daddy. But before I do, promise me you won't discuss any of this with Mom. It will only hurt me if you do."

"I promise you, my precious girl."

Closing her eyes to savor the sweet sound of his endearment, Sienna kissed her father's cheek. Duquesne hadn't called her these kinds of endearing names in a very long while. Hearing him using them so often now made her realize how much the two of them had been missing out on over the past years. Sienna had also come to realize that her mother had virtually separated her from her father by dragging her all over the country for a bunch of silly nonsense.

To keep from crying, Sienna held her head up high and squared her shoulders. "I'll see you later. Please do whatever the doctors recommend to you. Okay, Daddy?"

Duquesne blew his daughter a flurry of kisses. "Okay."

Seeing that Erique was still on his cell phone, Sienna headed straight for the elevator, wishing she had time to tell him goodbye. She was already going to be late and his phone call was obviously an important one. As she thought about her mother's earlier warning about her not being late ever again, she suddenly burst into a fit of laughter.

Sable may think she's in total control of me, but she's really not. And she won't ever be in control of me again if I stop giving up my free will to her. Sienna suddenly felt that she was strong enough to do that now. She was the only one who should be in control of her destiny and it was high time she took hold of the reins. *This was her life.* Waiting on graduation was just the excuse she had been using to get through each day confrontation free. This was no way for anyone to have to live their life.

With a warm smile gently curving on her full lips, Sienna gave a silent goodbye to one of her major weaknesses, the one that had allowed her to turn over her power to another human being, her mother. Sienna had always been mindful of the need to honor her mother and father. It was what God had commanded His children to do. She would still do that, but she had to become true to herself so she could be true to others.

Sienna had to learn to honor her own heart.

Instead of getting into the elevator when the doors slid open, Sienna went back down the hallway she had come from. She planned to wait until Erique got off the phone. Being late for class wasn't the end of the world. Besides, she had never been late for any of her college classes.

Sienna could tell that Sable was still on pins and needles. Her nerves seemed to be stretched to the absolute limit. Unlike this morning, when she had pretty much overeaten, Sable had barely eaten a quarter of the nice dinner Marjorie had prepared. She was also still talking about the missing money, but Sienna couldn't do or say anything to alleviate her anguish. It was odd for her to see her mother on edge like this. Finding out what had happened to the large sums of money withdrawn from Duquesne's bank accounts was driving Sable batty. Because her name wasn't on the business accounts, the bank clerk had told her over the phone that she was unable to give out any information to anyone other than the account holder.

Mrs. Control was never out of control. *Not* being in control was something Sable would have to get used to.

Both Sienna and Duquesne had vowed to take back from her the control of their lives. Although Sienna hadn't expected her rebellion to happen this soon, she was none-theless more than ready for it to occur.

Not only had Sienna gone back to talk to Erique at the hospital, she had walked down to the cafeteria with him, where they had had a cup of hot tea. It was during that time that she had decided not to go to any of her classes. Sienna had straight A's in all of her courses and she would have to miss the rest of the semester to even come close to failing. Of course, she didn't plan to do that, but missing classes had been her first attempt at gaining jurisdiction over her life.

Sable reached down and turned the tuner to another radio station when another song came on that she didn't like. It was only the tenth time she had changed the station. Sable appeared to grow more and more agitated with each mile she drove. Sienna couldn't wait until they got to the hospital so she could hurry up and get out of the car since her mother was also driving a little recklessly.

Duquesne had been asleep when Sienna and Sable had first arrived in his hospital room. Sable hadn't been too happy about his state of rest. She had nearly worn a hole in the floor while waiting for him to awaken. When she hadn't been able to stand it a second longer, she had shaken him until she had gotten him to wake up, only to begin drilling him about the missing money.

"Sable, why is the money in my business accounts so much of a concern to you?"

"It's not."

"It's not! You've got to be kidding me, Sable. The money

is all you've been talking about since I've been awake. Why are you checking on my accounts in the first place and how did you get hold of the account numbers?"

"I have my resources. Has the doctor been here today?"

"He came in to see me right after Sienna left this morning…" Duquesne could have kicked himself. He knew he had said the wrong thing, even before he saw the angry look on Sable's face. Giving up his daughter hadn't been his intent.

Sable hurried across the room. After grabbing Sienna by both her shoulders, Sable began to shake her daughter as if she were a rag doll. "Have I not made myself clear to you? You are obviously not listening to what I've been saying to you…"

"Sable," Duquesne shouted, "stop shaking her like that. Are you crazy?"

A hard slap right across Sienna's face caused her to rock from side to side for several seconds. Just as she put her hands up to shield herself from another hit, Sable cracked her daughter hard in the face again, causing Sienna to back up into the nearest corner. Fear was an understatement for what the younger woman felt. As if she expected another attack, she looked downright terrified. Her mother's nerves had been hanging by mere threads throughout the day and into the evening. It now looked as if the fragile strands had snapped, causing Sable to become totally unstable.

Duquesne couldn't possibly go to his daughter's rescue, not without causing serious damage to himself. All the tubing running from his body and the IV needle in his arm severely restricted his movements. It was just as well, because he wanted to hurt Sable badly. Seeing the petrified look on

Sienna's face had Duquesne crying out to her, anxiously coaxing her to come to him since he couldn't go to her.

Painfully shocked, with tears running down her face, Sienna began to run toward her father's bed, needing desperately to find protection and comfort in his arms. Before she could reach her destination, Sable grabbed hold of a section of Sienna's long hair and yanked on it as hard as she could.

As Sable jerked her daughter all around by her hair, Duquesne, knowing he had to do something to stop Sable's madness, picked up the water-filled plastic container and hurled it in the direction of his wife. When the pitcher connected with its target, its content splashing all over Sable's clothes, she screamed out his name but also loosened her grip on Sienna. In her uncontrollable rage, Sable then hurled several expletives at her husband, wondering what she ever saw in him in the first place. Money, of course.

In the next instant, Duquesne was clutching his chest, as if he were in unbearable pain. The excruciatingly painful look on his now-ashy face alerted Sienna to the fact that her father might be in serious trouble. When she saw that he was having difficulty breathing, she frantically reached for the emergency chain above his bed and pulled it down hard. The piercing sound of the emergency alarm startled both Sienna and Sable and it also brought several nurses running into the room.

Erique rushed into the hospital room right behind the nurses.

Chapter 7

It didn't take Dr. Erique Prescott long to assess Duquesne's grave situation. He wasted no time in calling a code blue. The crash cart would be there any minute, but in the meantime, he knew he had to administer CPR. Saving Duquesne's life was all that mattered to him at the moment. As he worked on the patient feverishly, he suddenly looked up. That was when he spotted Sienna shrinking away in one corner of the room.

Erique understood the horrific fear he saw in Sienna's eyes. He was fearful, too, afraid that Duquesne just might not survive a heart attack. A glance around the room brought Sable clearly into his view. She looked as frightened as her daughter. Had he not been aware of the problems between Sienna and Sable, he would have thought it terribly odd that the two women weren't finding comfort in each other at a scary time like this.

The crash cart was quickly wheeled into the room. Other medical personnel rushed in and immediately surrounded

Duquesne. Everyone appeared ready to assist Dr. Prescott in any way he needed them to. The E.R. doctor was also on his way up to Duquesne's room to assist in the emergency.

A good forty minutes had passed before Duquesne's condition was finally stabilized. He was then whisked up to the intensive care unit (ICU) where he would be monitored closely. Duquesne's medical condition had been upgraded to critical.

Now that the E.R. doctor had taken over Duquesne's care, Erique thought he should try to tend to the needs of Sienna and Sable. The formidable-looking Sable didn't appear to be an easy person to approach. Although both women were clearly in a state of shock, Sable also looked highly agitated to him, as though injustice had been done to her.

Before Erique could approach Sienna, she came up to him, timidly. Upon spotting the reddish swelling on her left cheek, he reacted instinctively, reaching out and touching the bruise, wondering how she had gotten hurt. Sienna quickly backed away from him, as though his touch had stung her hard. He knew better, though. It was more than likely her mother's presence that had caused her to react negatively. In fact, he was sure of it.

"Are you okay, Sienna?" he asked softly.

"I am the least of my worries. How is my father?"

"Let's step outside the door for a minute or two," Erique suggested. Sable's dark, mistrusting eyes had him feeling a little nervous.

Sable stepped in front of Sienna, intentionally blocking her exit. The lethal look in her daughter's eyes caused Sable to instantly back off. Sable wasn't sure what the look meant, but she quickly decided that it wasn't the right time for her to find out.

The last thing Sienna wanted was for her mother to make a scene in front of Erique. Had he been there earlier to witness what had gone down with her and her mother Sienna was sure he would have found Sable's actions unspeakable. Sienna really didn't know what to expect from Sable. Her mother had never hit her before, so Sienna knew she had to be careful not to antagonize her any further. She had grabbed and shaken her daughter quite a few times, but not nearly as roughly as she had done earlier. Sienna's face still stung something awful from the vicious slaps.

Sienna stopped just a few steps short of exiting the room, praying that Sable had the good sense not to attack her again. For a second or two, she wondered if she should present Erique to Sable. Sienna quickly decided that she should make the introductions, especially since she planned on keeping him in her life despite all obstacles. "This is Dr. Prescott, Mom. He's going to talk to me about Daddy's health."

Sable narrowed her eyes. "In that case, it's me that he needs to talk to. I'm the one who has to make the important decisions regarding your father's health. How well do you know Dr. Prescott, Sienna? I get the impression that this is not your first meeting."

As if Sienna needed protection, Erique moved closer. "It's not our initial meeting, Mrs. St. James. I took care of your daughter when she got sick at the university."

Erique had thought it necessary for him to intercede on behalf of Sienna. He couldn't help wondering if Sable had inflicted the bruise to Sienna's face even though she had told him her mother had never physically abused her. Physical abuse normally followed emotional and mental abuse, though it often occurred much later, once the abuser saw that the verbal and mental attacks were no longer working in their favor.

Sable regarded Erique with obvious distrust. "I see. What do you think my husband's chances for survival are?"

"I'm not a cardiologist, ma'am. I'm a general surgeon. You'll have to talk to Mr. St. James's primary doctor about his prognosis. I only assisted in your husband's emergency care. As his next of kin, the doctors will be glad to share with you all of his pertinent medical information. The ICU nurses can also assist you with that."

Sienna didn't dare tell her mother that Duquesne had given her power of attorney over all of his affairs, including medical and business. Sable would find that out soon enough, especially once she started throwing her weight around. Sienna was also the one who had withdrawn the large amounts of money from his bank accounts. All of it had been done on her father's instructions. There were still numerous requests she had yet to fulfill for him. Duquesne had given Sienna quite a lengthy laundry list to take care of.

Because Duquesne was determined to divorce Sable, he thought it best to start protecting his assets. He planned to offer his wife more than an adequate settlement, but he wasn't going to allow her to run roughshod over him. Sienna no longer had to wait until she graduated to obtain large sums of money because her father had decided to give her part of what she would inherit from him now rather than later. He didn't want his legacy to his daughter to end up as part of the divorce settlement.

In spite of what Sienna thought the consequences might be for her actions, she took Erique's hand. "Do you have time to sit down with me for a few minutes?"

"I'll make time. Do you want to talk here or up in the ICU waiting area?"

"ICU. I should make myself available just in case they need me."

"Good idea."

Although Sienna was aware that Duquesne's consequences for opposing Sable had resulted in his serious heart problems, she wasn't going to allow Sable to continue intimidating her. Sable would never take responsibility for causing her father lots of undue duress, but Sienna knew that her mother had been acting out horribly during both of his medical crises. She absolutely blamed Sable for what had happened to Duquesne.

Without bothering to consult Sable about her plans to go up to the ICU waiting area, Sienna left the room with Erique, leaving her mother shocked and furious.

Comfortably seated in the ICU waiting room, Erique risked touching Sienna's swollen face again. This time she didn't recoil. "How did this happen?"

As Sienna relived the horrendous incident between her and Sable, her eyes watered up. "A direct result of disobedience. I was warned not to be late again."

"You didn't answer my question, Sienna. How did you get the bruise?"

"My mother slapped me across the face, twice."

"Why was that so hard for you to say?"

"I don't know. It's embarrassing." Sienna lowered her lashes. "It hurts, Erique. It hurts a lot to have my mother physically harm me. I think she hates me."

Erique brought Sienna's head to rest against his shoulder. "She doesn't hate you, Sienna. If she loathes anyone, it's herself. You told me she hadn't physically abused you before. Was that the truth?"

Sienna nodded. "She has shaken me hard before, but she has never hit me."

"Does she come back later and apologize to you for her actions?"

"Never. Sable St. James apologizes to no one."

"That's very unfortunate for her,"

Sable entered the area where Sienna and Erique were seated, which kept Sienna from responding to his comment. Her attention was suddenly drawn to a gentleman wearing a white lab coat. The stranger had followed Sable into the ICU waiting area.

Dr. Grinage Ross looked down at the chart he held in his hand. "I'm looking for Sienna St. James."

Sienna got to her feet. "That would be me. How can I help you?"

Dr. Ross introduced himself to Sienna. "I'm the cardiac surgeon assigned to handle your father's case. Let's step away so we can discuss his care in private."

Sable moved toward the doctor. "Why are you talking to her about this? I'm the wife of the patient. Duquesne St. James is my husband. Sienna is *only* his daughter."

Only, Sienna mused. Sable had just made the loving relationship between father and daughter sound unimportant.

Dr. Ross looked down at the chart again. "I'm sorry, ma'am, but Sienna St. James is the only name on the medical power of attorney. I'm not at liberty to speak to anyone that's not listed on the paperwork. Not without permission from the patient to do so."

"That's absurd," Sable shouted, waving her arms about. "I'm the only person you should be talking to. You are violating my rights. I hope you know that."

Dr. Ross shrugged. "According to the legal document in the chart, I'm only to speak to the person named. I'm sorry, Mrs. St. James, but as I stated before, Sienna St. James is the only person I can speak with about Mr. St. James's medical issues."

Sienna made direct eye contact with the doctor. "I'd be happy to step aside with you." Sienna then smiled at Erique. "I know you're on duty, so can we catch up later?"

"It's okay. Handle your business. I can wait on you. We still need to talk."

"Okay, Erique. Thanks for everything."

Knowing that Duquesne was in critical condition had Sienna more fearful than she had been earlier. Her insides were shaking like a bowl of jelly. That her father just might die had become very real and very scary to her. She had understood most of what the doctor had said about her father's health, but there were a few things that had sounded foreign to her. Knowing Erique could clear them up for her made Sienna feel a lot better.

"When do you plan to operate?"

"We'll go in once he is a bit more stabilized, the sooner the better."

"What do you need me to do, Dr. Ross?"

"You just need to sign the consent papers." He covertly glanced over at Sable. "Do you think your mother is going to cause trouble for us?"

Sienna nodded. "More than likely. She thinks she should be in charge of his care."

"Well, the spouse normally is. I hope you can get her to understand that we need to do the surgery as soon as possible. The last thing we need is family interference."

"It might be a good idea for you to clue my mother in on what's going on medically. If she feels we've included her, maybe she won't be so hard to deal with."

"Are you giving me permission to discuss your father's condition with your mother? I can't do it otherwise."

"You have my permission, Dr. Ross. Dad wanted me to have control over this situation because he knew that I'd be easier to deal with. Sorry. But that's just the way it is with our family, unfortunately."

"I'll talk to her now. If you don't mind, I'm going to ask her to step back into your father's room so we can speak candidly. Are you sure this is okay with you?"

"I'm fine with it, sir. I will be praying about it. Good luck with my mother."

Sienna watched Dr. Ross as he approached Sable. When her mother got up and went into the room with her father's doctor without incident, Sienna sighed with relief.

Erique slipped his arm around Sienna's waist. "How are we holding up?"

"Pretty good. Daddy needs to have a bypass done. Dr. Ross mentioned that he has a good bit of blockage. Can you explain that procedure to me?"

"The blockage is in his arteries, where a plaquelike substance has built up. The plaque keeps the blood from flowing through the heart normally. It's a major procedure but a very common one. Dr. Ross is a great heart surgeon. Your dad is in good hands. Now, I think we should get you something to eat. What do you think?"

"I agree with you. The cafeteria?"

"Unless you want to leave the hospital grounds it's the only place close by."

"I want to stick close by in case I'm needed." Sienna looked anxious as she looked toward the room where her mother was talking with the doctor. "I probably should tell my mother we're going."

"I think you should do that."

After thinking about Erique's suggestion, Sienna shrugged with nonchalance. "I think not. She'll only protest and end up telling me not to leave. I rode here with her. If she leaves me, you'll have to give me a ride home. Is that a possibility?"

"It's a sure thing. You can count on me to take you home if it becomes necessary, but you'll have to wait until I finish all my hospital business. Are you down with that?"

"I'm down." Sienna grinned. "I like being around you. It's fun."

"We're on the same page, kid, 'cause I like being with you, too."

Sienna blew on her tea to cool it off before taking a sip. She had also ordered a blueberry muffin. Erique was busy hogging down the breakfast meal he had ordered, consisting of four turkey sausage links, two eggs over-medium and two slices of toast. His glass of milk and orange juice remained untouched, but he had already downed a glass of ice water.

Erique suddenly looked up at Sienna. "Who are you?"

The pointed question momentarily stunned Sienna. Then a blank look took over her expression. Not being able to tell him who she was with strong conviction made her feel downright stupid.

Erique studied Sienna closely, wishing he knew how to help her. "Does your silence mean that you don't know who you are, Sienna?"

Sienna's eyes started blinking rapidly. "I hate to admit it, but I'm not sure about who I am. I know who I want to be."

"Then tell me who *that* person is? I'm curious."

After a few moments of silence Sienna began to tell Erique about the person she wanted to be. Opening her heart to others less fortunate than herself was important to her. More important, she wanted to help free young women who felt hopelessly trapped inside themselves, much like she did. She wanted people to be able to see beyond her looks and see inside her compassionate heart. "I am a good person, Erique, with a great spirit. I need and want to be free to be me, whoever me is. I don't want to be what someone else wants me to be. I would like to be proud of who I am and not fearful of who I've been forced to become. Does any of that make sense to you?"

"Perfect sense. What stops you from being the person you want to be?"

"Fear is the biggest thing that holds me back. When your entire life is planned out for you, you never get the chance to find out who you really are. I'm a grown woman who is just now learning to voice my likes and dislikes. My entire wardrobe, including my undergarments and shoes, is selected for me. I'm told what hairstyles look good on me and I'm also forbidden to wear any styles that my mother objects to."

Sienna began to cry. It was hard for Erique not to take her in his arms, but he felt that he shouldn't do anything that would interrupt her flow. "I know now that I'm the only one to blame for how my life has been run. My mother couldn't just take away my control. I willingly gave it up. Why I did that is what I can't explain. Fear is the only answer I have for all of this. I spend every day of my life in fear of one thing or another."

"Fear is not only crippling, Sienna, it's paralyzing. You probably feel that your heart is damaged beyond repair. It's not. Your heart will heal in time. Your great spirit is the one thing about you that stands out for me. Your spirit is still intact. If your spirit was broken, you probably wouldn't want to wake up each morning. But you do get up and you have made the most of each day despite your odd circumstances. I'm glad to hear you taking responsibility for what has happened to you. You are the only person in this world who is totally responsible for you. It's not too late for you to take back what you've freely given up all these years, Sienna. It's not too late for you to take control."

"I know that, Erique. That's why I've already begun to take back what belongs to me. Reclaiming my dignity is already in progress. I will be free sooner than you think."

"I'm eager to see you unleashed. Free your spirit first. The rest will follow. I can already imagine how much more beautiful you'll be when your spirit is flying free."

Sienna arrived early to the hospital the next morning. She got a chance to see her father before he had been taken down to the surgical suites. They had prayed together and had warmly embraced each other right before the attendant had arrived.

Sienna, now seated in the waiting room right outside of the surgery area, couldn't help worrying despite it being a sin. Erique was observing the operation, but that didn't make her feel any better. He was in there and she was outside waiting and praying. She had asked him if he could keep her posted by cell phone, but cell phones weren't allowed in surgery since they could cause major electronic interference.

Seeing Erique coming through the door had Sienna leaping out her seat. She ran up to him and grabbed hold of his arm. "How he is? Please tell me he's okay."

Erique gently kissed Sienna's forehead. "Your dad came through with flying colors. Actually, his heart wasn't in as bad a shape as was initially thought. He definitely had some serious blockage, but it wasn't to the extreme. His prognosis is great."

Sienna let go of her breath, which she had been holding for several seconds. "When can I see him?"

"He'll be in recovery for at least a couple of hours. Let's go grab something to drink from the cafeteria. I'm through for the day. I have three glorious days off."

Sienna looked terribly anxious. "Are you sure it's okay for me to leave?"

Erique took Sienna by the hand, feeling sorry that she needed to have permission for everything she did. Sable had really brainwashed her daughter. Old habits were hard to break even when someone wanted to break them as badly as Sienna did. "We won't be that far away. Your dad will be knocked out for quite a while. Trust me on that."

Sienna still didn't look like she was convinced, but she began walking alongside Erique. She had a million questions she wanted to ask him about the surgery, but at the moment she couldn't think of a single one. Confusion had her over a barrel. At least she didn't feel as uptight as she had been only moments ago. Knowing that her father had come through the surgery okay had her ecstatic, but she was still slightly worried.

Chapter 8

A week after his operation, Duquesne looked very well. His color was back to normal and he appeared a picture of health. His arteries were now free of plaque and the doctors had said that his overall prognosis was very promising. He had lost a few pounds, but that wasn't anything unusual. He had been given a restricted diet upon his discharge from the hospital two weeks ago, but the forbidden foods weren't something he couldn't live without.

As Sienna carefully carried Duquesne's breakfast tray into the first-floor guest bedroom, versus the upstairs suite of rooms he had occupied before the hospitalization, she was extremely pleased to see how much her father was continuing to improve.

Duquesne beamed up at Sienna, his smile both warm and endearing. "Morning, sweetheart. You are right on time. I'm starving. What you got good for me today?"

"Oatmeal, fresh fruit topping, soft scrambled eggs and

one turkey sausage link. I decided on the herb tea over coffee and the orange juice was just squeezed." Sienna placed the tray on the portable stand and then pushed it closer to the bed. "Good morning, Daddy!" Sienna leaned over and kissed Duquesne on the cheek.

"Sounds great! Thank our wonderful cook for me the next time you see Marjorie."

Sienna smiled smugly. "You can thank the cook yourself since I'm she." Sienna dragged the rocking chair over to a spot where she could easily converse with her father.

Duquesne raised an eyebrow. "I'm impressed. I didn't even know you could cook. Who taught you how?"

Sienna settled down into the rocker. "Marjorie. Who else?"

Duquesne grinned. No one had to tell him that the cooking teacher wasn't Sable. Cooking wasn't her cup of tea. In the early days of their marriage he had done more of the meal preparations and the household chores than she had. "Marjorie should get a certificate in teaching. The food is really good."

Sienna cracked up. "Save all that praise for after I cook something complicated. Anyone could have accomplished this simple meal."

"I'm sure you'll do well with anything you take on in the kitchen." Duquesne laid his fork down on the tray. "How are things going with you and your mother, Sienna? Are you two still having a hard time of it?"

Sighing, Sienna shrugged her shoulders. "Things are still strained with us after all this time, but I'm trying hard to begin a new relationship with her. It's hard to get over everything she's done." Sienna pounded her fist down on her thigh. "I just can't wait to move out of here. That should kind of help things along. As soon as you're better, I'm gone."

Duquesne wasn't happy with Sienna's statement. He didn't want her to suffer through another day of misery because of him. All of the horrible things that had occurred in her life had him feeling very guilty anew.

"All I can suggest is that you keep trying to make a go of it with your mother, sweetheart. She's really hurting and I truly believe she's sorry. We've been having a lot of good conversations lately. To forgive is to be forgiven. I'll leave it at that."

"Have you forgiven her?"

"I have, Sienna. I don't know if it will please you or not, but we've decided to try and save our marriage. We've both done our fair share of wrongs. If I didn't believe Sable was trying to change, I would be leaving here right along with you."

"I believe you," Sienna stated.

"Good. Where do things stand with you and Erique?"

Sienna appeared to beam from head to toe. "We're having our official first date as a couple this evening. He's taking me out to dinner and I'm so excited about it. Can you believe that life is just beginning for me at twenty-one years of age? This is so surreal."

Tears sprang to Duquesne's eyes. "I *can* believe it and I couldn't be more thrilled about it. My lovely daughter is having her very first real date. Will wonders never cease!"

Sable suddenly popped her head into the doorway. "How's it going in here? Mind if I come in and sit down for a minute or two?"

Duquesne looked to Sienna for the answer.

Sienna smiled at Sable, a genuine smile. "Please come on

in, Mom. Dad and I were just discussing my first official date with Erique. I was telling him how excited I am about it. How do you feel about my dating Erique, Mom?"

Sable came on in and took a seat. "I'm truly happy for you both, Sienna. I hope this is the beginning of a wonderful relationship between you two. He seems to have your best interest at heart. I wish you well. He's a fine young man and a dedicated physician."

"Thanks, Mom." Sienna was sure that Sable had done her homework on Erique.

Sienna actually believed that Sable was happy for her. Because her mother was desperately trying to stay in touch with God on a daily basis, Sienna knew that Sable would eventually be okay. She then made the commitment to work as hard as she could on getting her relationship right with Sable. It was important to Sienna to live her life in the best light possible. Removing all dark clouds was the only way to do that.

Sienna was ready to let the bright sunshine beam its light on the St. James family.

Erique leaned in closer to Sienna. "You've been smiling a lot this evening. What all have you been thinking about?"

Sienna reached up and laid her hand against Erique's face. "How happy I am. Things in my life are finally moving in the right direction. Graduation is just a few weeks away and I'm so happy about it. There have been a lot of changes in my life."

"Yeah, there have been. Most of them have been positive changes. Your life is totally different now. Now that you don't have any extracurricular classes or any pageantry stuff, period, do you miss it?"

"Not for a second. I'm freer than I have ever been in my life." A tear escaped from the corner of her right eye. "You know what the best thing about all this is?"

"Please enlighten me."

Sienna grinned. "I like being an adult. I have finally taken responsibility for myself. Another good thing is that I get to hang out with you whenever we have time."

Erique was moved to tears. "That sounds really nice, Sienna. How are you enjoying our first romantic date so far?"

"It's awesome. I can't wait for us to do it again."

"How about dinner out again tomorrow evening? You get to pick the place."

"I'm free."

"How about the next night after that one?"

"I'm free."

"What about every night for the entire upcoming summer months?"

Feigning ignorance, Sienna giggled inwardly. "What about them?"

Erique chuckled. "I guess I took that one a little bit too far."

Sienna leaned over and kissed Erique softly on the mouth. "What if we take our budding relationship slow, one fascinating date at a time? Will that work for you?"

"It works for me, Sienna, very well, I might add."

"This girl is just learning how to honor her own heart so I'm going to need a little patience as we further develop our personal relationship. I also vow to honor your heart."

"I promise the same. As long as we honor each other's hearts, we'll both be okay."

Smiling broadly, Sienna and Erique raised their glasses to make a toast. "Here's to honoring our hearts."

The softly spoken vow was then sealed with a sweetly passionate kiss.

The inspirational sequel to

He's **FINE**...*But Is He* **SAVED?**

Acclaimed author

KIMBERLEY BROOKS

He's
SAVED...
But Is He
FOR
REAL?

An entertaining novel about men, dating, relationships and God.

Sandy, Michelle and Liz are three single girlfriends who are each struggling with their own issues with men. As each faces confusion, jealousy and loneliness, they look to the one Lord and Savior of all for help.

"Heartwarming and engrossing...
He's Fine...But Is He Saved?
engages you from the first page to the last."
—Bestselling author Jacquelin Thomas

Coming the first week of February wherever books are sold.

www.kimanipress.com

KPKB1230208TR

Because even the smartest women can make
relationship mistakes…

ACCLAIMED AUTHOR
JEWEL DIAMOND TAYLOR

You
DESERVE
MORE

A straight-to-the point book that will empower women
and help them overcome such self-defeating emotions as
insecurity, desperation, jealousy, loneliness…all factors that
can keep you in a destructive cycle of unloving, unfulfilling
relationships. Through the powerful insights and life-lessons
in this book, you will learn to build a relationship that's
strong enough to last a lifetime.

"Jewel Diamond Taylor captivates audiences. She moves the spirit."
—Susan L. Taylor, Editorial Director, *Essence* magazine

Available the first week of January, wherever books are sold.

www.kimanipress.com

A volume of heartwarming devotionals
that will nourish your soul...

NORMA DeSHIELDS BROWN

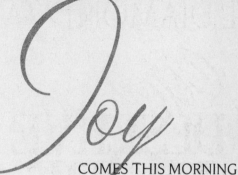

Joy

COMES THIS MORNING

Norma DeShields Brown's life suddenly changed
when her only son was tragically taken from her
by a senseless act. Consumed by grief, she began
an intimate journey that became
Joy Comes This Morning.

Filled with thoughtful devotions, Scripture readings
and words of encouragement, this powerful book
will guide you on a spiritual journey that will sustain
you throughout the years.

*Available the first week of November
wherever books are sold.*

www.kimanipress.com

A soul-stirring, compelling
journey of self-discovery…

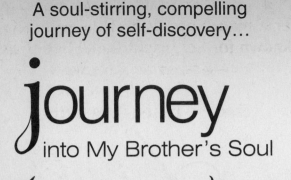

journey
into My Brother's Soul

Maria D. Dowd

Bestselling author of
Journey to Empowerment

A memorable collection of essays, prose and poetry,
reflecting the varied experiences that men of color face
throughout life. Touching on every facet of living—love,
marriage, fatherhood, family—these candid personal
contributions explore the essence of what it means to
be a man today.

**"*Journey to Empowerment* will lead you on a
healing journey and will lead to a great love of self,
and a deeper understanding of the many roles we
all must play in life."—*Rawsistaz Reviewers***

Coming the first week of May
wherever books are sold.

"Ms. Hudson-Smith is well-known for her romance novels, but she will soon be well-known for her inspirational fiction as well."
—*Rawsistaz Reviewers*

Essence **bestselling author**

Linda Hudson Smith

FIELDS *of* FIRE

A novel

Newly engaged and working in professions dedicated to saving lives, Stephen Trudeaux and Darcella Coleman differ on one important decision— whether to start a family. Then tragedy strikes and they know it will take much reflection, faith and soul-searching for their relationship to survive.

Coming the first week of April, wherever books are sold.

Visit us at
www.kimanipress.com

KPLHS0270407TR